THE RAGE OF
ACHILLES

TERENCE HAWKINS

CASPERIAN
BOOKS

This is a work of fiction. All the characters and events portrayed in this book are either fictitious or are used fictitiously.

www.casperianbooks.com

Cover image by K. L. Gaffney

ISBN-10: 1-934081-20-5
ISBN-13: 978-1-934081-20-4

For Sharon,
who takes me to every opportunity,
around every pitfall,
and over every obstacle.

PROLOGUE

Thetis is her only name. It's the only name she's ever had. Some of the other slaves have family names, because either they were born free and taken in raids, or born of parents who at least remembered freedom. Not Thetis. Her grandfather couldn't remember his grandfather being free. So far as she knows, Peleus' family has owned hers since Cronus ate his children.

Peleus comes to her at night. Her father is asleep and has been since the sun went down, since the pigs he tends bedded down in the dung. The rags at the hut door are suddenly thrust aside; she wakes to see Peleus filling the doorway, and her heart sings. She is his only child's mother, and he has come for her as she knew he would. Without speaking, he raises a hand. Moonlight gleams from the gold at his wrist. His finger crooks. She rises from a bed recently enriched by filthy linen, leavings from the big house in which he lives. She ignores the pain in belly and loins, reminders of a birth just a week past, the boy she squeezed out after three suns' coming and going taken away to the big house where the linen and the gold came from.

He holds a thick finger to his lips. She nods. Pulling her excuse for a chiton around her, she comes to him. He inclines his head and smiles. She smiles back. She will precede him to the big house where she will take her place: her place as his child's mother.

She could find the trail even without a moon, but tonight it is full, so she walks without hesitation. When it forks, she takes the path to the big house and is startled when his big hand grips her shoulder. The other way. She is confused but soon relaxes. This fork must lead to a private shrine, secret from the slaves, known only to the family and its gods.

The trail is not well worn. Ah, the family is not pious. She thinks how she must change that when she lives in the big house and is in charge of the worship of its gods. She wonders for a moment why he does not speak at all, but realizes that silence must be part of her consecration.

They come to a bend in the trail, the pines through which they have climbed suddenly gone: bare rock on her left, hard moonlight and a cliff on her right, the crashing sea below. His arm snakes around her and she is amazed by the cold bite of bronze in her throat. She tries to speak, but blood bubbles through the new mouth gaping just below her chin.

Peleus curses his clumsiness. He draws the knife again across her throat, thinking of her as a sacrificial ox rather than a bedmate, and this time hits the big artery in her neck.

She is astonished again. Blood spurts before her. It squirts like his seed: first jetting far, then less so, finally dissipating itself in copious dribble. She sags against his restraining arm and, just as she dies, turns to him and mouths: "Why?"

Peleus does not answer. He knows what to expect after her last moments. Holding her upright, he adroitly moves his feet away from the flow bubbling down her twitching legs.

She is still at last. He cradles her for a minute. He croons into her ear: wordless love sounds with which she can comfort herself in Hades. Careful to spill neither blood nor filth on himself, he sidesteps right to the edge of the path where the cliff careens away down to breakers whose salt he can just barely smell. He whispers a little prayer and throws her aside.

The body bounces and rolls, and as it rolls, gathers momentum, its arms flung wide like a maenad in ecstasy. One outthrust arm catches in the crotch of a scrubby pine sapling grown twisted from an outcropping and the body hangs suspended. Peleus, horrified, stares. Was she still alive? Was she trying to save herself? Will she hang there forever to shriek his shame to every passerby?

The body does not move except in time to the wind. Peleus sighs. She is dead, but caught. New anxiety gnaws at his entrails. He sees he cannot reach the body without plummeting to the surf himself. As he forms the first words of another prayer, he hears the creak and crack of the scrub giving way and laughs with relief as the body bounces twice off rock before losing itself in the glowing surf where flesh will feed fish and bone pound itself into sand.

He stands at the cliff edge and stares at the sea. He hopes for another glimpse of his immortal wife, the baby's real mother: the Thetis who cannot die.

⌒

Peleus sat all alone in his hall, a bowl of undiluted wine at his hand, retainers all kicked away, uncomprehending of his weeklong rage. He stared into the fire of a single brazier and wondered why it was that his only son, the child of his old age, should have to be born of a swineherd's slave daughter.

Then the doors flew open as though forced by a great wind, but without a sound. Phosphorescent sea foam poured through and covered the flagstone and rose to lap around his ankles on his dais two feet above the common floor. As he stared at the incongruous wrack, a wave crashed at his great threshold and rolled into the hall.

She rode a dolphin bridled with gold. It surfed to his feet and turned its forever-grinning, bottle-nosed head to him as though in inquiry. Afraid to look at her, he stared at it—until he had no choice.

PELEUS, the voice spoke without words. Terrified, he held the dolphin's gaze—more human than its rider's, for dolphins at least die like men.

PELEUS, the wordless voice spoke again in his head, louder, so that he feared that a third repetition would make blood flow from his ears. He tore his eyes from the dolphin's.

He could not meet hers. The best he could do was to stare at the door and take her in through the corner of his eye. He trembled and knew that if he looked at her directly, he would die, or worse, be transformed into something other than a man. He thought of Actaeon, who had seen Artemis bathing and had, in her rage, been turned into a stag. Would he, seeing a nymph, be turned into an oyster? But through the corner of his eye he saw as much as man could: pure and translucent as marble, garlanded with plaited kelp, sceptered with a bar of light.

PELEUS. YOU ARE MY BELOVED. Fool that he is, he is tempted to look at her directly. As his head turns, he catches it, and jerks his eyes back to the dolphin grinning through its golden bridle. Yet in the periphery he

7

sees her glowing nimbus, a pearly halo shot through with lightning, whose crackle can be felt but not heard. His hair and beard and even the light fur on his arms stand on end in time to its discharge. His heart hammers in his chest so hard that he fears the ribs will spread and split to let it fly to her.

BELOVED PELEUS, FATHER OF OUR SON. *Again his head almost snaps to face her, and again his desire to remain living or simply human is a little stronger.* FATHER OF OUR SON, ACHILLES, WHOM THE GODS LOVE. THE GIRL WITH MY NAME WAS I, BORROWING HER FORM TO TAKE MY LOVE WITH YOU, AS MY FATHER ZEUS AP-PEARED AS A SWAN TO LEDA. *The words fill his head. His mouth hangs open and spittle runs into his beard. The dolphin's grin, fixed by nature though it is, seems to grow a little wider.* WHEN YOU THOUGHT YOU FUCKED THE GIRL, YOU FUCKED ME. HE IS OUR SON. I AM YOUR WIFE.

He will not allow his head to move. The hand he can see jumps and trembles as though with fever or the falling sickness. He prays for death and the dim, cold peace of Hades. This is too close to Olympus. As he stares at his hand, he realizes that he has heard no sound other than her words fill-ing his head. He risks rolling his eyes left and right. Sea fills the room up to the foot of the throne and roils and foams, all without noise. The dolphin's tail beats lazily against the silent tide.

I AM YOUR WIFE, PELEUS. I AM ACHILLES' MOTHER, AND I WILL LOVE AND PROTECT HIM AND SEE THAT HE HAS GLORY IF NOT LONG LIFE. WILL YOU HAVE A SON BY AN IMMORTAL MOTHER WHO WILL DIE YOUNG AND GLORIOUS? OR WILL YOU HAVE HIM A SWINEHERD'S DAUGHTER'S SON WHOSE LIFE WILL BE AS OTHER MEN'S, AND WHOSE MOTHER WILL BRING YOU SHAME?

Peleus does not even think to speak. When men adress the immortals it is through spilled blood and greasy smoke.

PELEUS, IF YOU WOULD HAVE ME AS YOUR WIFE AND MOTHER TO OUR SON, YOU MUST SACRIFICE THE GIRL. IF SHE LIVES SHE IS HIS MOTHER AND YOU MAY TELL OTHER MEN SHE IS YOUR WIFE IF YOU SO CHOOSE. BUT CHOOSE, PELEUS, MY BELOVED.

The dolphin holds his gaze as the water around it begins to ebb. Does it wink? Can it nod? But its great head slips out of his field of vision before he can be sure what it has done.

Staring at the wall, he watches the waterline sink. When it is halfway down from its crest, he dares to turn his head to the door. The vanishing tide has carried them to the threshold. The dolphin splits her legs, just as he did those nights she loved him in flesh-and-bone disguise. Her naked back ripples with muscle and her golden curls just brush the great door's lintel as a final wave sucks the last of the water from the room and propels her away. As she vanishes, her head turns toward him, and he buries his face in his lap before he catches her fatal eye.

It is a long time before he dares to raise his head again; so long that his back creaks as he straightens. The hall is as it was before she arrived: doors closed, single brazier guttering, wine bowl half full at his elbow. Stunned, he looks for any sign of the sea. A lobster flailing in a corner, perhaps? Seaweed clinging to the throne's lion feet? But wherever he looks, he sees nothing but dry land and mortality.

First assuring himself that no retainer has crept back, he drops whimpering to the floor and on hands and knees scuttles for evidence of her presence. Nothing. He forces thick fingers between the flagstones and draws them out dry. Sobbing with frustration, he licks the stone hoping for a hint of salt, and rises to his knees spitting out dust. Eventually, he resumes the throne and rinses his mouth with wine. Then, with both hands, he raises the bowl to his lips and drains it in three gulps. He wonders for an instant whether she was ever here. Remembering the dolphin's grin, he thrusts the thought aside and wonders instead what choice he will make.

No choice at all. He howls for more wine. Tomorrow night, he will sign his marriage contract in blood.

PELEUS'
PERFECT SON

Flat sea. Flat sky. In the minutes after night has ended but before day has begun, the world is light, but the sun not yet risen to bring it color. So the sea and sky are shades of gray: silver above, lead below. At the edge of the sea a few miles away are the Achaean ships. They lie like whales, canted at odd angles and settled into the sand over the years they have reposed at the limit of vision.

They stand apart on the rampart over the Scaean Gate. In a few minutes they will rejoin their family and the court, but for now they can talk unheard, just the two of them. Neither wishes to speak. Last night the spies brought them news they could not believe: Agamemnon had stolen Achilles' prize, the girl Briseis. Compensation, said the king, for his own girl, repatriated to Troy to placate Apollo and so stop the plague the god had sent. And Achilles had roared like a sacrificial bull when his own prize had been taken to replace the king's.

Not believing their luck, the Trojans took the auguries at first light, confident that the sacrifice would confirm divine favor and quick victory. Instead, the goat bolted and kicked when the knife was raised—usually the worst possible sign. The only thing worse was what the animal's split, steaming belly revealed: a liver shrunken with disease and bowels choked and churning with worms. Horrified, the royals shielded the goat from the priests' view while nicking so many arteries that its abdomen swam with obscuring blood.

But they knew what they saw. Prince Hector edges closer to King Priam and bends to his ear, his dyed horsehair plume trembling as it dips. He whispers. "We are so fucked," he says.

Priam nods. They do not speak more.

෧

Patroclus has heard the talk in the camp. Now he hears the heavy steps crunching sand at the entrance to the tent, followed by a guttural snarl as a Myrmidon too slow to move aside hits the dirt in a clatter of armor and babbled apologies. There is a hiss of silk as two slave girls come to the tent flap, the older offering a bowl of wine cut with water and flavored with pitch. She does not cry out when the first backhand knocks the bowl flying and the second dislocates her jaw. She or her sister has been through this before. So has Patroclus. Face down on the bed, he pulls up his tunic and tries to relax.

He hears fabric rip. A whimper. Booted feet shift on the canvas floor. He recognizes the grunt and turns his head. A girl too young to bleed is on her knees, chiton pulled down to her waist, breastbuds covered by modest elbows, the back of her head caught in his massive paw as Achilles violates her mouth. Patroclus sighs. For the moment, at least, Achilles has found another outlet.

Grunting again, Achilles thrusts his pelvis forward, and the girl, unable to help herself, gags. Achilles yanks her head back and spends across her face as she retches. Not backhanded, but with a leather-cased fist, he clubs her once. She falls away from the blow and does not move. Her eyes are half open; her breathing is loud, almost a snore. Soon it stops. Achilles takes no notice. He stands blind as a statue, eyes straight ahead. Finally, he speaks. "Look at me," he says.

Patroclus does. Achilles is nearly two yards tall, among the biggest of the Achaeans. The muscles outside his armor stand out like a ship's cables. Nine years into the war he is almost thirty, but still he has all his teeth. His chest heaves; golden beard bristles; eyes amber as a lion's hold Patroclus fixed. He is as much a beautiful animal as a goddess' son.

"Did you know he would do this?" Achilles asks.

"Do what?"

"Take her." Achilles' voice is surprisingly level. "Take my prize. *My* prize. My Briseis. My *Briseis. My Briseis.*" He is howling now. "You knew, you *knew.*" Patroclus, alarmed, sees that Achilles' rage is making him hard again. He rises up a little on his knees. "You treacherous bastard, you were laughing at me with the rest of them! *You handed her over yourself!*" A fist strikes his shoulder and Patroclus closes his eyes.

෬

Twice in ten minutes is too much, even for godlike Achilles. After a dozen savage thrusts he admits defeat and withdraws his sagging cock. Sobbing with rage at this fresh humiliation, he cuffs Patroclus' head into the pillow, but not hard. Or not as hard as he can—even warrior Patroclus would not survive.

Achilles sprawls across Patroclus' back and continues to weep. Patroclus, taking courage, dares to turn his head to the right. The girl's face is a yard from his. A thick rope of blood trickles from the corner of her mouth and mixes with the seed on her chin. Her eyes are open and fixed. At the tent flap are two women. They have seen his head move and clasp their hands and mouth: "What now, what now?"

Achilles sobs so hard that Patroclus fears he will break both their hearts. Shame will leave him oblivious for a while; perhaps a long while. Patroclus winks hard with his exposed eye. The women advance and sweep up the dead girl in their arms. Only as they bend to pick her up does Patroclus see that their shoulders shake with weeping as violent as the great warrior's, but silent. Then they are gone.

Achilles' tears will not stop. Whenever it seems as though they will end and Achilles will sleep, some imp whispers in his ear, "They laugh at you," and he howls and pounds his lover's head and hiccups. Finally, it is enough: when Achilles at last sleeps, Patroclus rolls away.

Patroclus waits a long time. First for the breathing to become deep and regular, then for the exhausted snore. When the light through the tent walls has grown dim and golden, he eases out of bed. Standing in the center of the tent, he pulls his tunic back into place. He rubs his hands over his buttocks and smiles because he need not wince. Hands above his

12

head, he stretches heavenward and hears his back crack. For a moment he thinks about a bowl of wine and crawling back into bed, forgetting about all this until morning when it will be just another one of the big man's rages, gone with next light. But he knows this one is different. He knows what has happened. And worse, he knows he was a part of it. Briseis had to go back. Though he had no choice, neither betrayal nor shame is any less for their necessity. Disgrace takes him back to boyhood, where for today at least he allows himself to be the bully's toy.

He looks at the bed. Sprawled on the silk, Achilles still wears his mother's armor. On his right hand is the blood of a dead girl whose name neither of them ever knew. Even in Morpheus' arms, Achilles rages. He twitches and mumbles like a dreaming dog suckling in its sleep. Patroclus looks at his sleeping lover and smiles, though he knows he is looking at a dead man. He turns to the tent flap and watches the sun sink behind the black ships that brought them all here. Well, he thinks, who can look at his lover without seeing a man soon to die?

A breeze blows up from the west, colder than it should be. He rubs goose bumps covering his arms. The wind turns icy. It blows straight from the sun. He knows it to be a message from Apollo. "We all look at dead men wherever we turn," he says. The wind, now colder than anything he has ever felt, tears the words from his lips and scatters them unheard. "Young or old, all are dead soon," he shrieks, but cannot hear himself.

BUT THE MAN ON THE BED IS DEAD SOONER STILL. AND YOU BEFORE HIM. The voice is just a whisper, but it echoes in his head like a gong.

His face is wet with freezing tears; his beard is soaked. He wants to scream to the sinking sun, "No, you lie," to the wind, "You are not cold," but the wind is howling now, and his breath smokes in its frigid grasp. He runs a hand across his face and feels frost around his mouth.

He turns away from the tent flap, his eyes wide with terror. One of the women who bore away the dead girl stands behind him. She stares at him confused. She hasn't heard the wind or felt the cold. Shuddering, he takes the wine bowl she raises, but it does nothing to warm him.

The man on the bed snores and twitches still. Patroclus drains the bowl, crawls under the sheets, and wraps his arms around him, trying not to think about what it will be like to be dead.

ACHILLES
ON THE BEACH

The sun has been up a long time, but Paris is still in bed. Light streams in through windows generously large in his house far from the walls. There is no fear of arrows or stray javelins here, high up in the citadel.

He scissors his legs lazily through a tangle of silk sheets still damp from dawn's lovemaking. He likes watching his legs move. He runs his hands over his thighs and traces with his fingers the big muscles' divide. He stares at his belly: sometimes it reminds him of his warrior brother's breastplate, rippled and ridged like a god's. As he stares at his belly and thighs, the snake between stirs, needing no attention but his.

But it has attracted another's. She stands at the window wrapped in a robe his mother embroidered a long time ago. "Somebody's awake," she says. She has a little lisp. He once thought, long ago, that it would drive him crazy. It never has.

She comes to the edge of the bed, near its foot. He smiles lazily and, holding her eye, runs the tip of his index finger down his shaft. The snake leaves its bed on his thigh and starts to strain upwards. Her eyes leave his and drift down. The wall behind her is painted with a garden that never existed on this earth; her head is garlanded with pigment lotus. "No war today?" she asks. A painted fingernail traces his instep.

"No war today." The snake is throbbing and he admires it. "You haven't heard the news?"

"I won't know till you tell me what it is." The lisp gets a little stronger when she grows petulant. Her head dips and her tongue takes her finger's place, slipping between his toes and finally down the arch. He whimpers.

"Achilles is out of the war."

Her head snaps up. "What?"

"Come on," he laughs, "don't stop." Her head stays up. "Don't stop or I won't tell you."

She dives back to his foot and splayed fingers start working their way up his calf. "The spies told us last night. Agamemnon stole Briseis from him. He said it was only fair because he was king and he had to give up his girl to save the Achaeans. Achilles went crazy. He swore he wouldn't raise a hand again for Agamemnon. Or his brother, your husband. Did you do this for him?" His voice is suddenly sharp with anxiety.

"Never," she slurs around his big toe.

"Good," he says. Relaxing against the cushions, he wraps his hand around himself and squeezes. "So this is very good. The Achaeans don't know what to do, and soon we will drive them into the sea." He starts to pump himself. "Let me see them."

Obediently, she releases his toe and sits up at the edge of the bed. She slips the robe off her left shoulder. Shrugging, she exposes it entirely. Even now, near ten years later, her breast affects him as it did the first time he saw it. It is like a mountain, like Olympus itself, pure white and thrusting arrogantly from the plain of her ribs, its crest a peak of coral that tightens and darkens as he watches. Any larger and it would sag to her waist; big as it is, on a woman nearly thirty, its continuing firmness is widely viewed as a sign of divine favor on the Trojan cause.

He moans. "Both." She shrugs the robe off the other shoulder and it falls to her hips. "Touch them for me." She smiles and reaches for the pot of oil beside the bed. Filling her hands, she anoints herself, delicately at first, then with a two-handed grip that makes the coral crests an impossible blood red that he has never seen on another woman. Her breath begins to labor and whistle.

She stops and reaches for the oil pot again. She hands it to him, smiles crookedly. "Touch yourself for me." He grins and fills his hands with unguent.

15

The sun is directly overhead. The only shelter is in the lee of a canted ship. Two veterans have found it, as veterans will always find comfort when it is there to be found.

One, Cephales, mends the strap of his shield. It does not need mending. The old soldier just wants to be sure; he does not want to go out to face the Trojans tomorrow to find himself with an unguarded left one minute, and the next paying the boatman to take him across the River Styx. As he works, he wonders whether he is weakening the strap with his constant attention, and he gnaws his beard with anxiety. He knows he has been in the lines too long and that his heart is going if not gone. He prays that he will die before his friends know.

Lacademon, not so long in the lines but long enough to find shade when he can, does nothing. He sits on the sand with his back flush against a hull out of water so long that the barnacles might be fossils. He watches Cephales work the braided leather without guessing his purpose or his fear. Once, he glances at his own shield pitched beside him, and decides that the strap will do.

A third, Polycrates, approaches. He plants his javelin point down in the sand and leans his shield against the long, immobile ship, then drops on his ass in the shade and plants his back against the hull. "Hot," he says. His friends grunt. "Heard the news?"

The man doing nothing says nothing. The man fixing his strap must ask. "What news?"

"The boy wonder."

"What about him?" Cephales has stopped his busy work; Lacademon turns his head.

"You heard that King Agamemnon took his girl?"

"Right. Big deal."

"Fucking right it's a big deal. Achilles is acting like he fucked his father. He's running around screaming that he's out of the fucking war and he'll just sit on the beach and get a nice tan while we get our asses kicked."

"No shit?" says Lacademon.

"No shit," Polycrates says.

They sit in silence for a while. At last, Cephales puts down his worri-

16

some shield and speaks. "What does Achilles care about one piece of ass more or less? He has a dozen girls and Patroclus, too."

Polycrates shakes his head. "Brother, this isn't just some piece of ass. I haven't seen her, but one of my buddies did. Fifteen years old if she's a day, tits like melons that stick straight out, and a face like Pallas Athena." He shakes his head again. "What do you think it means?"

Cephales considers. "I think we will have a very hard time without Achilles."

Polycrates nods. He turns to Lacademon. "You?"

"I think I'm glad I'm not Patroclus."

All three laugh. Cephales stops before the others and starts working at his shield again.

The kings' tents are pitched on hills, or the closest thing—dunes whose sand is anchored by tenacious, long-rooted grass. Still, each can sit on his little eminence and look down on his ships and men and see the other kings on their own dunes.

There is an ox-hide and olivewood stool at Odysseus' canvas door. From where he sits he can look east to Achilles and west to Agamemnon. Last night he heard the gored-heifer bellowings from the east. This afternoon he looks west and sees Agamemnon, crowned with a wreath of field flowers, strolling with his arm around Briseis' shoulders while a piper flutes behind them.

Odysseus sits alone and watches. He looks towards Achilles' tent, from which no sound comes now, nor has it all day. He looks back to happy Agamemnon. He raises a bowl to his lips and takes a swallow of watered wine flavored with resin. He spits it onto the ground before him. "Nice work, shithead," he says.

Achilles has been on the beach since just after the sun rose. As he raved and wept it traced its long course across the sky and now verges on drowning itself at the rim of the western sea. No one has dared disturb him in this rocky little cove a mile away from the farthest outpost of the shore-hugging Achaean fleet. A few Myrmidons, his very best, nervous equally from Trojan presence and their lord's despair, at first followed him covertly as he made his way up the coast. His storm troopers, they thought themselves invisible even from him, dropping soundlessly to their faces or fading into brush whenever he even appeared to sense their presence. They thought they could post guard without his knowing. But just as he was about to climb down to the strand at the beginning of the rocky descent from the trail, he turned without a word and loosed one of the twin javelins he carried. It landed quivering between the two men in the lead. They stood open-mouthed, staring at their lord. He raised his arm and pointed wordlessly back down the trail. One by one, his commandos left rock clefts and trees and shambled back to camp.

He has spent the day in grief. He would not let his men hear again what they heard last night, so he kept silent until he drove them away. Certain of his solitude, he howled. At first he raged. Big rocks were raised overhead and shattered into gravel against unyielding cliff. The roaring surf could not hear itself crash over his shrieks. An unlucky octopus, caught in a tidal pool, found itself Agamemnon's effigy: its eyes plucked out, each foot-long arm torn off slowly as ink jetted down Achilles' chest, its bag of a head sloppily vivisected with fingers and teeth.

Finally, everything that could be broken had been broken and everything that lived had been killed. He was alone with himself. It was past noon. Achilles turned on Achilles. At first he was crude. He tore at his face and splashed salt water across the bleeding tracks. Shells crunched in his mouth to lacerate gums and tongue, but he could not make himself swallow. He stripped and ground his crotch across a boulder crusted with mussels, watching blood drip from his scrotum into the water. When he shat he rubbed his own filth into his hair and beard and cried out to Olympus to make it all end. The gods remained stubbornly silent.

Twice, he battered his head against rock, not because he wanted to die, but because he wanted the shame to stop. Yet he lives, and so does his shame. He is exhausted, but he cannot stop. Finally, he sits in the sea and stares at the sun, now an orange semicircle gilding fat clouds. He is slumped, his forearms resting against his thighs half submerged in surf growing colder with each wave. He feels sand shifting beneath him and knows that if he sits here long enough, the tide will rise and take him out to sea. This is not how it is supposed to end.

18

Finally, he speaks the words he knows he must. "Mother. Mother, please. Please. Please help me, mother." He waits. He waits a long time.

The sun is down to a quadrant, less, an octant, just one segment of an orange. The world before him is twilight, the world behind him dark. His head throbs with last night's wine and today's multiple stony traumas. He has given up hope and waits for the waves to take him away. He takes comfort in the knowledge that he will be asleep when the big fishes take off his toes and work their way up his legs. The cold water is now up to his sternum and its icy kiss makes him tired. He tries one more time. "Mother, please."

The water is over his nipples. He thinks about getting up, running back to his clothes and arms, and walking back to the camp where there is a fire and wine. But there is shame there too, and he is tired anyway, and now he is beginning to feel warm rather than cold. So perhaps the glorious death he was promised is here in the water, with his last enemy an octopus not three feet across.

The water is at his collarbone. He raises an arm out of the surf and notices that his fingers are blue. He is about to lean back, to recline as though at a banquet, and inhale salt water and drown his shame. But just as he rises up for a last backstroke, the water in front of him erupts. Twenty yards offshore a geyser rises, steam curling a hundred yards into the air, water boiling all around it. Suddenly he is in a whirlpool. Alive again and astonished, he sits up. "Mother? Mother, is it you?"

He stares straight into the heart of the geyser now subsiding into a boiling fountain, knowing that that is where she is. Then, just back from Hades' grasp though he is, he remembers what it means to look at an immortal, even if he slipped into the world from between her thighs, and throws a forearm over his eyes.

The water boils. He can hear it. He steals a glimpse down past his forearm and sees that thighs livid from cold a minute before have grown boiled-lobster red. If the water gets any hotter, the flesh will blister and part from bone. But it does not. The roiling has stopped; so has the geyser's jet and crash. So too has the surf. Again he peeks at the water and sees it flat as a bath in which he has fallen asleep. He waits.

19

He thinks an hour has passed, but he knows enough not to expose his eyes. Never curious about anything other than war, he finally notices that no matter how many times his heart beats here in the surf at sunset, the sky grows no darker, as though the movement of the sun stopped with the surf. He knows then that he is no longer in time. He waits.

Finally, he can bear it no longer. His back shrieks with his prolonged half crouch; his arm trembles with the effort of shielding himself from the divine. Eyes screwed shut, he drops his right arm into the water and begins to raise his left into its place. Something thick and wet and rubbery wraps itself around his left leg. Circles of cartilage hard as bone bite into his skin. His eyes pop open as a tentacle thick as his own arm wraps its way up to his groin and tightens hard enough to make him cry out.

As though awaiting that signal, the tentacle tightens further and pulls. He jerks forward against submerged sand and his head disappears under water. His mouth, still open, takes in water like a siphon. He claws at air and light. With another yank from the tentacle, his hands submerge as well.

The salt water bites his lungs. He flails and panics and coughs, expelling the last of his air in a few pathetic bubbles that race to the shimmering surface and break and are gone. He does not notice that the dark has yet to gather in his eyes, and so he fights, clutching at the sand and rocks speeding below him and kicking at the tentacle.

He snaps his head forward. Lungs and ears full of water, his groan is something he can only feel. He sees he has been taken by an octopus that must surely be the great-great-grandfather of this afternoon's victim, fifty feet across with a head as big as an ox, eyes the size of platters, human as his own, that stare at him with neither pity nor reproach. He thinks that he has offended his mother by killing one of her creatures and knows himself to be a dead man taking the long way to Hades. He stops struggling.

The octopus descends. The dim light roofing Achilles' new world fades. He wonders whom he will see, whether those he sent there himself will mock him, whether the friends who preceded him will welcome him at whatever tables the dead can keep. Still, the octopus dives. The light, rather than disappearing entirely, seems only to have shifted. Now it comes from below, a hazy point of brightness ahead and down. The octopus flexes and jets and pulses towards the light.

They arrive. The tentacle around his leg relaxes and Achilles drifts down to find a seat on a submerged rock. The octopus flaps once more and is gone. Ahead of him is what looks like a roofless temple: a dozen columns of coral, pink and white, arranged in a circle twenty yards across. Within is the source of light: a ball of lightning that rolls and dances from pillar to pillar. Knowing himself dead, he dares to look directly. Inside the ambient electricity he sees what seems to be the shadow of a human form.

He draws his eyes away. What looked like a temple now seems a military camp. Around it circle hundreds of great fish, orderly as cavalry patrols, each bigger than the biggest man, armed with serried ranks of white teeth and festooned with dimly glowing lights hanging from scalloped lips and fins. On the sand around are ranks of infantry: lobsters big as hunting dogs, crabs like wild boar. Clams the size of chariot cars snap open and shut in rhythm like bacchantes banging their cymbals.

Achilles sits and waits. Water seems to nourish a dead man's lungs just as well as air, and now that he has died, he has plenty of time. He stares at the rolling light in the roofless temple. At length it stills and a voice fills his head. I KNOW WHY YOU WEEP, ACHILLES, MY SON.

Achilles is startled. He had expected the voice of Charon.

I KNOW WHY YOU RAGE. *The voice comes from the fireball. Achilles weeps, his salt tears blending imperceptibly with the water around him. His mother has come through after all.*

The fireball grows brighter. He is bathed in warmth, not of water boiling from the divine presence, but the radiance of her love. SPEAK, ACHILLES. YOU CAN.

He opens his mouth. It is an effort for lungs and diaphragm to push water rather than air, for teeth and tongue to form words in this new medium, but she is right. "I hurt," *he says.*

I KNOW. I KNOW, MY SON.

"He has shamed me before the fleet, before all the kings, before all my men, before the Trojans, before the gods."

I KNOW, I KNOW.

"How can I make him pay?"

The fireball is silent. POOR BOY. MY POOR BOY. I BORE YOU FOR A SHORT LIFE BUT PROMISED YOU GLORY. NOT THIS. NOT SHAME BEFORE YOUR FRIENDS. BUT DON'T BE AFRAID. YOUR MOTHER WON'T LET THIS HAPPEN. I WILL SPEAK TO MY FA-THER, YOUR GRANDFATHER, THE LORD OF LIGHTNING. HE WILL BRING AGAMEMNON GRIEF BEYOND TELLING. AND

21

WHILE THIS HAPPENS, YOU MUST REST BY YOUR SHIPS. STAY OUT OF THE WAR. LET AGAMEMNON KNOW WHAT LIFE IS LIKE WITHOUT MY BOY.

The fireball has grown brighter by degrees until he can barely look at it. The figure inside stands out in sharper contrast. This is as close to seeing her as he will ever come. Though the glare around her makes his head throb, he forces himself to look anyway. DON'T WORRY, SON. DO AS I SAY AND AGAMEMNON WILL REGRET THIS. AND I PROMISE YOU THAT YOU WILL HAVE GLORY BEFORE YOU DIE.

He is about to speak again, but the light winks out. For a fraction of a second, he knows himself to be alone at the bottom of the sea. Then darkness enfolds him as well.

It is night when he awakens on the beach face down in gravel and sand, fifty yards from the water line, half covered with slimy weed. For a few seconds, he lies there without moving. The beach is bright with a full moon. Little crabs like spiders dance a few feet from his eyes, wondering whether he is dead enough to eat. So does he. Not until the bravest scuttles close and brushes his ear does he move. He rolls fast and crushes it with his fist, then crazed with rage and disgust, spins and pounds three more into twitching pulp before the others scatter.

Weaving and stumbling like a boxer in his last rounds, he staggers to the water and, kneeling in the surf, rinses shell fragments and guts from his hands. Then he vomits gallons of seawater back into its source. Only then does he remember. He walks into the water until it has risen to his waist and splashes his chest and face. When he can stand the cold no longer, he walks back onto the shore and towards the rocks where his clothes and weapons wait.

He will do as his mother told him.

THE FLOWER
OF THE
HOUSE OF ATREUS

The lords of Achaea await Agamemnon's pleasure. Agamemnon has developed a way of keeping them waiting. They stand outside his tent in the midmorning sun.

Diomedes turns to Odysseus. He is a full head taller than the Ithacan. He loves Agamemnon, but only because he loves war, and Agamemnon has given him a long one. "You'd think a man his age would be worn out by now," he says.

"Pardon?" says Odysseus. He knows exactly what Diomedes means.

"Man's over forty and he's had that little piece working him over for a couple of days now. You'd think this morning at least he'd say, 'Hey, wait till lunch, sweetheart.'" He laughs and shakes his head. "Seen her?"

"Only from a distance. Pretty enough."

"Pretty? I'll say. And if she's still getting juice out of that old bull, she must know a couple of things they don't teach 'em back in Mycenae— whoops, here he is."

His last words are almost drowned out by the discordant blast of horns. Agamemnon swaggers out, resplendent in a fresh robe of Tyrian purple embroidered with white flowers. His redheaded brother, just a notch less grand, is a respectful half step behind. Always a half step behind. As Odysseus watches, he realizes that it can't be easy being Menelaus. It shows in his face, heavy and immobile as an actor's mask, enlivened only by eyes that burn with hatred. The younger brother, old husband of a beautiful young wife stolen by a beautiful young man, turning to big brother for help. Then, for nine years, waking up every morning to realize that you are where you are because someone else is fucking your wife, and your friends are dying every day because of it. No, not easy at all.

The brothers walk forward. Years ago, Agamemnon would have mingled with his boys, clapped shoulders, joked. Now, he looks neither right nor left but somewhere in the middle distance. Menelaus tries to do the same but cannot. He knows that if he fails to meet eyes and nod it will be thought he does so for shame.

Agamemnon stops. Still the half pace behind, Menelaus does as well. The Achaean lords, not as well trained as Menelaus but still respectful, form a half circle around him. Their chatter drops to a muted buzz. Agamemnon draws himself up like a bad actor. "Allies," he says. "Friends, brothers. Last night Lord Achilles sent an envoy to my brother. He did not come himself. Judge from his message whether he should have, whether propriety and respect demanded it. But his message was this: despite his oath, despite the sacrifices of those who have gone down to Hades here before the walls of Troy, despite the great wrong done us, he will have no more of war." Odysseus doubts that that is exactly how Achilles put it. "We must fight on without Achilles."

A slave on his right steps forward with a wine bowl. Agamemnon raises it, and just as he is about to swallow, a voice from the assembled lords speaks. "Thirsty, king? Hot work this morning?"

The lords erupt in laughter.

Agamemnon shouts: "Who said that? Who said that?" Spilled wine covers the front of his purple robe, a fortunate choice of color. The Achaean kinglets laugh louder; even Menelaus seems about to smile.

Odysseus knows it is time to act. He steps forward, halfway into the dead space between Agamemnon and his laughing vassals. "Shut up! *Shut the fuck up!*"

The laughter dies fast, but not fast enough for Odysseus. "I said shut up!" He draws his sword. "Does someone want to die right now instead of next week? Because next week we're all dead men!" Sword exposed but threatening no one in particular, he faces the circle. "Don't get it? What, confused? Listen, boys, our wives may be widows right now. Just keep laughing at your king."

The last snort and chuckle has already died; he has their attention. "Listen, we were outnumbered five to one when we got here, right? And we've lost a lot of good men in nine years, right? And we're still alive, and we've still sacked their allied towns, and we've kept them bottled up all this time, right? And why is that? Because we're *Achaean!* Because we're an Achaean *army!* Because we're led by an Achaean *king!* And the minute we forget we're Achaean, or forget we're an army, or forget we've got an Achaean king, we're dead! Right?" He stares at the half circle of warrior kings. They shuffle and look anywhere but at him. *"Right?"*

First Locrian Ajax responds: "Uh...right."

Then Telamonian Ajax: "Right."

Nestor: "Right."

Idomeneus: "Right. Right!"

Odysseus hears the mutter gathering strength, but not nearly enough. "I can't hear you!"

A ragged chorus replies: "Right!"

"I still can't hear you!"

"Right!"

"I still can't hear you!"

"Right!" It is a full-throated chorus now. The lords are grinning, shaking their fists in the air.

Odysseus grins back. "So Achaeans, listen to your Achaean king!" He turns to Agamemnon and bows. He pretends not to notice that the king's lip quivers and his hands shake. "Lord, you were speaking, I think," he says. He sheaths his sword and backs slowly into the ring.

Agamemnon has recovered. "If an Achaean army is nothing without an Achaean king, an Achaean king is nothing without an Achaean army!" He raises his arms wide and then elevates his fists to heaven. The lords roar. Agamemnon raises himself up on the balls of his feet. "And if an Achaean king is nothing without an Achaean army, an Achaean army is nothing without its Achaean lords!" The nobles' roar is like a tidal wave crashing on a beach. "And so, lords, if you are nothing without me, I am nothing without you! We are one! Together! Invincible!"

Odysseus, back in the big half circle of little kings, can barely believe what he sees. Grown men, lords of thousands, men who made their first kills before their beards sprouted, weep and embrace. Odysseus backs away from Eurepylus as he staggers forward sobbing, snot soaking his beard, but cannot avoid his bear hug. "Athena speaks through you again, Odysseus," he whispers in his ear. "I saw her standing just above your shoulder when you spoke."

Odysseus hugs back, though it makes him queasy. "Oh," he says.

The lords are starting a war chant. Grinning, Agamemnon makes patting motions with his hands, asking for silence. Finally, he gets it. "Thank you. Thank you. This war has been hard. And I will tell you a thing that you already know: without Achilles it will be harder." Reminded of their loss, the lords groan. Agamemnon, now in his stride, half grins and cocks his head—he even raises a finger. "Harder for him when we divide Troy's gold and women and boys!"

Another roar. Odysseus is fascinated: they are like children. When he thinks of children, he thinks of his own Telemachus and hopes he is not this stupid.

Agamemnon waits for the roar to subside. "I know you have asked yourselves why I took Briseis, why I caused this trouble." A groan, a few shouts of "No, no." Agamemnon laughs and shakes his head. "No, you have. You would not be men if you had not. I will tell you: *it was not my will but the gods'.*"

Silence. Some of the lords fix their eyes on heaven and hold out their hands in supplication.

Agamemnon speaks again. "Three nights ago the Lord of Lightning came to me in my sleep." The lords murmur; more look skyward. "He came to me not in disguise as a speaking bull or my father, but as himself, King of Olympus, seated on clouds, thunder in his hands." Odysseus wonders briefly how you can hold a sound, but lets the thought go. "He spoke to me as his son, a child of the House of Atreus he fathered. 'Great Agamemnon,' he said. His voice was like the lightning. 'Great Agamemnon, dearest grandson. You have sacrificed for those you rule as I sacrifice for those I rule. For do you not think that even I, Olympian Zeus, am thwarted in my desires by the other gods, my children and brothers? Oh, I am.' And he laughed and his laugh was like an earthquake, and I wonder that its noise did not make me wake. But his servant Morpheus kept me

26

in his embrace, so I slept, and he continued to speak. 'But no matter how I sacrifice for those I rule, I must always be he who rules. So when I sacrifice at one moment, I see that I am compensated at the next, for if I did otherwise, I would no longer rule.' "

The lords are silent. Odysseus stares at heaven with the others, not out of reverence but because he knows that if he met Agamemnon's face so strained with piety, he would no longer be able to control himself.

Agamemnon continues: "Brothers, I did not know what he meant. Though I was afraid, I told him so. You know the gods on Olympus, when they speak, speak as they will. Sometimes we do not understand them until it is too late, when we have acted on what we thought they meant and sit in our ruins and only then see what they were saying. But because it concerned not just me but all of you, I risked a question of the Lord of All."

A gasp. A rustle. The lords of Achaea are duly impressed by their king's temerity on their behalf. " 'Father of the gods,' I said, 'how can your sacrifice compare to mine?' At first I feared I would not awaken, that my slaves would find me in the morning with blood running from my eyes and ears and mouth and that you, my brothers, would have to sue for peace with Troy, but Zeus answered me."

A gasp again, this time louder. Words of wonder ripple through the mobbed kings. "No. God respond to man? How he must love Agamemnon. How he must love us." Odysseus, seeing his friends watching him, murmurs and looks heavenward.

"He answered, brothers. 'Great Agamemnon, beloved grandson,' he said. 'I did not send you and yours to Troy because death gives me pleasure. I sent you because the Trojans broke one of the laws I gave the world, and without those laws, the world is a formless void and the men who sacrifice to me are no more than the animals they give. And even though the Trojans have given me many fat oxen, they harbor the one who broke my law of hospitality when he stole his host's wife. And though I love them as I love you, I cannot abide their crime.' "

Odysseus stares at his king. Agamemnon stands rigid; his eyes are fixed straight ahead. His words jerk out of his body in an unaccented rhythm.

"In my dream I was silent and Zeus spoke again. 'And if in the order of the world as I have laid it down there are kings, and those kings make sacrifices for their people, then the order of the world requires that the people make sacrifices for their kings. And so, beloved grandson, if you gave up a woman for your men as I required you to do, then in the order of the world your men must give you back a woman, and that woman must be the best because you are the best. And that woman is Briseis.' My terror forgotten, I spoke. 'Lord,' I said, 'how can I take her? She is Achilles' prize. Achilles, son of your daughter, and I would shame him.' And Zeus forgave my outrage of asking him a question and answered. 'Greater shame to you, grandson, if you did not take her. And because you are a king, part of my order in the world, greater shame to me. So if you do not take her, you shame me. And if I am shamed by the Achaeans, I must forgive the Trojans' crime.'

"Even if I had wanted to speak then, I did not have the manhood. Great Zeus reached forward and touched my face and I slept without more dreams. I awoke and took the woman Briseis, and the rest you know." He stands rigid for another instant before the god leaves him. Then he jerks, sags, rolls his eyes; his hand crosses his face and he looks confused as if thinking, *What am I doing here? Who are these men?* Then Agamemnon is king again. "That, my lords, is how it was. That is why I took the woman Briseis. That is why we are where we are."

The Achaean lords stand in uncommon silence. For a moment, Odysseus wonders what to believe. Then he remembers that when the gods speak to his friends, they usually tell them what they want to hear. He is careful to hide his smile.

The silence persists. Odysseus inclines his head to the right and steals a glance out of the corner of his eye. Locrian Ajax is weeping openly, but without sound. Other lords have their hands outstretched, palms open, lips moving in prayer. Odysseus risks an open twitch of his lips: Agamemnon is doing all right.

"And so, my lords," says Agamemnon, "that is how it is. Now what shall we do? Shall we leave Troy unraped because godlike Achilles will sit this one out? Shall we go home and tell widows and orphans, 'Oh, your husbands and fathers fought like lions and died heroes, but when one of our number sulked, we counted his loss greater than yours'? That we ran like puppies when we had no Achilles to save us? Is that what we should tell the widows?"

Still silence, more than silence: the absence of sound, like the surf receding before a tidal wave. The answer is shrieked, full throated, by all voices at once. "NO!"

Agamemnon has them and he knows it. "Shall we tell the orphans that their fathers lie at Troy and they live in poverty because we were afraid to avenge them without Achilles?"

"*No!*" Odysseus surprises himself by adding his own voice to the chorus.

Agamemnon flings his arm in the direction of the walled city invisible behind his tent. "Shall we leave that untaken because we are afraid?"

"No!" shriek some. "Never, never!" say others. "Troy today!" others still. And one voice, louder than the others, pounds like a gong, over and over, "Fuck Achilles, anyway!"

Agamemnon, delighted, laughs. He picks up the words from his lords and threads them together in a dactyl. He chants: "Never, never, Troy today, fuck Achilles, anyway." He repeats it. "Never, never, Troy today, fuck Achilles, anyway." He pumps his fist up and down in rhythm to his words.

The lords pick it up. "Never, never, Troy today, fuck Achilles, anyway!" Their fists pump up and down in time with Agamemnon's. They sway in cadence. Arms are thrown around shoulders and they begin to circle in a ring dance. Then Agamemnon runs to the head of the half circle and leads them into a line: each man's hands on the shoulders of the man ahead, all prancing in an awkward step. "Never, never, Troy today, fuck Achilles, anyway." Agamemnon leads his lords around his tent three times and then breaks away to resume his place in the center. The little kings laugh and pound each other on the back. "So, lords," says Agamemnon. "Are you with me?'

"Yes!" they bellow.

Agamemnon looks to Odysseus, winks broadly, and raises a cupped hand to his ear.

"*Yes!*" Odysseus has never heard men raise their voices like this before without spears in hand and Charon just around the corner.

Agamemnon smiles. "Then, lords, tomorrow we will talk about what we do, but now you are thirsty. Drink my wine today, and tomorrow we will talk about Troy." He raises both arms to their cheers. He drops them, spins, and walks fast towards his tent, Menelaus a half step behind.

Diomedes' big hand drops onto Odysseus' shoulder. "Hey," he says. "Thanks."

The impact nearly makes Odysseus drop the wine bowl Agamemnon's slave is filling for the third time. "You're welcome," says Odysseus. "For what?"

"For saving my big dumb ass, that's what. When I shot off my big dumb mouth. If you hadn't grabbed the stage an hour ago when I made my big dumb joke, I'd still be kissing Agamemnon's ass in Hades. He was looking right at me."

"Oh," says Odysseus, raising the bowl to his lips. "Was that you? I didn't know."

Diomedes snorts. "Fuck you didn't, but thanks. And listen, I know who my friends are and I don't forget." The big hand drops on his shoulder again. Just as Odysseus begins to dread the teary bear hug that his comrades can't seem to live without, one of Agamemnon's squires bursts into view.

Achilles and Patroclus sit on ox-hide stools on their little eminence half a mile from Agamemnon's tent. They have seen the lords gather, they have heard their cheers, they have watched their dance. They have not spoken. Achilles because he will not, Patroclus because he knows he should not.

At last, Achilles breaks the silence. "They'll be sorry."

Patroclus nods. It is the safest thing to do.

The spy has just left. Priam stands on the Scaean rampart with his two big boys, pretty Paris and strong Hector. He is very old. He does not want to die with Troy besieged, not knowing what the future holds for his sons. Less still does he want to die on the end of an Achaean spear, certain that his sons are moments dead or minutes away from death. He wants to die on this rampart looking at a beach clean of Achaeans.

Hope makes him speak. "Is it time now?" He is ashamed of the quiver in his voice. Just yesterday it would not have been there.

Paris rubs his chin thoughtfully. If he is to die on an Achaean spear, he doesn't want it to happen tomorrow, or even this week. Next week or the

30

week after will be more than soon enough. "I don't know," he says at last.

Hector can't restrain himself. He spits over the rampart and shoots his brother a look of pure hatred. His father raises a shaking hand as though to stop a boys' fight, and drops it when Hector plants his elbows on the rampart and buries his face in his hands. Hector shakes his head back and forth a few times and speaks to his palms. "I don't believe it," he says. "I don't believe it."

"Believe what?" says Paris, ever the younger brother.

Hector spins and faces brother and father. "'I don't know, I don't know,'" he minces. "You steal that big-titted slut from your host and the gods let you live. You fuck that big-titted slut for ten years and the gods let you live, even though they don't let a thousand men better than you live. Why, I don't know, but I don't question the gods. And now, with the Achaeans at our walls and right on their side, the gods—again, why, I don't know, but it's not up to me to question the gods—take out of the war the one man who can kill *me,* and of course kill you and the thousand better than you, and you rub your chin and think about tonight and tomorrow morning and next week with that big-titted slut, and say, 'I don't know.'" His face is now an inch from Paris'. Priam's hands are up again. His lips tremble as he struggles for words.

Paris tries to face his brother, but he can't. His eyes dart to the side. He looks back and looks away again. "You're right," he says.

"Right? Right how?" Hector's overmuscled chest, cased in crude linen, is pressed against his brother's silk. His hands twitch at his sides. Priam smells fratricide and whimpers, clutching at an arm thick as his own waist.

"Her tits *are* big," says Paris, still afraid to meet his brother's eye.

For a long moment nothing happens, then Hector's laughter erupts. He wraps his brother, now laughing even harder, in big, scarred arms. Priam titters feebly but weeps at the same time with real vigor. He puts either hand on his sons' heads and through his tears thanks the gods for this moment.

Agamemnon looks pleased with himself. After Odysseus has refused a fourth bowl of wine, he waves the slave away. He sits in a chair, one of the few in the camp, carved of olivewood and inlaid with ivory and silver. His brother, of course, stands. Odysseus wonders whether Menelaus can lie down to sleep, or if his rage makes him dream upright.

"So," says Agamemnon, once it is just the three of them. "So. How did I do? Did I pull it off?" He answers his own question. "Of course I did. No small thanks to you, Odysseus. Rough moment there, but you came through. You always do. Don't think it's not appreciated by me and my brother."

Odysseus is startled when Menelaus not only nods, but smiles. "We do," he says. It is perhaps the thousandth time he has spoken in nine years of war.

"Yes," says Agamemnon. He swirls the wine around in his bowl and takes an appreciative swallow. "Good work today. And let's not forget that my great-grandfather Zeus showed his favor yet again by taking me when I spoke of my dream." He shakes his head. "Do you know, Odysseus, when Athena will speak through you?"

Odysseus, not trusting himself to speak for fear the truth will fall from his mouth, just shakes his head.

"No," Agamemnon agrees. "If we knew when the gods would speak, we would be like them, and of course we're not. Oh, well. So do you think I pulled it off? Pardon, that *we* pulled it off?"

Odysseus has had three bowls of uncut wine and knows what his king wants to hear. He knows he cannot tell the king what he really thinks, or Penelope will be a widow soon, and he also knows that if he listens to the wine and speaks as harshly as it commands, the king will never hear him again. "Lord," he says. "You spoke well, I congratulate you. I congratulate you for having been visited by the Thunderer. And I know the other lords will stand by your side whatever happens, just as I will, for you are our king by right and by your virtues, and by the blessing of your great-grand-father whom we heard today. We will follow you to death."

Agamemnon's chest swells as Odysseus speaks. He straightens in his chair and assumes a regal demeanor, like an Egyptian statue of a god-king with a forked beard halfway to its waist. His eyes fix on the middle distance and his chin lifts ever so slightly: the very model of royalty. Odysseus knows that he will laugh if he looks directly at him, so he shifts his gaze to Menelaus. "But lord," he says, eyes still fixed on Menelaus, "if we follow you to death, the way things look, that takes us to next week."

Menelaus understands. He surprises Odysseus with another smile.

Agamemnon, lost in his dream of divine right, takes a little longer. "What?"

"I mean just what I said: we are in trouble. With Achilles out of the war, the Trojans could roll us up like a cheap carpet."

Agamemnon's face floods with blood as his anger rises, then pales as the words sink in. "How can you say that? Achilles is just one man! The Myrmidons aren't even one in twenty of our men! And didn't you just say, Lord Odysseus, that you and the other lords will follow me to the death?"

"I did," says Odysseus. He is pleased that the king has been shocked out of complacency.

"So how does that get us to death next week?"

"Perhaps not next week, lord, but certainly next month. And above all else, forget taking Troy any time soon. First, let's concentrate on staying alive."

Agamemnon's mouth gapes and snaps shut like a fresh-caught mullet dropped onto the deck. Odysseus meets his bulging eye and waits until he has recovered himself. "Lord, you say the Myrmidons are but a twentieth of our men. Actually, they're a bit more. But still, we were only ten thousand against fifty thousand when we arrived here fresh and young. And now we are many fewer, and those who survived are older, and each of us who lived to grow old bears wounds from the Trojans as well as time. Are you, lord, the man you were when you snatched me from Ithaca? No? Nor am I. Have you ever counted our men? No? I have. Even with the new boys who come here with the ships bringing wine and arms, we are less than eight thousand, and many of us veterans—old and wounded. So losing one-twentieth of our number against a walled city that was five times our strength when we were fools enough to land hurts. It hurts a lot. When you have a big belly, a week's fast means nothing; when your navel presses your backbone, missing breakfast means death.

"But forget the loss of men and the number of men. Think instead of the minds and hearts of men. Sure, the lords are with you. We know Achilles for what he is: a spoiled boy grown up to be a spoiled man. If he were my son, I would have whipped the piss out of him before he grew his first beard. But the men think of him as a god—not the great-grandson of gods, but a god—and they already know he's out of it. And without their godlike Achilles in armor made by gods, these boys will start thinking, 'What's the use?' And they'll stand for the first Trojan rush, and the third, and the fifth, because they're good boys, but when the seventh or ninth comes, and they've seen their best friends split open from balls to breastbone dying whimpering in a pile of their own bowels, they'll think about home. And when men think about home, when their backs are to the sea and they know the enemy will come again, that's when the ships look good. And when the Trojans see men in panic knocking out the chocks and trying to find oars and uncasing sails we packed ten years ago, they will come with everything they have and we will all be dead men."

Odysseus thinks he has said enough, for the moment. Beads of sweat decorate Agamemnon's brow just below his laurel crown. Menelaus' face has resumed its usual rigidity, though perhaps just one degree harder as its owner contemplates death without revenge. The silence persists. The beads of sweat under the laurel crown become trickles. Agamemnon shifts in his beautiful chair. His robe seems too heavy for him; he plucks at it and fidgets. His breathing grows ragged and his eyes fixed. He cocks his head like a dog listening to its master's voice, one only he can hear. At last he speaks in the rhythmless voice with which he recounted his dream: "What can we do?"

"Don't worry," says Odysseus. "I have a plan."

It is past twilight but not quite night. They have left the shade of the ship in which they spent the day. No longer needing shade but still in search of comfort, they have built a fire against the sudden cold of the Illyrian night.

"Some party the big guy had," says Polycrates.

Oiling his shield strap, Cephales grunts. "He's entitled. He's the king."

"Right," says Polycrates. "He's the king. Bet he'll be on his nice big king's ship headed back to Argos when the dogs are eating the balls off our dead asses in front of the Scaean Gate." He spits.

Lacademon laughs. "Don't worry, junior, the Trojans let soldiers burn their dead. Anyway, when did anyone have balls on his ass? Mine are pretty much under my dick. Where you from, Crete or something?"

All three laugh, Polycrates loudest.

Paris is asleep, and well he should be. She has outdone herself tonight. Just before she lost herself as she rode him, she saw her own shadow on the garlanded wall, cast by the dozen flickering lamps she had lit so her husband could see what he was doing. Or what she was doing. Just as both their backs arched, for a moment, she could see her shadow twinned. Behind her was Aphrodite, her hands on Helen's shoulders, pushing her down to take Paris' hungry thrust, her own pelvis thrusting into Helen's buttocks to force her forward on his grinding hips. She felt nipples hard as spear points jammed into her back, and forgetting herself, glanced over her shoulder to face the goddess who had driven her since before she first bled. And saw nothing.

She stands by the side of the bed and pulls the robe his mother embroidered around her. Doing so, she smiles; how that woman hates her! She looks at her husband. Flat on his back, arms spread, legs crossed—his mouth is wide open and the snore echoes. His shoulders are broad, his hips narrow; the snake of which he is so proud limp and exhausted against his thigh. Even with all those muscle and long limbs and golden hair and big cock, he still looks just like a little boy.

They all do when they're asleep, even Menelaus with his funny Spartan beard and thick muscles and scars and misbehaving midget penis. When he slept his face relaxed and all the anger went away and he looked like the boy his mother must have suckled. Thinking of Menelaus, she smiles. Whatever else she has taken, she has given him something: someone to hate, someone to soak up all that rage. Perhaps when he sees her dead body, he will forgive the gods for making him the younger son. Perhaps he will forgive himself for having taken a thirteen-year-old to his bed and finding, when after weeks he was finally able to fuck her, that someone else had been there first.

Thinking of what will happen, she shudders. She draws Hecuba's robe close around her. She stares at her shadow on the wall. Just hers, not the twin. Thinking still of what is to come or what may come, she holds out her hands, palms upward. "Aphrodite," she says to herself. "Please tell me what will happen. I won't tell. Just tell me. Just me. Just so I know when to kill myself."

Helen squints at her shadow. A little blurring, maybe? Another figure behind her? The goddess refuses to appear. Of course. She is a presence only at the worst of times: when her eyes meet a man's or drift to his cock.

Then she is a sudden heat drifting down from Helen's navel and growing in wetness between her legs. She makes herself seen only in shadow behind her, hands on her shoulders or coiled in her hair, fucking Helen as Helen fucks.

There have been a few times Helen has seen her face; perhaps now is one of them. Her husband is still snoring, dead to the world. She picks up a hand mirror, polished silver in an ivory frame, opens her robe, and sits, legs spread. Murmuring a prayer to her goddess, she runs nails down her thigh. Her heart beats faster and blood courses to her sex. She cups her left breast and pinches a nipple already hard. She holds the mirror between her legs. Her southern lips, still wet from her husband's seed, swell immediately as they have always done, no matter how many times she has commanded otherwise, no matter how many times she has thought of beating them into submission before they rule her again. Her lower mouth gapes toothless in the middle of her woman's golden beard, and she touches herself. Men call it silky but to her it feels like finest lamb's wool. Men say what they will say.

She raises the mirror and sees her own face: lips puffy, pupils broad as saucers, nostrils wide. She knows this is how men have seen her and she hates it, but this is the only way she can reach the goddess. As her right hand works, the mirror shakes in her left. She stares at her face, slackening and tightening as she gets closer, and as she reaches the edge, she whispers another prayer. "It's just me. Please."

A flash. Another face in the mirror, a voice in her head. NOT NOW. SOON. I WILL TELL YOU WHEN IT'S TIME TO DIE.

WHAT SHALL WE TELL THE TROJANS?

Though still morning, it is already hot. The three veterans are again in the shade. Polycrates has just come back from the Myrmidons' camp and is drenched with sweat. "No shit," he says. "They're having a fucking Olympics over there. Javelins, discus, horse races, foot races, wrestling." He laughs. "Wine's flowing, too. They gave me a couple of blasts after I beat one of their boys in a sprint."

Cephales ignores his worrisome shield strap. "Guess they don't have much else to do."

"Guess not," says Polycrates. "But shit, what are we doing? Just sitting on our asses while the big boys hoot and holler and dance and tell each other how rich they'll be once we take Troy?"

"Right" says Lacademon. "Except we have to worry about fighting, and the Myrmidons don't. At least as long as the boy wonder wants to sit it out."

Polycrates is about to speak again when Sinon, one of Diomedes' commanders, arrives. Though he is old, he is not very good and will never rise higher unless everyone better is killed. He carries in his arms a bundle

37

wrapped in burlap and tied with twine. It looks heavy and clanks as Sinon walks. Cephales wonders whether it is a bunch of short swords.

Sinon stops and drops the bundle in front of them. A wooden handle sticks out of loose cloth. No, not swords. "What is this, boys, a circle jerk?" says Sinon. "Nice. Figured I'd find you assholes in the shade. Brought you a present." He grins. "Come on, open it."

Polycrates breaks the twine and the bundle falls open. Shovels.

"What the fuck is this?" asks Polycrates.

"Shovels," says Sinon.

"I know that," says Polycrates. "What for?"

"What the fuck do you think they're for? Oh, wait. Sorry. I forget, you're from Macedonia or someplace like that, where they haven't discovered fire yet, right? Well, listen, bright eyes, when this fucking war is over and you're back in the cave with the tribe, you can say, 'Look what I brought back, it's for *digging*.' Hey, you'll be a hero. Any luck you'll be able to get them to stop hanging out of trees by their tails right after that." He snorts. "Listen, you get confused, ask one of your philosopher buddies here."

"So," says Cephales. "Why are we supposed to be digging?"

"Because Lord Odysseus told the king we'd fucking better be thinking about what happens if the Trojans hit us while our best troops are smearing oil on each other and reading love poems. So the king says we're going to have a nice wall around the ships, and in front of the wall a nice ditch with stakes in it. And Lord Diomedes is in charge of the ditch, and I said I knew the men for the job. Pick 'em up and move out."

The men don't move. Polycrates speaks. "That's slave work," he says slowly.

Sinon claps a hand to his forehead in exaggerated consternation. "You are *so* right! I am *so* sorry! But you know what? We forgot to bring slaves. Sure, we picked up plenty of women and kids and whatnot when we sacked their towns, but we kind of killed everyone who could hold a spear, which means everyone who could hold a shovel. So, tell you what, you just trot over to King Priam, he's a good guy, and ask him if we can borrow a couple hundred big bull workers for a day or so. And just ask him if he'd hold off on attacking until we're all done. And give Hector a big, wet kiss for me while you're over there."

Still, the men don't move. Sinon sighs. This is an army, but it is an Achaean army. "Listen," he says, "does everyone think he's fucking

38

Achilles? Just cuddle up with the boyfriend and let the other dumb fucks do the work and get killed? Do you assholes think the fucking ditch is going to dig itself? Or that Olympian Zeus is going to dig it for us? Why don't we all just put on all our armor and walk right into the fucking sea and get it over with?"

Cephales stands. "Right," he says. He bends over the shovels and hands one to Lacademon, who slowly takes it, and more slowly still gets to his feet.

Polycrates stares in disgust at the offered shovel. He does not move. "Take it," says Cephales. Still, Polycrates does not move. "Take it or you're as big an asshole as Achilles."

Polycrates is silent for a second, then he grunts and gets to his feet, reaching for the shovel as though he's found it in a dung heap. "Right," he says. He turns to Sinon. "Where do we dig, chief?"

Sinon does not smile. He is not so bad after all.

"This is good," says Hector. "This is very good."

They stand at the top of the wall, facing their distant enemy. The Achaean camp is alive with movement, visible even here.

Paris nods solemnly, his face set in what he hopes are soldierly lines. Eventually, his desire to understand overpowers his wish to appear to. "Um...why?"

Hector laughs sourly. "Let me explain, little brother. First of all, this is an easy thing to do, and a thing that makes sense to do. But in the nine years they've been here, they haven't done it, because up until today, they thought they didn't have to. Today they do. So we know that today is the day they're more scared than they've ever been, which is the first good news.

"We know why they're scared: they're scared because Achilles is sitting it out. We all assumed that he'd get over it once he screwed Patroclus stupid, or does whatever he has to do to get it out of his system. But it looks to me like whoever decided to put up that wall knows Achilles is out of it for a long time, and their information is a lot better than ours. So I guess that wall tells us we can write off Achilles for good."

Paris is silent. He does not know whether his brother is right. He hates admitting that he can't think this way. No god speaks to him, at least not

39

about anything that matters. So he keeps his peace and frowns as though he's weighing it all, when all he thinks about is whether this means that he can have another night, or another week of nights, with Helen.

Priam speaks. "So the time truly is now," he says. "When they are weak and afraid and the wall isn't finished."

Hector snorts. "No rush," he says.

Paris almost breaks into a grin, but stops himself.

"They'll stay weak and afraid for a while," Hector continues. "Maybe a long while. And let them finish the wall. It's a piece of shit, anyway. Rush job. Someone over there, Odysseus probably, figured out that we'd heard about Achilles by now and that we'd strike. So he's just covering against a surprise attack. No, let's sit tight a little while and do something they don't expect."

"Like what?" asks Paris. He is a little giddy. As long as his brother doesn't propose a two-man commando raid with himself as spear-carrier it looks as though he's won some time.

Hector does not respond. He turns to the rampart and rests his elbows on the battlement. Priam and Paris have only Hector's back to consider. At length, they approach, one to either side. Hector acknowledges neither. He simply stares at the Achaean camp three miles distant, now ringed with half-raised walls. Occasionally, a shift of the wind carries sound from the ships: an ax striking wood, metal striking metal, once a shouted curse. Finally, he speaks. "Tired of this war yet, brother?" His voice is low.

Paris laughs. "Shit, are you kidding? Of course I'm tired of this war! Who isn't?"

Hector's smile could curdle milk. "Well, I don't mind it, but I don't think it's the best thing for Troy. Let me ask you something: would you stop this war today if you could? If you could see the Achaeans sail away in a month and look around and see your family and friends and say, 'Well, at least they won't die with bronze in their guts?' would you do that?"

Paris is getting a little nervous. That two-man commando raid is starting to sound like a real possibility. "Of course," he says as manfully as he can.

"Then give up Helen."

Hector has turned to face him. Paris can't believe what he sees. He had expected a wide grin at this uncharacteristic joke, a wink of merriment to break the tension of war and fraternal hatred. Instead, he is looking at a face hard and expressionless as a turtle's. Still, Paris laughs, hoping to

40

provoke a response in kind. "Ha, ha, brother," Hector would say, clapping him on the shoulder. "Got you good there."

Nothing. Hector's face doesn't change. Paris peers around him to his father, who looks anywhere but at him.

☙

"A truce? A *truce*? You've got to be shitting me." Telamonian Ajax starts to laugh but sees Agamemnon's face and stops himself. "What the fuck for?"

Agamemnon is in his olivewood chair, the only man seated. His brother stands behind him, half a dozen lords stand before him. He likes being the only man allowed to sit. "As I told you," he says slowly, "to consider their peace proposal."

Diomedes has even less self-control than Telamonian Ajax. Or perhaps not, perhaps he just loves war more. He snorts and spits, turning his head just enough to hit sandy soil rather than the carpet under Agamemnon's beautiful chair. "Fuck that," he says. "We've been here nine fucking years and they want a *deal*? What's the deal? They watch while we fuck their daughters and then we watch while they jump into their own pyres? Sounds okay to me. Nothing less."

Odysseus does not speak, nor will he while this plays out.

Agamemnon raises a majestic hand. "Please. I'm just trying to tell you what they propose. First, a truce while we talk."

Nestor is far too old to be here in the first place. He can no longer fight, but remembers the days when he could. "King," he says, "your grandfather knew the honor in talking. 'Talk,' he said, 'to your enemy when he is the slave cleaning the shit from your worst horse's stall. Talk to your enemy when he is dead and he can't answer you. Talk about your enemy to his daughter when you fuck her in your kitchen while your wife is asleep.' That is what your grandfather said about talking to the enemy."

"The king's grandfather talked a lot," says Odysseus.

The lords laugh. Nestor sputters and starts to speak again, but the lords laugh harder and he stops. He glares at Odysseus. He would kill him if he could. He can't. Thus he falls into furious silence.

"Anyway," says Agamemnon. "They have transmitted a proposal. Not all we could wish for, but a proposal. They will give back Helen's dowry."

Odysseus came to the tent wondering whether Menelaus knew the

41

terms. He sees his face and knows he did not. The man convulses as though he has taken an arrow in the throat; he gargles and clutches the back of his brother's chair, wild eyes darting from lord to lord, imploring, *No, you can't think of this.*

Agamemnon, knowing the commotion his words will cause behind him, plows on. "Not just the dowry, my lords, but much more besides. Treasure from Paris. All he has, or says he has. Treasure from Priam, too. Reparation for all we have suffered for having to come here. Or so they say."

As he speaks, Menelaus has left his place behind the chair. He stumbles as he walks. He knows he cannot leave his brother's side to stand with the lords, for he has always stood apart from them at his brother's back. Abandoned now by Agamemnon, he must stand by the door by himself.

The lords are silent for a moment. Then they erupt.

Nestor: "Fuck that!"

Diomedes: "Do they want to fuck my wife, too?"

Telamonian Ajax: "Nine fucking years and that's it?"

Locrian Ajax: "War isn't about gold!"

But Idomeneus, over and over, until the other lords fall silent and begin to listen: "How much? I said, *how much?*"

Still, Odysseus does not speak. He watches Menelaus who has by now fallen to his knees sobbing. "No, *no,* NO!" He drops to his belly and crawls forward into the lords' circle, and throws his arms around Diomedes' knees. "Don't do this to me. Please. *Please.*"

Agamemnon stares, horrified. "Get up. Brother, get up. I said, *get up.*" Menelaus does not move; he clings to Diomedes' knees, weeping like a brokenhearted child. Diomedes stares at his king while patting and rubbing Menelaus' shoulders, looking like a father with his first newborn, wondering what to do next. "Brother, get up!" Menelaus buries his face deeper and sobs harder.

Agamemnon looks to his lords. They will not meet his eye. They study their sandals, each other's sandals, the sandals of the slaves at the door. Menelaus' tears stop only for occasional hiccups. Agamemnon sweats. "Brother, I command you, get up!" But Menelaus drops his arms from Diomedes' legs and lies flat, shoulders heaving, legs twitching.

Odysseus wonders what the king will do. He has wondered since before he entered the tent, since he saw that something like this would have to happen. He thought he knew, but the king surprises him.

Agamemnon abandons his beautiful chair. He walks the four steps to where his brother lies and drops to one knee. He touches Menelaus' shoulder, rubs his back, croons in his ear—words the lords cannot hear. Soon Menelaus is silent. After a moment, he curls to his knees again and stands. He will not look at the lords, instead looks to his brother. His brother wraps his arms around him and they embrace for a long time. More words are spoken, each to each, that the lords cannot hear. When the brothers release each other, Menelaus returns to his place behind the chair and Agamemnon sits again.

"Well," he says. "Of course we're not taking it." He meets each lord's eye. "Of course. You knew that. We're here for Troy."

The lords roar, Idomeneus loudest of all.

"But I must tell you, my lords," says Agamemnon once the noise has subsided. "There is another part to their offer: if we don't accept the first part, they ask that we settle this once and for all with a battle between our best men before the two armies. Each side, one champion, winner takes all. And now I must ask your opinions."

The offer has left the lords stunned and murmuring.

First Diomedes: "Ask Odysseus."

Nestor: "I fight. I don't think, I fight. Let the Ithacan ask Athena."

Telamonian Ajax: "Right. Odysseus will know."

Odysseus knew what to say before he came here, but watching his king and his king's brother roll in the dirt has left him shaken. He wonders how much sense speaking sense will make, but he decides he must speak it, anyway.

"My lords," he says. "Brothers. Boys. Don't waste your time thinking about the peace offer. Think instead about the fact that it was made. Think about why it was made. Think about when it was made. When the Trojans made it, what did they know? They knew that Achilles had decided to sit on his godlike ass, that we were so scared that for the first time in this war we built a wall around our ships. And it was then that they asked for peace, that they offered us gold for peace. What does that tell us?

"That we're weaker than we thought. They're no fools; they know that if they offered peace when we were at the walls of Troy we'd know their weakness and we'd want more. Now, in our weakness, they offer generous terms hoping that we'll be happy to take them. So I say, let them come, fuck 'em. We'll live. And we'll live to kill them all and take everything they have.

"The single combat idea? Forget it. Let the bards write it into a story a hundred years from now. This is war: I didn't come here to lose it all because one good man had one bad day. All it says is that they know that our army can beat their army and, given a little more time, *will* beat their army. Otherwise, why would they want to settle it in single combat?"

The lords murmur again. This time, however, in hope confirmed rather than threatened. Even tearstained Menelaus risks a smile and Agamemnon beams ear to ear. "So lords," he says, "you have heard our gray-eyed goddess speak through her favorite son!" He drops forward in his chair, resting forearms on knees. His voice drops as well, a confidential whisper. "Now what, my lords, shall I tell the Trojans?"

AN ARROW
IN THE BALLS

Three soldiers: two lie against their ship, backs pressed against a hull now dry as tinder from more than nine years out of its intended element. Cephales is at work on his strap again. Lacademon just stares at a fire, smaller than usual on an unusually warm night. Neither speaks. Polycrates runs towards them. They have not seen him all day. They do not remember having seen him like this. He runs in a half crouch, his arms outstretched and flapping. Though his knees pump like a sprinter's, it takes him a long time to cover the ground between them, perhaps because every third step takes him backwards or to one side.

He's ten yards away now. The men at the ship still do not speak. They are soldiers; they will do nothing until they have to. Polycrates circles the fire, legs firing like an Olympian, half crouch now exaggerated so that his trunk is parallel to the ground. His arms flap wildly, his lips are pulled back from his teeth, his eyes glare fiercely into the distance, and from his mouth come crazy little shrieks. He orbits the fire three times. A wineskin, nearly full, bounces from his hip. At the end of the third orbit, he tilts back his head and cries out like a rutting fowl. On the fourth orbit, he speaks. "Hey, look at me, boys, I'm an eagle!"

His friends roll their eyes and laugh. Polycrates completes a fifth orbit,

45

crowing as though about to stoop on an unsuspecting wren, and spirals into the side of the ship. Roaring with laughter himself, he doubles over, forearms on thighs. He straightens up, remembers his wineskin, raises it, and holds it an arm's length from his gaping mouth. White wine squirts out: half a pint swallowed, half a pint filtered through beard to drip to thirsty sand.

Then Polycrates remembers his manners. "Want some?" he asks, extending the bag to Cephales. As he reaches for it, Polycrates' eyes light on the shield now left leaning at the ship's side. He grabs its top and raises it one-armed to critical inspection. "Hey, I don't like the look of this *at all*," he says. He takes its sides in both hands and examines the inside, the soldier's side, with exaggerated care. "What the fuck are you thinking about?" he says. "Look at this fucking strap! Do you want to get killed or something?"

All three laugh, Polycrates the hardest. Exhausted, he spins around and flops to the ground next to the fire. "Tell you what, boys," he says. "Best I've felt since I got to this fucking place."

"Where the fuck have you been?" says Cephales. He can't stop himself from nervously checking the strap.

"Where have I been? Oh, I don't know, checking everyone else's shield straps. What the fuck do you think? I've been over at Achilles' camp. Been trying to find out whether what I hear is true. And it is."

From the ship's side, Lacademon, who is neither drunk nor afraid that his shield will let him down, speaks. "Spending a lot of time at Achilles' place," he says. "Auditioning? Want to take over for Patroclus? What happens, someone says, 'Oh, dropped something here in the sand, help me find it,' and there you are all bent over and next thing you know the tip of Achilles' dick is poking out your throat." He pauses to consider. "Know what? Noticed that you don't make a lot of noise when you fart these days, and tell you what, you fart a lot."

All three are laughing so hard that words are an effort. "So," says Polycrates, "if I don't make noise, how do you know it's me?" He flops onto his back and wraps his arms around himself in anticipation.

"Because no one's farts stink like yours."

All three roar. This is how it has been for nine years. This is how it would have been if they had stayed at home: most nights around the fire, drunk, sometimes for a grand finale pissing the flames into sodden, stink-

46

ing dark, and every so often spilling blood in sudden anger. Now, however, the blood is spilled for their king in the name of the gods. So those who live to piss out their fires at home will remember the days when they and their friends righted the balance of a universe gone terribly wrong with one man's theft of another man's wife.

When they recover themselves, Cephales speaks. "So what did you hear?" he says, wiping streaming eyes. "I mean, when Achilles' thighs weren't pressed against your ears?"

At this they all lose themselves again. Polycrates says, "Well, I tried to ask him what was going on, but he couldn't understand *because my mouth was full.*"

At this rate, the sun will be up before they actually talk. Lacademon says, "What's this shit about the truce?"

Polycrates is suddenly grave. "No shit, brother. Truce for sure. Talked to Patroclus' squire. Good-looking boy, by the way, not that you'd be surprised. Anyway, here's what's going to happen: tomorrow the heralds come to the army. They'll say, 'Take off your armor, line up, sit down'—same thing in the Trojan army. So that's what you'll see tomorrow. Heard it here first." He nods solemnly.

His friends regard each other for an instant. Finally, Cephales speaks. "Uh...what the fuck for?"

"What for? What *for?* Why, so we can watch the big guys slaughter a couple lambs and swear oaths and then talk us all back to Argos. With lots of extra gold and women and boys that we didn't have before we came here."

Lacademon asks, "And why should the Trojans do that?"

"Easy, chief. They came to Agamemnon yesterday. They said, 'Hey, give you whatever you want just to go away. Except Helen.' Well, you can imagine how Menelaus and big brother took that. So they said, 'Okay, let's all of us stop killing each other. How about we each pick one man, winner takes all.'

"Well, I gotta tell you, I'm not a big fan of Agamemnon, but he didn't spend a lot of time on that. 'Uh,' he says, 'your best man, I bet that'd be Hector, am I right?' and they say, 'Well, yes.' And he says, 'And I guess you know our best man, Achilles, he's kind of indisposed right now?' And they scratch their heads and look embarrassed and say, 'Well, we heard rumors and whatnot, but no, not until you told us, no.'

47

"So Agamemnon says, 'Oh, you didn't? Well, tell you what: I like this idea. Winner takes all is good. All, by the way, means Helen too, right? Right. But let's make it fair. Instead of Hector versus a stand-in for Achilles, let's leave it to the guys who really have a problem here. Your Paris versus our Menelaus. Deal?'

"And the Trojans piss themselves and say, 'Well, we like this truce and everything, but we have to check with the king and whatnot, so how about we meet tomorrow in front of both armies and make a sacrifice and swear to keep the peace while we're working this out?' And Agamemnon likes that and everybody kisses and hugs, and when the Trojans are out of earshot, Lord Odysseus laughs his ass off."

Cephales is confused. "Why? Don't get it. If Menelaus loses we've come here for nothing."

"You *are* an asshole," says Polycrates. He says it pityingly, so the older man takes no slight. Of course he doesn't mention how many times this had to be explained to him in Achilles' camp. "Paris is one good-looking boy, sure, but fire-eating warrior he's not. Menelaus will kill him on the third throw, if not the first or second. The Trojans know it. So they're stuck. They offered this single-combat deal in the first place, and if they turn down Paris versus Menelaus, they shame Paris, shame Priam, and admit their shame to the gods. Can't. So they can't turn down the deal, and they can't have Paris fight Menelaus, which means they have to give us almost anything we ask, including Helen. That leaves them a little dignity."

The older men sit in silence. They glance at each other once or twice. Cephales nods. "Lord Odysseus is a smart man," he says. "Athena loves him; this is her doing."

"Maybe," says Lacademon. "Maybe. Or maybe one of the gods who hates the Trojans suggested this to them and now he's laughing until he pisses himself—if the divine ones piss at all. Do they? I never thought about that until now. I mean, they don't bleed, why should they piss or shit?"

"Bet they don't fart like me, that's for sure," says Polycrates. He screws up his face with effort and lets loose a rattling burst that makes the fire burn brighter and bluer while his friends laugh and gag.

The rampart over the Scaean Gate is a terrace wide as the wall itself and stepped in three levels. The king and seven elders, bastard half-brothers or the legitimate sons of bastard uncles, sit on the highest level: a chair of rosewood and silver for the king, stools of richness varying with rank for the others. A silk canopy striped purple and white shields the king from a sun already up three hours; slaves hold brightly colored parasols over his aging paladins. Still more slaves wave horsehair flywhisks: it is late spring in the Aegean, and the war has given the maggots much meat in which to breed.

On the step below them are the lesser princes of the blood and greater nobles, noncombatants by virtue of age or infirmity or plausible excuse. Each must do with only one slave. Seeking shade and shelter from the fat stinging flies, they jostle and elbow; from the folds of their silk or linen, gorgeous in primary colors but too heavy for this heat, rise blasts of mingled perfume and sweat.

The third step, the lowest, is reserved for the royal women. Queen Hecuba isn't there; she cannot bring herself to watch this. Pride of place has thus gone to Priam's aunt, ancient at seventy, desiccated and sweetened with myrrh and painted with an impossibly serene regal face like one of the dead god-kings of the Nile that travelers have described. She sits beneath a canopy even thicker and grander than Priam's, a breach of protocol he indulges and even encourages, for it is clear that one kiss of the sun would reduce her to a smoldering pile of bone and ash. Around her are other court women, their robes less rich than the men's on the step above but still beautiful enough to break the heart. The royal women occupy only half of their step. They bunch to one side, leaving room for the woman who is yet to arrive. They will say, if pressed by a man of Priam's family, that it is out of respect for their lovely princess, but among themselves they admit that it is because they fear the whore's contagion.

The low murmur of the princes on the first step, cackle of the lords on the second, and hum of the women on the third all stop when Helen mounts the rampart. She is preceded by a girl whose head is garlanded with wildflowers and accompanied by two noble virgins who hold over her head broad fans of peacock feathers. Even after ten years of monthly public appearances, her presence stuns. Priam, over sixty and weak in vision and the manly sap, still gasps whenever he sees her. They say her face is that of a goddess. Of this Priam is not so sure; his gods are rarely more

49

than voices in his head, and on their rare appearances, he has known not to look on them directly, so the goddesses he has seen are only painted marble or clay, one sculptor's idea of beauty, no more.

But perhaps what they say is right: Helen's beauty cannot be described, and so it is like that of Olympus. But however divine her features, her eye is as knowing as the oldest dockside whore's, and what is below the face has nothing of Olympus. The silk in which she is robed is so fine that she seems naked. However heavy, her round melon breasts jut proud over a flat belly, nipples always crinkling in welcome. As she faces the breeze, the robe blows flat against her muscled loins. Priam can just make out the triangle between them and imagines it just one shade darker than the gold curls piled on her head, and for the first time this year feels the snake stir.

At Priam's right is Xantithap, lord of the household, his father's son by his favorite concubine. He leans forward. "Worth fighting a war for, lord?" he asks, smiling.

Priam nods. "Worth fighting for, yes. Not worth losing for, though. And not worth losing a son for."

At Priam's left is Zeritherem, chief priest, his father's brother's son. "Then don't speak too loud, lord," he says. "Each of us has lost a son for her, and each man below us has lost two."

Priam starts as if slapped. His mouth moves but he cannot speak. He thinks of his big boy Hector and the glory he has won defending the family. He thinks of Paris lying with the girl and what it must be like. The snake stirs again in its sleep. "I am the king, Zeritherem," he says. "The king's words are always heard." He allows himself a half smile. He has spoken without saying anything; that, he has found, is when the king speaks loudest.

Polycrates' eyes might have been carved from beets. He sits in the sand with his knees drawn up, arms folded, head resting on his arms. "Sure hope I don't puke again," he says.

"Should've thought of that when you were draining that wineskin instead of sharing with us," says Lacademon.

"Hey, I offered . . . urrr. Sorry." Polycrates turns his head to the left and retches like a dog. His shoulders shake for minutes. He turns back and

50

wipes bile from his beard with his forearm. "Uh...got something wet?" His friend passes a skin, weak wine cut five to one with sweet water. Polycrates drinks thirstily. "Oh, man. That's better. Thanks, I won't forget this. Whew. Well, what did I tell you, anyway? Here we are. No armor, on our asses. There they are." He waves at the Trojan line three hundred yards away. "And there the big guys are, in the middle." He points at a dozen men resplendent in plumes and silk under a canopy between the lines.

As they watch, two little animals twitch and die under sacramental knives. "One black lamb, one white. Just as I said."

They sit in silence for a moment. Smoke rises from beside the canopy. "Well, I guess the deal is made," says Polycrates. "Pass that skin again, would you?"

Pandarus has never been happy. He is the Trojans' best archer, but he is an archer in a war of chariots and spears. Skill at killing men at a distance is something neither side reveres. The unfairness of it all weighs him down like a second set of armor. The big men treat him decently, but the decency is always alloyed with something close to contempt. It is as though he is a boy who violates the unspoken code of the schoolyard in a fight. "He won, yes, but he *kicked*." Yes, he's killed a lot of men, but always with a bow. Which is all right, sometimes, if you have to, but real men kill face to face.

He has never been happy, but he has always loved Paris. The prince is ten years younger than he. Pandarus was already a soldier, eighteen, when he first saw the golden boy scampering around the royals' pavilion at a sacrifice. His heart fluttered when the king laughed at insolence that would have brought a beating to a boy less beautiful. After that, Pandarus made it a special point to be at every public occasion at which the youth would appear. Each time he saw him, his love deepened and became more carnal, until the dream of Paris came to dominate his nights with his slave boys—to their benefit. While his friends and other men of rank bent their boys over and buggered them screaming, Pandarus anointed his with perfumed oils and was as likely to fill his own mouth with their seed as to plant his in their barren furrows. It got him talked about, but then, what do you expect from an archer?

51

Pandarus has heard the rumors flying through the city. Yesterday, the Trojan lords came back from the Achaean lines with their news: Paris against Menelaus, to the death. Or give up Helen and all the treasure Paris took with her and much more besides—impossible. And if they fight, winner takes all, which Pandarus and every other man who can hold a spear knows means losing Helen, losing the treasure, and losing Paris as well—equally impossible. So today the Trojans sit facing the Achaeans hoping a better deal can be struck. For nine years they have sat within their high walls inviolate from raping Achaeans, but have watched as their tributary towns have fallen, one by one, each loss meaning fewer slaves for their houses and less grain when Troy's own fields blow away in the droughts the gods send whenever too few animals have died under the priests' dull knives. They will not tell each other this in daylight and armor, but at night when the wine flows, they whisper that much more war will kill them. So they are stuck.

Pandarus stands in the second rank, right of center. Last night he thought of the battle between Menelaus and Paris and wept salt tears and took his best boy to his bed. He had even let the slave fall asleep afterwards. Not for long, of course; even if he could fuck his master he was still a slave. So the archer beat him for half an hour, and after the slave crawled out weeping, he returned alone to his bed and wept himself. Squinting through his tears at the fat, dull flame of a single oil lamp, his vision clouded, and from the brightness at the center of the haze came the clear, hard voice of Apollo, who told him what to do.

So Pandarus stands in the second rank, right of center, without his armor like the others, but still with his bow. He is, after all, Pandarus the bowman. From where he stands he can see the fires of sacrifice lit. Soon, twin columns of sooty smoke heavy with animal fat carry their burden of supplication to the gods.

The Trojan lords are trudging back to their ranks. From where he stands, Pandarus thinks their heads are bowed in defeat. The Achaeans stand where they stood, watching the Trojans retreat. At their center is a glorious orchid, Agamemnon; to his right, a little removed from the others, is a squat tree trunk—Menelaus. An easy target, and the time is now.

The men around him stare curiously as Pandarus plants the bottom of his great ibex-horn bow at the outside of his right foot. He braces his right hand at the center of the bow, and with his left forces the top down so that the bow assumes its curve. He slips the string into its notches. No one around him raises the alarm. Not for long, Pandarus knows. He reaches into the quiver behind his back and pulls out a single arrow, one never shot before. It is five feet long, tipped with barbed bronze, fletched with goose quill black as death. He kisses the bronze tip and its razor edges cut his lip. The tastes of salt and iron fill his mouth and he laughs.

No time now. The men around him buzz. He nocks the arrow and raises the bow. As he does, he draws a deep breath and pulls back the arrow until its feathers just graze his ear.

The hideous little tree trunk man who would kill his beloved stands alone. Pandarus holds the bow taut, the disproportionately big muscles on the right side of his back bunched and quivering. Then he knows that it is time to let go, and he does. The fletching draws blood from his cheek, the snapping string thwacks against the leather on his left forearm, and the arrow is on its way. A blow between his shoulder blades knocks him to the ground as soon as the arrow has left his bow. Behind him, Zarithex, an officer of the king's bodyguard, raises his staff to strike again. "What have you *done*?" he screams. "Do you know what you have done?"

Face in the sand, Pandarus smiles. He knows.

There is much Pandarus doesn't know. He doesn't know that there are only twenty million people in his world, not that many more than when all men lived in caves, huddled in furs against the cold breath of glaciers that had begun their retreat just five thousand years before. Though he once saw black men with flat noses and thick lips brought to his king when their ship washed ashore and has heard of yellow men and men with no heads and their faces in their bellies, he thinks the whole world is Trojan and Achaean. And though he does not know that everything that is curves the space around it, he knows enough about gravity to shoot high. And though he does not know that the world is round, he knows enough about the Coriolis force to shoot a little to the left for a target to the right.

Menelaus watches the departing Trojans. Their backs are twenty yards away as he turns to Agamemnon to speak. He blinks; something must be in his eye. Suddenly, he feels a pinch in his groin and curses. An armor strap caught in his kilt, must be. Still looking at his brother, he reaches down to adjust himself and nearly faints with pain as his hand collides with a shaft in his upper thigh. For a second, he stares stupidly at the arrow. It sticks out like the monster erection that he has never quite been able to manage. From where it is buried between plates of fancy king's brother's armor seeps dark red venous blood that has dripped halfway down to his knee.

No one is looking at him. He clears his throat and no one notices. He flutters his hands at his sides. Still, the lords talk to one another around the king, oblivious. He takes a halting step forward and almost falls. "Uh..." he says. Louder. "Uh..." It is the best he can do; he has never been good with words.

Diomedes is facing him, talking to the king. He looks up at Menelaus, and his jaw drops. Wordlessly, he claps his hand to the king's shoulder and spins him around. Agamemnon is still talking as he comes nearly face to face with his brother. "Well," he is saying, voice rich with satisfaction, "not a bad day for us, still—" He falls silent as his eyes follow Diomedes' trembling hand. "Oh, no. Oh Zeus, Father of the World. Oh, *no*." He takes two stumbling steps forward and moves as if to embrace Menelaus, but at the last instant realizes that if he does, he will drive the arrow deeper. "Oh Zeus, Father of Us All." He spins towards the retreating Trojans who, curious and confused, have stopped and face the Achaeans. "You *bastards*!" he screams. "You treacherous, murdering, truce-breaking bastards!"

Even at this distance it is clear that the Trojans know something is wrong. One of them points to Menelaus. Hector stares and takes a step forward. He stops dead and looks back at his own lines. They are only fifty yards from him and he can see the knot of men and hear the raised voices from the right flank, from where the arrow must have come. He faces the Achaeans again and walks slowly forward, hands outstretched, head bowed so that the horsehair plume on his best helmet almost sweeps the ground before him.

Agamemnon skips forward and picks a stone from the sand and throws. It clangs harmlessly from Hector's armor. "Truce-breaking motherfucker!" Agamemnon screams. "I'll burn your house with your filthy kids inside! Your father will eat my horse's shit! My slaves will fuck your wife!"

"Uh," says Menelaus. "I think I'm all right."

Hector has accepted the blow and continues to approach. His humility

54

drives Agamemnon into a frenzy; he tears at his beard and spins to his squire. "Give me a spear! Give me a fucking spear! I'm killing this piece of dog shit now!" He lunges towards his lords who stand frozen with shock. Not at Menelaus' wound, for death slow or sudden holds no capacity to surprise them; rather, they are stunned that a people already guilty of a breach of hospitality would compound their sin with truce breaking.

Odysseus is at Menelaus' side. The king's brother's arm is draped across his shoulder as he bends to examine the wound. "Stop him," growls Odysseus. "In Athena's name, stop him. It's a flesh wound. *Stop him.*"

Agamemnon has taken a javelin from a squire and, still ranting, has planted his right foot for a throw at the advancing Hector. Diomedes places a rough hand on his shoulder. The king overbalances, swears, and struggles to right himself. Diomedes wraps thick arms around him. "He's all right. He's all right," he says. "Don't do it. Athena has spoken."

Agamemnon, trapped in bronze and leather and muscle, thrashes and raves, but more for show than purpose. Odysseus snaps an order to his own squire. "Tell the heralds to get Machaon the physician. And you, get my bodyguard and get them up here fast to cover us. Go." He turns to Ajax. "Can you get him behind us?" The Telamonian slips Menelaus' arm over his own shoulder and starts him back to the rear of the negotiators.

Odysseus steps forward. Behind him are a dozen lords and their servants: fifty men, half unarmed. Dead ahead is Hector, who Odysseus knows could kill him. Behind Hector is the Trojan team, and behind them, the Trojan army—proven liars yet again, ready to break a peace when its sealing sacrifice is still burning on the altar. He takes half a dozen steps towards the now immobile Hector. Head still bowed, the Trojan drops to one knee. "I didn't know," he says. "You have to believe me. It was no doing of mine."

Even on his knees Hector's head nearly reaches Odysseus' shoulder. "I have to believe nothing, Prince Hector," he says. "And I believe nothing from the Trojans. Go while you can." With that he turns on his heel and walks back neither fast nor slow, keeping secret his fear. The muscles below his neck and between the shoulder blades, hidden by his embroidered ceremonial cloak, writhe and tense in anticipation of a spear or arrow from the Trojan lines.

Then he is back with the Achaeans and still alive. The lords murmur and pat his back: that Odysseus, the brightest *and* the bravest. What brains it took to seize the moment when the king was foaming at the mouth. What balls it took to walk out into no man's land alone and call great Hector a liar to his face. Odysseus allows himself a half smile but not a glance back at the Trojans—not now, anyway. His bodyguard is pulling up. Odysseus barks orders and the spearmen deploy to screen the lords while the charioteers crisscross ahead, teasing the Trojan ranks while kicking up enough dust to cover the retreat.

Time to face the king who stands apart, watching as Machaon works. As Odysseus approaches, the physician takes pincers to the stub of the arrow he has already clipped short. He is on his knees before Menelaus, who is held upright and immobile by a lord and two slaves. Glancing upwards, Machaon says, "Sorry about this," and pulls hard. The point does more damage coming out than going in; dark blood spurts in Machaon's face and Menelaus, tough as he is, bolts like a gelded colt. Machaon takes a clean cloth and presses it against the wound. "Look at the bright side," he says. "Two inches to the right and you wouldn't care about getting your wife back." He laughs. Menelaus doesn't.

Odysseus stands beside the king. The king stares at his brother and will not speak. Finally, Odysseus must. He hates this and despite himself shows it. "So," says Odysseus. Still the king will not speak. "So," says Odysseus. "My lord."

Agamemnon's eyes still do not leave the doctor's work, but he speaks. "So," he says. "My Lord Odysseus. A question for you: why did you stop me from killing Hector?"

"A couple of reasons, king. First, you probably couldn't have, forgive me for saying it, but it's true, so what's the point? Second, even if you had, we were cut off from our own lines, nearly unarmed, only a hundred yards from at least one man and probably more who were ready to break the truce to kill us. Third, while no one would have blamed you for killing him after he broke the truce, we look better if we wait a couple of hours, send out a herald to announce the truce broken, and then kill the truce-breaking sons of bitches to the last man. Then there's no doubt as to who's in the right and you'll be remembered when the last bard is dead."

Agamemnon holds onto his anger for another minute still. Odysseus knows it is only for effect, just to remind him who's boss. And it is just for a minute. Then his shoulders sag and he runs a shaking hand across his face. "You're right, of course. Tell me, doesn't your head ever get tired?

Do you ever have thoughts of your own or is it always Gray-eyed Athena talking in there?" When Odysseus opens his mouth to speak, Agamemnon shakes his head. "Never mind. No matter. You and the Gray-eyed One keep your secrets. Now, what do we do?"

Odysseus, relieved of the king's anger and his presumed communion with the divine, speaks quickly. "First, we stay here for a little while so that our boys don't panic. Spread out so we look casual. Next, send runners back to the lines to tell them to put on armor and fall back inside the ditch. Diomedes and Telamonian Ajax go back first to start forming up the defense and then we go back in the chariots. Menelaus around the long way, so that as few as possible see him. Then, as soon as we're ready, send out heralds with as insulting a message as possible and let them bring it on." He pauses. "Oh, for the moment at least, the story has to be that they shot at Menelaus and that's it. Don't tell them that they missed because they'll catch us in a lie. Just don't tell the boys that he was hit. It won't do much good, but as soon as the first Trojan charge is coming, they'll forget about it."

Agamemnon's eyes are childlike. "Are you sure they'll come?'

Odysseus grins. "No choice. They stole your sister-in-law and then broke a truce sealed with sacrifice. If they don't wipe us out to the last man, their shame will never end. And they're not ready." He laughs sourly. "If we live through today, that bastard with the bow just did us the biggest favor we could ask for."

Agamemnon pulls himself together. "Of course."

"Of course," Odysseus says. "Now, my lord, if I may suggest, let's get out of here."

From his new vantage point atop heaving shoulders, Pandarus can see the Trojan lords' return. Not steadily; the men holding him aloft pitch and sway with the chant carrying the Trojan right flank. "Pan-dar-*us*! Pan-dar-*us*!" But he clearly sees great Hector, his beloved's protector and tormentor, abasing himself before an Achaean savage whom he guesses to be Odysseus. His bowels writhe with shame and satisfaction at the same time. As he watches, Hector and the lords turn and limp back, only recovering their arrogance as the lines open to admit them.

Despite Odysseus' best efforts, Pandarus can see what is happening among the Achaean delegation: Menelaus dragged to the rear, a crouching physician, even the gout of black-red blood. And he knows that he has done what he had to.

And so, for once, do the Trojans. After he was knocked into the dust, a ripple ran through the ranks, then laughter, then cheers. Next, Zarithex himself was beaten down, then his teeth battered down his throat with the butt end of a spear. Then Pandarus was lifted to the shoulders of dancing men, his hands kissed, wineskins pressed to his lips and squeezed dry. Whenever the furor seems about to die down, he raises the great ibex-horn bow above his head and shakes it towards heaven. Then the men cheer again and the dancing continues.

As he drains his third wineskin, Pandarus turns to the center and rear of the lines where the royal pavilion stands. He imagines for a moment he can see Paris, tall and slender, turning his lavender-plumed head towards the right flank. He thinks he sees him wave. Weeping, he waves back and drops the great bow as he blows kisses with both hands. He grasps the shoulders of the big man carrying him and squeezes his eyes tight as he strains to catch the words in his head. It is Apollo, the god of archers and plague and Troy. It begins as a whisper, but rises to drown out even the cacophony of his own name on a thousand lips. YOU DID WELL, PANDARUS. NOW ENJOY WHAT YOU HAVE WHILE YOU HAVE IT. Pandarus laughs again with joy. This moment is all he has, and he revels in the promise of what is to come.

He opens his eyes just in time to see the approach of Hector's bodyguard, and the god repeats his last words in a roar so loud that Pandarus is astonished that others do not turn as his skull reverberates with the divine words. Bizimarko, captain of the bodyguard, laughs and raises both fists in exuberant salute as he approaches Pandarus' entourage. "Pandarus the bowman!" he shouts. "Pandarus the great!" At this Pandarus's new friends roar. "Come with us, Pandarus, and tell the royal family how you did what you did! Prince Hector himself commands it!"

Pandarus' bearers laugh and drop him to the ground, where he spins and stumbles dizzy with wine and long elevation. The boys laugh indulgently and clap him on back and shoulders. "Remember me when you're a prince, Pandarus!" shouts one. "Don't forget where you came from, Pandarus!" cries another, holding his own bow aloft. Pandarus laughs and waves and grins at the bodyguard as they close around him. They grin back, forming a tight circle, clapping him on the back even harder than the boys in the ranks. Soon arms snake themselves around his own arms and hold him tight. Pandarus thinks they must be eager to be so close to a hero. Perhaps too eager, for the men on either side have now pressed so close he can barely breathe, though he keeps laughing and shouting to every curious face, "I'm the one! I'm Pandarus, the king-killer!"

The bodyguard has stopped talking to him. They have broken into a slow jog without the grip on his arms relaxing. He stumbles twice and is rudely pulled back to his feet. He has begun to wonder what kind of hero's welcome this is.

As they approach the city walls, he begins to weep again. Any minute now, he'll be face to face with Paris. His tears stop as the bodyguard takes a hard right and picks up speed towards the Scaean Gate. Pandarus is lifted off his feet as they break into a trot. He looks up at the rampart over the gate more than ten yards above him, hoping to catch an admiring eye or even a neutral one as the great bronze-bound oak doors swing wide to admit them. But on the rampart he has no friends. Splendid nobles scowl and look away; one spits, but he has taken too long bringing up his phlegm, and it lands inoffensively behind the hurrying party. At least the commoners and slaves on the mud streets offer a cautious cheer. Pandarus has little time to enjoy it; his keepers dash to an anonymous door in an otherwise blank wall that pops open at their approach.

Pandarus still hopes to be led up rather than down. Somehow, he thinks, that would be a good sign. In this he is disappointed. The narrow stone stair is not wide enough for three abreast. Fast and single file his guards march him into an earthen-floored basement lit by the guttering flame of a single lamp filled with cheap oil, rancid and smoky. He has a second to realize that it is the house of a very minor noble, rich enough to keep only two man-sized jars of grain against inevitable famine, and just one small barrel of wine. Then, for the second time that day, he is knocked face down into the dirt.

At first he stirs and struggles to rise. A booted foot hits the small of his back, a spear butt lands between his shoulder blades, and his mouth fills with dust. He cries out, "But I'm Pandarus! Pandarus the king-killer!"

Bizimarko's laugh is short and harsh. "That's right, buddy. That's why you're here. Now shut up and wait."

59

He has to wait a long time. How long, he cannot be sure; the oil lamp is the only light in the basement. He knows it is a long time because he becomes painfully aware that all that wine has made its way to his bladder. He prays to Apollo, first for deliverance, then for self-restraint. When he can stand it no longer, he says, "Uh...I really have to take a piss."

"Oh?" says Bizimarko. "You're not moving. Orders."

Pandarus prays harder. Apollo remains silent. He tries to distract himself with thoughts of his glory that morning. That makes him think of the wine and the rhythmic bobbing up and down on the soldiers' shoulders. He whimpers and tries to stop himself, but it is too late.

Bizimarko notices the puddle spreading from beneath him. "Nice, king-killer. Piss yourself when you were breaking the fucking truce, too? I'll bet—" He is interrupted by the sound of a door flung open and many feet on stone. He laughs. "Perfect timing, too. Here come the royals. Just keep your head down or I guarantee I'll split it."

The head that Bizimarko threatened now roars with a heart pounding a hundred times a minute and blood singing so loud in his ears that he cannot at first make out voices.

Finally, Hector's bull tones, a bellow even when he tries to whisper, penetrate his hearing. "Pissed himself? Gods above us. Don't blame him. Only thing I don't blame him for."

Pandarus didn't think it possible to be more afraid than he is. He finds he is wrong. He hears a quavering voice, an old man, and his breath stops when he realizes that it is the king. "We can't just kill him," says the thin voice. Pandarus breathes again. "The priests say we should impale him on the walls." Pandarus' heart stops. "And Cassandra says we should burn him alive."

A third voice, not as deep as Hector's and somehow effeminate, interjects, lazy and insolent. "Goes to show," says Paris. "She's never right."

Despite his predicament, Pandarus' heart flutters. He knows enough not to move his head until the royals give him leave, but he can roll his eyes. Before him is a pair of feet: beautiful feet, long and high-arched, encased in the most elegant interpretation possible of a soldier's heavy sandals, the straps tooled leather, the bronze chased with gorgon's heads. With a start, Pandarus sees that the toenails have been painted lavender to match the crest on the helmet, and despite everything, he feels his cock stir in the urine-soaked mud beneath it: it is his beloved, closer than he has ever been, so close that he could lick his perfumed feet.

"Um, say," Paris drawls. "Should we be talking in front of this turd?" A purple-tipped foot lashes out and the painted nails catch Pandarus' cheekbone, drawing blood as the kick drives his head to the right.

Everything inside him breaks and Pandarus sobs so loudly that Hector's laugh can barely be heard. "Why not?" he shouts over Pandarus' tears. "He's a dead man anyway, one way or the other."

Even Bizimarko is bold enough to join in the general amusement. Pandarus' shoulders continue to heave, silently now, as the laughter subsides. Hector's voice is suddenly serious. "We're fresh out of choices, I'm afraid. Thanks to this fool." Another kick, Hector's halfhearted one this time, or Pandarus would have died then and there rather than just losing his breath and then puking up two quarts of wine and bile. "Some god tricked this bastard into breaking our truce, or maybe some god made him break the truce to show us what to do—no difference. We have to hit the Achaeans. Now, today, while they're still disorganized and we still have some kind of chance. If we burn this shit on the walls we admit we were wrong. We can't. We have enough trouble like that already." He pauses. Eventually, Paris clears his throat and audibly shuffles his feet. Hector continues, satisfied. "So we attack. And if we win the gods have shown their favor. And if we don't, well, we don't."

There is the crunch of feet on basement dirt. A second pair of feet enters Pandarus' vision. Big feet: soldier's boots whose only ornament is hard wear and cracked nails without paint. "We're not ready. They're entrenched. It won't be easy," says Hector. "But thanks to the foreign minister here, we can't talk anymore." The big feet shift and Pandarus tenses. A kick to the head from Hector will certainly kill him. "Oh, but that gives us a way to deal with this problem. Guess who's leading the first wave into the ditch without his bow? Dies like a hero or like a sacrificial lamb, and either way, he's dead and so's Troy's shame." Bronze and leather creak. A hand grasps Pandarus' plaited hair and snaps his head to the side. Hector bends and thrusts his face into the archer's. This is the first time Pandarus has seen him close: his features are a caricature of his divine brother's, thick and heavy, split with scars from wounds left unattended. A rough hand grabs Pandarus by the back of his neck. It raises his head and twists so that he is face to face with Hector, who speaks in a blast of garlic and bad teeth and intestinal parasites even worse than the average Trojan noble's: "Welcome to the infantry."

Polycrates has just rejoined his friends. They are falling back and Sinon is a rank or two ahead. "Pick 'em up," Sinon yells. "Show's over, assholes! Now back to the fucking war! Let's move!" The ranks begin to move at a fast walk. A dozen paces away, a trooper throws his sword into the sand and, eyes rolling, strips off his armor. The rank around him gains speed and loses order as he starts to run. His flight is interrupted when Sinon drops him in his tracks with a spear butt to the base of his skull. He swings the limp soldier over his shoulder. "Straighten the fucking line," he snaps.

Polycrates has been running for a lot longer than his friends. As soon as the arrow flew he took off for Achilles' camp. Though it is over a mile away, he was back before the retreat to the ships was fairly begun. "I heard," says Polycrates, panting harder than the others but at least able to talk. "Poor bastard, an arrow in the balls. Lord Zeus and Lady Hera, does it get worse than that?"

"Who?" says Cephales. "*Who* got it in the balls?"

Another soldier, running a little faster than the three, hears the question and answers over his shoulder as he passes. Like any soldier he can answer any question, whether he was asked, whether he knows the answer. "Menelaus, dumbfuck," he shouts, and with a short laugh, picks up the pace and is gone.

"Oh no," says Cephales. "Not Menelaus. Not in the balls."

The three soldiers are part of a larger contingent, one that is now coalescing behind Sinon. For a while they surged and bolted with the vast anxious mass of the army, but now that they are behind their shepherd, they are sheep and fall into a slow trot just faster than a walk, almost placid.

"In the balls," says Lacademon. "The gods do play with us, don't they?" He shakes his head and, still at a slow run, spits to his side and makes a protective gesture from a Minoan mystery cult that neither of his friends knew he honored. His hands fly to anus, genitals, nipples, mouth, eyes, ears in quick butterfly touches, and are finally crossed on his chest, all in a second. "In the balls," he says again, as though nothing has happened. "Are you sure? What did you hear?"

"If it didn't happen, how did that fucking Thessalonian or whatever he was know about it?" says Polycrates, irritated. Their element of the line has been held up as others flow through the gates of the brand-new palisades around the ships, giving them plenty of time to talk. "No, I heard it from a runner from the delegation. Our guys are standing around saying the Trojans are about to cave in and all of a sudden Menelaus yells "ouch" and then he has this yard-long boner. One of those arrows from a big horn bow, a mankiller, only kind that can throw them over that range and hope to hit what they're aiming for. It was one of those big-headed mankiller arrows with a point nearly three inches across, sharp and barbed. But the thing is, that big point hit exactly the wrong way. It was level to the ground, three inches horizontal, when it hit him in the sack, right under his dick, which I guess was tucked up or he was pissing off to the left or something. So it went in right there and it sliced his balls clean off. They land on the ground, plop, right in front of him, and then the poor bastard is standing there trying to pull the arrow out and pick up his balls at the same time." He shakes his head. "Last I heard, Machaon the surgeon was trying to sew his balls back on. Good luck to him and a quick death to Menelaus." He spits and makes a mystic sign, the same as that made by Lacademon, who winks in response.

The lines have started to move again. The timber walls around the ships are just ahead, and behind them is the unmistakable sound of an army gathering to advance. The assault is still an hour or so away, but as inevitable as the progression of a distant swell that forms into a wave that beats in a man's brains when he runs from its curling crest.

Cephales tests his shield strap. "Good luck or quick death to us all."

THE BATTLE
FOR THE SHIPS

The royals leave after half an hour, each pausing to give him a few kicks, even feeble Priam. The king, in fact, prays aloud to Zeus that he will accept Pandarus' suffering and death as atonement for the sins of Troy as he drives a foot into Pandarus' bruised ribs and grinds his heel into his neck. Hector satisfies himself with a measured blow to the side of his head that leaves Pandarus conscious but barely so, and lovely Paris drives his foot so deep between his cheeks that Pandarus is sure he will shit blood for a week.

But that is not enough. As Pandarus lies there, gagging with pain and weeping with grief and humiliation, he hears booted feet shuffle and a muted laugh behind and above him. He risks a glance back and sees a lavender-nailed foot planted just outside his left hip. He knows the other foot is at his right and he guesses what is to come. Hot liquid, body temperature, strikes him between the shoulder blades and runs in a rivulet down the center of his back. As Paris guffaws, the stream dances in time, sometimes staying centered between his shoulder blades, sometimes soaking his hair so the urine runs into his mouth, which is wide open as he sobs wordlessly.

"Hey, king-killer, like the bath?" Paris is laughing so hard that he is missing Pandarus altogether, soaking the cellar's dirt floor.

Hector hasn't been laughing. "Put it away, boy," he growls. "Hasn't it caused us enough trouble already?"

Suddenly, Paris isn't laughing either. "Boy? *Boy?*" he shrieks. "You call me that in front of this garbage?"

"What does it matter what I call you in front of him?" says Hector. "What will he do at sunset, tell all the other dead in Hades? Relax. Down there they have plenty more to gossip about."

Paris laughs shrilly and squeezes out another few drops; he must be shaking it. Pandarus throttles the impulse to turn his head. In a minute there is the sound of sandals on stone and then silence, broken only by his mud-muffled sobs.

Before he has completely exhausted himself, Bizimarko and two of his men pull him upright. "Let's go, soldier," says Bizimarko. Pandarus is surprised at his tone; it is less unkind than he would have expected from the bodyguard of sons of gods who think him garbage. He is dragged up the stairs, feet grabbing futilely at steps he can't quite catch, and out into the light.

For a second, he is blinded after his afternoon's captivity. Then his head is wrapped in a rough cloak and rough hands pick him up. Carried like a slaughtered ram, he hears Troy: his bearers' feet squishing in streets muddy even in times of drought, the curious mutter of passersby suddenly stilled as the royal bodyguard is recognized, and the relieved clatter and jabber of soldiers suddenly safe inside the walls. Then wood shrieks and bellows as the great gates open, and he is engulfed by the sounds of a wide world full of enemies: horses protesting the whips across their withers as the bronze-rimmed wheels behind them crunch in dry, sandy soil; the urgent rhythm of drums calling troops to their ranks; the creak of leather and bronze as armored men obey, and their curses as they smother the urge to do anything but.

They are not long in this world of urgent noise before the bodyguard stops. Pandarus hears a muttered conversation just ahead of him, barked laughter from two different voices, and then he is set on his feet. The cloak is pulled from his head and Bizimarko fills his vision. "Here you are, soldier," says Bizimarko, again not unkindly. "Sorry about this. All this. You're with this unit now. I'll say a prayer that it's quick. You deserve that, at least, after all the shit you've taken today." He turns to leave and pauses. "Hey, nice work on Menelaus. Hear you got him in the balls. Way to go." With that he is gone.

Pandarus stands where he has been left, blinking. Ahead of him stands an officer who tugs at his beard, oiled and ringleted, and paces back and forth as he issues orders to a steady stream of runners. Pandarus looks over his shoulder: fifty foot soldiers are forming up for an advance that from their looks is imminent. They nervously pull at armor straps and re-settle helmets; they roll their necks and shoulders; they run whetstones across spear points and sword edges already sharpened feather thin; one takes a step back from the ranks and pisses into the sand. Just ahead of the officer are half a dozen war chariots, each drawn by a double team, each chariot holding two men, a driver and an archer. As the bowmen ready securing their quivers and testing spare strings, Pandarus' right arm drops back as he mimics the firing and longs to be in their place.

Pandarus steps to his left to look between the chariots at what is before them: a beachy plain broken by nothing but a few scraps of war. A helmet no one has bothered to claim in triumph, broken spears, chariot wheels, dead horses, some freshly killed and bloating in the heat, some long ago picked clean and bleached by half a generation's sun and rain. Far behind the plain is crashing sea embraced by outstretched arms of harbor rock, and spread across the sheltered sand, the Achaean fleet.

For as long as Pandarus can remember, the Achaean ships have been part of his life, beached out there just at the limit of clear view from the walls, a hundred black-prowed hulls whose presence shadowed every thought and haunted every dream, whose destruction or departure was the object of every prayer and the purpose of every sacrifice. And throughout that time, the ships and their crews have left themselves arrogantly open and exposed, defended only by arms and valor, mocking the Trojans cowering behind high, thick walls, penned up in their homes and slowly starved while men from a thousand miles distant leisurely nibbled away at an empire built up over centuries.

But today is different. Today the Achaeans crave the comfort of walls, however hastily built. A thousand yards from where Pandarus stands is the outer perimeter of the Achaean defense, a ditch three yards wide and two deep, its bottom planted with sharpened saplings hard to come by on the Illyrian plains.

Pandarus cannot see all the details from where he stands, but he sees earth thrown up from the excavation formed into a thick, low rampart all around the Achaean side of the ditch. And beyond that, twenty-five yards back, is the wall itself. Owing to the rarity of timber and the scarcity of time it could not encircle all the ships, but it fronts more than half. It curves around them all the way to the protecting surf. The wall is ragged; ten feet high in some places, six in others, pierced by gates in half a dozen places, mostly lashed together with what Pandarus guesses is ship rope. That thought fills him with sudden, crazy pride; if the Achaeans are cannibalizing their beloved ships that way then they must truly be fouling themselves with fear. As he watches, a thousand Achaeans sally from the biggest gate. Their rhythmic chant carries this far, marking time to their slow jog. As they reach the rampart, their column splits, half right, half left, to take up position behind the earthen barricade.

At last, the officer speaks to him. "What did you do?" he asks. "Shit in a temple? Rape Andromache?"

Despite himself, Pandarus laughs. "No, nothing like that. I just shot an Achaean. Why?"

"No reason. At least no reason that will matter in an hour. It's just that my orders are to bring you with us unarmed. Not that that will make a difference."

"Why not?"

The officer smiles sourly. "We're the first wave. We advance with the chariots at a walk into archery range, straight towards the main gate. Then we get to twenty yards from the ditch. Then the chariots stop and we charge into the ditch. We kill as many Achaeans as we can in the ditch before we're killed. Then the first wave of chariots rides over our dead bodies across the ditch." He nods. "Good plan. Great plan. We're all volunteers. Every man here has had a mother or a daughter or a son raped by an Achaean, so we don't care. Just wanted to know why you're here, that's all."

"As I said," says Pandarus, "I shot an Achaean."

The officer nods. "Broke the truce, right?"

Pandarus grunts.

"Menelaus, right?"

Pandarus grunts again.

The officer laughs. "Thought so." He draws his sword and extends it hilt first, holding the naked blade. "You're not going in there unarmed. You'll die like the rest of us, but you'll die like a man. Like the rest of us."

A discordant blast of trumpets sounds. "That's it," says the officer.

67

"We're going in." He grabs a javelin from a passing runner. "Sell your life dear," he says. "Behind me now!" He raises the javelin high. "All right now," he bellows. "Let's *go*! Die for Troy, boys, but kill for her first! *"Now!"*

෧

Agamemnon and Odysseus perch unsteadily on the head of a wine barrel. Their heads just clear a gap in their wall. "You're sure?" Agamemnon asks for the twentieth time that hour.

"Not sure, lord," says Odysseus, again. "Just as sure as I can be."

"Athena told you this?"

"Yes, lord," says Odysseus, trying to keep the fatigue out of his voice.

"I still don't like it," says Agamemnon, nervously chewing his beard. "Keeping half our troops inside. It might not work, despite what the Gray-eyed One says."

Odysseus chooses his words carefully. At times like this it is hard to play the game. "She hasn't lied to us yet, king," he says.

"Tell that to my brother."

"Athena didn't lie," says Odysseus. "The Trojans did."

Agamemnon's eyebrows crawl to his hairline. Despite himself, he smiles. "Good point. What? What's that?"

"Battle trumpets, lord," says Odysseus. "Soon enough we'll know whether Athena spoke the truth."

෧

Three soldiers are on the earthworks directly before the main gate. Sinon passes behind them and claps each on the shoulder. "You guys are assholes," he says. "But you're the assholes I want around me now."

Lacademon replies: "Sinon, you're an asshole, but that's it." A dozen men on either side up and down the line erupt in laughter, including Sinon.

"Maybe," he says. "Tell you what, Lacademon, let's live through today so we can beat the shit out of each other tomorrow."

The troops laugh again. The rumble from Troy makes anything funny.

"Right, boss," says Lacademon. "Hey, the Trojans don't take prisoners, right?'

68

"Right."

"Just wanted to make sure. So I guess I have to kill them all, right?"

"Right."

"Right. Single-handedly?"

"Right."

"Hey, if I get tired, you guys help me out, okay?" he bellows.

"*Right!*" Javelins and swords are shaking in the air and men are laughing and Sinon stands back beaming. "Hey, thanks," says Lacademon. "Hey guys, good news, here they come! Now don't forget, you fuckers, kill every last fucking son of a bitch of them! *Got it?*"

"*Right!*"

Pandarus trots forward with the rest of the troops behind their officer, just ahead of the foot soldiers. He has always thought himself better than the infantry and does not want to die this way. He prays to Apollo the Bowman, hoping that one of the arrows now dropping around them will find him as its mark so that he can at least go out like an archer.

Apollo is silent. But as he looks past the charioteers ahead towards the Achaean lines, Pandarus sees the clouds above them roiling in the late afternoon sun. A beam of light shines down on the Achaean earthworks. A beautiful young man stands on the ramparts, ignored equally by Achaeans and Trojans. He is naked, holding aloft a bow, his whole body haloed in iridescence. Apollo.

Forward, then, to live or to die. Around him, the rain of arrows grows more intense, the whir of their passage now punctuated by the various sounds of impact: tinny clunks against bronze armor, twangs against the layered ox hide of the shields. Sometimes he hears the wet hiss of an arrow point burying itself in the soft hollow spaces of bowels or lungs, other times, the flat crack of bronze on bone. Though the men behind him rarely cry out, halfway across the killing field, Pandarus looks behind to see that at least a dozen have fallen.

The chariots ahead have slowed. Their leader looks behind at Pandarus' officer, who raises his javelin in reply. The head charioteer raises his whip and the chariots pull ahead and slightly apart, leaving a gap of two yards between each. The officer turns, his spear still high. "Now, boys! *Now!*

Make those fuckers die for Troy!" He laughs like a happy child and turns to run into a gap between the chariots, Pandarus right behind. When they clear the chariot line, an Achaean javelin pierces the officer's chest so deeply that its point pops out of his back plate. Pandarus catches him falling. As bright red blood pumps from both front and back, Pandarus lifts him to ask his name, but the officer's eyes have gone hazy and his jaw slack as Hades drops his purple cloak.

Pandarus drops the sword he has been loaned and picks up the javelin the officer no longer needs and raises it above his head. "Follow me!" he cries. "Follow me, boys. *Follow Pandarus the king-killer!*"

He knows enough not to look behind. It is twenty yards of open ground to the Achaean ditch. The arrows fall like hail in a winter storm, and striking bronze, they sound like it as well. Pandarus drops his head and charges.

Cephales hunches over his shield; he has laid it flat on the ground to give both straps that last touch of oil and each a last reassuring tug. Lacademon's hand lands heavily on his shoulder. "Come *on*, brother," he shouts half an inch from his ear. "If it's not ready now it's too late, anyway!"

Cephales laughs nervously in agreement, and as he rises, shifts the shield's comforting weight onto his left shoulder. The top strap wraps his biceps like a friend's fist; the bottom fits just right, loose enough for play, tight enough for precision. His head just clears the rampart when he straightens up.

The Trojan vanguard has taken a beating. The chariots, most now with a single occupant, have opened their ranks and stopped dead. The infantry behind have been halved in number since they started their advance. Behind them, also immobile, is another, larger rank of chariots, behind which rumble and chant what sound like a thousand men.

Through the hole in the cavalry line pops a single man, shrieking like a Fury, his javelin held high and level to the ground. Lacademon, at Cephales' right, laughs and grabs his friend's shoulder to steady himself for the throw. The spear barely has time to rise in its short arc before it buries itself in the officer's chest. He stands there, dumbfounded as men always are when they themselves are suddenly part of the day's casualties, before he is caught in his slow turning fall by another Trojan, elegant by infantry standards, who has thrown aside a naked sword to stop him before he hits the earth. Lacademon crows in triumph as the new man picks up the fallen officer's javelin and, in something that sounds like a distant cousin of Achaean, urges his troops on. "Got him!" cries Lacademon. "*Got the Trojan fucker!*"

Lacademon is still standing full upright, laughing, as the Trojan line hits the ditch. As the first arrow whines past his ear, he screams, "All *right* now, boys, let's *get* the bastards!" To Cephales' horror, he vaults himself up and over the lip of the rampart and into the ditch.

If they waited, the Trojans would simply fill the ditch and die like dogs under a quick torrent of spears and arrows from above. But the Achaeans can't let that happen. While one man standing alone might be able to figure that out, a dozen standing side by side are ruled only by the scent of blood and thirst for glory. So over the ramparts they go, sliding into the ditch on their asses or jumping in feet first to contest a hundred square yards of dirt for no better reason than to deny it to their enemies.

Cephales cannot allow himself to be the last over the top, but he comes close. No fool, he slides rather than jumps, his knees pulled up so that his big harboring shield can cover most of his body. When his feet hit the trench floor he retains his fetal crouch and exposes only his face.

Ahead are Trojans and Achaeans, swords rising and falling like woodsmen's axes, chunking into shield frames or meat. Straight before him is the Trojan who took up the spear when the officer fell. Cephales draws his sword and surges forward two feet, shield raised high, still crouching, ready to sweep the sword down and back to cut the tendons behind the Trojan's knees, to drop him to the ground for an easy finish.

The Trojan stands like a stone—waiting, it seems, to die—and at the last minute, swings the butt of his javelin against Cephales' shield. It is a stupid gesture; a symbolic effort of self-preservation at the instant of death. Cephales snorts his contempt, not noticing that rivets pop at the trivial impact. Unsecured now at its top, pivoting from the bottom strap in his left hand, the shield falls limply forward. Cephales freezes. The earth all around rumbles. The other men in the trench move in slow motion, like ants in honey. At the Trojan edge of the ditch, ambient day congeals into a milky rolling ball of light from which comes a voice. WE WARNED YOU, CEPHALES. WE THOUGHT YOU HEARD.

71

The light disappears; the men around him resume their fight in real time. He cranes his head toward where the light had been and, in doing so, exposes the full length of his unarmored throat. The Trojan raises the javelin high in both hands and drives its leaf-shaped tip downward through Cephales' neck, severing the windpipe.

Cephales stands for a moment, coughing, amazed that bright red blood jets not only from nose and mouth, but the hole in his throat as well. Death's mist covers him as he falls; the last sound he hears is the tidal rush of blood pouring into his lungs.

As Cephales falls he drags forward the Trojan, who clings to his fatal javelin and tries to pull it free of where it has lodged in cervical vertebrae. He plants a foot on Cephales' chest and has nearly worked it out when Lacademon edges through the bleeding crowd. "Killed my friend, Trojan fucker?" he roars.

When the Trojan turns as though to offer a reasonable reply, Lacademon's sword comes down like a cleaver and separates the Trojan's right arm from its shoulder: the big arm, the archer's arm that still grasps the javelin in Cephales' throat. Suddenly freed at one end, the spear swings forward, taking with it the arm suddenly disembodied. Some reflex has tightened its grasp. The Trojan stares as it rocks back and forth at the end of the spear shaft. He turns to the stump from which surprisingly little blood flows. With his remaining arm he pulls off his helmet. "I love you, Paris," he says, just before Lacademon's sword splits his head down to his upper lip.

Hector has been between ditch and wall for an hour; he is a killing machine. When his wheels first hit the corpse-filled ditch, his chariot sank lower than expected, and his horses worked too hard to pull him over the Achaean rampart, their hooves shattering first feeble earthworks and then ineffectual foreign skulls. But then he was over it. His bow made arrows fly a dozen a minute, and each dropped an Achaean defender. Arrows soon gone, he dismounted and led the infantry into a bloody half hour's work against the demoralized defenders. Five men fell to his javelin's thrusts; incredibly, two in the same throw, the point completely through the first man and buried deep in the second, sewn together with a giant needle. Then he fought with just his sword, clearing around him a three-yard circle from which any Achaean soon found himself next on the banks of the Styx.

A beautiful backhand cleanly severed the head of an Achaean lord. The trunk remained upright, battle-ax still poised over its right shoulder, as its head lay between its feet, teeth chattering and eyes rolling. The headless body dropped its ax and stumbled away, its legs pistoning clumsily, arms flailing in a crazy pantomime of flight, until it flopped onto its side and quivered like a decked fish. Then Diomedes, apparent commander of the shadow force outside the Achaean walls, came screaming at him on his chariot, arm raised to drive a bronze spear point through Hector's breastplate, his driver bent double restraining crazed horses. Hector threw his sword aside and raised a rock heavy as a man in both hands, and hurled it crashing through the fancy front of Diomedes' chariot. He laughed as it spun away on its broken axle.

Now he is with his men at the Achaean gate. Another axle taken from a fallen chariot is their battering ram. A dozen men swing it harder and harder as their friends mop up the hundred Achaeans who still survive the crossing of the ditch. Hector grabs the ram in his own hands and with his efforts doubles its effect.

When the smell of burning pitch and timber reaches his nose, though, he stops and looks left and right. A dozen ships outside the timber walls are in flames. The parties he had detailed off with torches cheer. He drops the axle and raises both fists clenched in the air. The other men on the battering ram do the same. In less than a minute, all the Trojan troops within the ditch, except those actually finishing off Achaean stragglers, have raised their fists and voices. Their wordless roar rolls across the plain to the walled city and back to them, amplified by forty thousand cheering countrymen.

Hector gestures to two of his men who bring a shield. At Hector's instruction, they and two of their fellows lift him on it, upright, to their shoulders. So close to the Achaean wall it looks like suicide, but Hector trusts the fate that has brought him this close to victory. "Trojans!" he cries. "Men of Troy! This is it! This is the time! *Are you with me?*"

The men who survived the ditch answer like thunder: "*Yes!*"

Atop their wine barrel, Odysseus turns to Agamemnon. "Now," he says, just above a whisper. Agamemnon nods, first to Odysseus, then to two runners who disappear in opposite directions.

Hector raises himself to his full height a little unsteadily. His platform is narrow and his great size strains even the four strong men supporting him. "Prince," shouts one, "please come down. Any Achaean with a bow can take your life!"

Hector waves him into silence. "Trojans!" he cries again, voice deep and clear as the great, curved trumpet that blows in his family's private temple whenever sacrifice is finished. "The sea washed up filth on our beach! Do you see it?"

"*Yes!*"

"It looks to me as though great Poseidon himself has taken a shit on our shore! Does it look like that to you?"

Laughter. Not one man in the thousands between ditch and wall wonders how they can laugh this close to an enemy that has kept them prisoners in their own city so long that children born midway through the siege have grown old enough to play with their fathers' swords. Hector joins them. He echoes the laughter in his head. It belongs to his own god, Ares, deep and cruel and full of rage. "So, Trojans, will you clean this filth from our shores? Will you rinse it back to the sea that cast it up?"

As the Trojans roar their answer, Agamemnon can barely contain himself. "Shit?" he says. "*Shit?* Do you hear what that oath-breaking bastard is calling us?"

"Look behind you, lord," says Odysseus.

The half circle of the wall encloses at least eighty of the ships and most of the army, seven thousand strong. It is almost half a mile from where its southern end meets the sea to the northern. The timber at either end is almost submerged at high tide, but it is not high tide now. The water at the wall's ends is barely knee deep.

There are men at either end of the wall, bunched in the sand, some in surf to their hips. Five hundred on either side: Achaea's best archers and behind them her best spearmen and swordsmen. They stamp and snort and pray, waiting for the order that will send them through the surf and wet sand, around the seaward edges of the Achaean walls and into the Trojan flanks. The Trojans are not sailors. To them the sea is a wall as strong as any stone. The Trojans would never have thought to get their feet wet.

As Odysseus and the king watch, the force on the Achaean left begins to move. The right, as ordered, waits. First a force of a hundred light infantry slogs through water as high as its waists and then disappears behind the wall's curve. It is followed by the lead archers, behind whom come the main force of mixed archers and regular infantry.

Hector, wobbling on his shield, pumps his fists into the air. "The gods are with us, Trojans! The gods drank the smoke of our sacrifice and bless us! Can you feel the gods' love, Trojans?" For a while now, the Trojans have chanted Hector's name, but their howled rhythmic answer is broken by the screams of horses and shouts of men coming from Hector's right. The connection between himself and his audience broken, Hector steals a glance over his shoulder. "Hera's cunt," he says.

On the walls, Odysseus watches the Achaean advance guard on the enemy right. The Trojans there are standing on tiptoe, straining to catch Hector's every word, their backs to the light infantry that is methodically spearing their horses and then setting up to screen the archers. Safe behind the infantry's shields and spears, each bowman drops to one knee and gives every Trojan in view an arrow in the back. A hundred Trojans are dead before Hector has noticed that something isn't right.

Hector sees the panic spreading on the right and thinks fast. "And now, Trojans, the shit is flowing. Follow me! To the right! The bastards have tricked us! Kill these treacherous, raping fuckers!" With the flat of his sword he beats the shoulders and heads of his bearers until they have dropped him to the ground. Rough-handed, he thrusts each of them forward to the right, to the Achaeans, screaming his orders to kill them all, and then dashes towards one of the few chariots to have made it over the ditch and through the battle behind it intact. Its owner, a noble whose name he should remember but can't, bows in homage and is thrust aside for his pains. The driver, ashen-faced at his proximity with royal celebrity, gapes at Hector, trying to form words but failing. "To the Achaeans, you stupid fuck!" Hector roars, slapping him openhanded. Half concussed and bleeding from both nostrils, the driver cracks the reins.

After a hundred yards, the horses tangle in the press of the Trojan retreat. There are wounded men prickling with arrows like porcupines, mouths agape and eyes dull with the certainty of death by day's end; men merely terrified, their weapons dropped in the dust as they scream towards the center, those who can speak mouthing to any who can hear, "All is lost, save yourself."

The Achaeans advance like a machine. Light infantry kills stragglers and then falls into formation, shield to shield, as archers fire just above their heads to drop another Trojan rank. The stink of defeat fills Hector's nose. It is a real smell, acrid fear over slaughterhouse stench. His head is still full of Ares' laughter, but now he hears its edge of mockery. "Trojans!" he roars. "Come to me! To Hector! To Hector!" To his surprise, the cry carries the field, and within minutes, the survivors of his flank have coalesced around him, men suddenly ready to die for Troy, laughing again as they form up behind him.

On his wooden parapet, Odysseus watches as the Trojan right falls apart and its center and left move to support it. As the entire Trojan force leaves its left flank undefended, he nods again to Agamemnon.

The force at the other end of the Achaean wall is differently composed. Without screening infantry, the youngest and fastest of the archers splash around the wall and sprint into position fifty yards behind what is now the Trojan rear. At the Trojan front, the Achaean light infantry and archers have fallen back behind heavy infantry that has planted its shields and spear butts in the sand, men shoulder to shoulder, waiting for the advance of Hector's rallied troops. As soon as the Trojans begin their charge against the Achaean line, the archers to their rear let fly, dropping the Trojan back rank to a man. The archers run forward, fire again, and another rank falls.

Hector is deaf to the commotion behind him. Both his horses have fallen to Achaean javelins and so he dismounts and screams forward, a yard ahead of the Trojan vanguard, swinging a battle-ax he has found in the borrowed chariot. The Achaeans bunch up before him, men in the front rank dropping to their knees and raising their shields, those behind rushing forward to cover their comrades with another layer of overlapping ox hide, the shields gapped only to permit spears to thrust forward, like a hedgehog with armor skin. Hector bellows in rage and swings futilely against a wall of bronze-bound leather; it bends but will not break. His men hit the wall a second later. Their javelins can't find breaks through which to thrust; swords batter futilely against shields.

Hector turns to urge his reinforcements up, but he sees nothing, then worse than nothing. In the twenty yards behind him, there are no Trojans, just Trojan weapons dropped in flight and Trojan armor shed to lighten flying feet. Twenty-five yards away, shrouded in dust clouds and a dry storm of falling arrows, is a mass of men, Trojan and Achaean, distinguishable from one another only in that the dead littering the ground all seem to be Priam's subjects. The Achaeans have started their rhythmic, barking battle chant, which grows louder and more regular even as Hector stands there. The Trojans only scream and pray.

Hector drops his ax and staggers backwards, again facing the Achaean hedgehog, which wavers and trembles as though ready to surge ahead. A Trojan officer grabs his shoulder and thrusts his face to Hector's ear. "Prince," he says, "we are finished. You must live to fight another day. Let us die covering your retreat."

Hector's mouth moves, but no words come. As he tries to speak, he tastes the blood flowing from his nose and an arrow cut across his cheek that he never noticed. In his head Ares' laughter booms again. IS THIS HOW YOU WANT TO DIE, BEST OF THE TROJANS? MEAT IN THE JAWS OF AN ACHAEAN TRAP? LET THESE MEN DIE FOR YOU, AND IF YOU MUST DIE LATER, I PROMISE THAT YOU WILL DIE LIKE A HERO. NOT LIKE A FOOL. Hector's vision flickers and the battle around him stops. The Achaeans before him are so many statues covered with the crawling fire of divine aura. Only his own hands move, quivering and trembling as if with febrile palsy. The clouds above him curdle and coalesce and crackle with internal lightning, and from them comes the god's voice again, this time reaching his ears instead of sounding within his skull's silence. YOU DON'T DIE HERE, HECTOR. RUN.

Suddenly, the Achaeans are unclothed of fire. They move forward a half step, still keeping hedgehog formation. From behind them arrows whicker and streak skyward to fall on the Trojan rout. From within the hedgehog erupt guttural snarls. A voice yells: "What are we waiting for? Kill the fucker and end the war right here!"

Hector turns to the officer who has offered his life. "All right," he says. He turns on his heel and runs, almost colliding with troopers who charge ahead to cover his flight.

He will not turn to watch them die; there is plenty of death ahead. He crossed the ditch with a thousand of Troy's best. Now, perhaps three hundred survivors desperately try to drive through Achaean infantry blocking their path to the corpse-filled trench. As Hector runs he picks his way through Trojan dead, some piled three deep. Men pierced with multiple arrows; men lying in piles of their own bowels freshly spilled by Achaean swords; men with arms and legs shattered by war hammers or amputated by axes. Enough still live, croaking like frogs for water, and as Hector stumbles through their fallen ranks, he thinks of a swamp at dusk.

He has reached the rear of the retreating Trojans. He raises his fists in the air. "It's Hector!" he shouts. "Now for Troy and home!"

Some faces turn and one or two cheer. Most, busy with staying alive, don't bother to acknowledge him. Hector stands there, fists in the air, and thinks he hears laughter—human, not divine—from his right. The Achaean wall is a dozen yards away. He keeps his fists in the air until he is sure that his men are ignoring him and he has heard the laughter again. He sprints towards the main gate, where less than an hour before, he and a dozen men battered the invading timber with a chariot axle.

There. There it is, half buried under the dead. He throws corpses aside and takes up the log and swings it into the gate. "Come on now, boys," he cries, striking wood with wood. "Troy's not beaten yet!" He hits the gate again and looks over his shoulder. The Trojans have not rallied to him. Some have made it across the ditch now so choked with the dead that they have to climb over them. Those who remain are desperate to follow.

Hector is not sure whether the laughter he hears is the god in his head or the enemy behind the gate. It doesn't matter. Weeping with rage and shame he grabs the axle at one end and swings it like a club against the unyielding wall. "Stop laughing at me! Stop laughing at me!"

One Trojan, the grandson of a royal bastard, the noblest of the survivors still on the wrong side of the ditch, runs to his prince's side. He still has most of his armor, but the sword he holds was taken from a dead Achaean. The kohl with which he painted his eyes that morning ran into black streaks down his cheeks hours ago. "Lord," he says. "Run. Run with me now. Run with me now or die here."

Hector drops the axle. He looks up and right. There, in a gap in the timber walls, he sees two Achaean nobles, one so grand he can only be Agamemnon. The king's head is thrown back in triumphant laughter; he claps as though he were at a play. The other, less grand, just smiles sourly and nods. Hector catches the sour man's eye. The Achaean points towards Troy, then raises a horn to his lips and blows. In less than a minute, the hail of arrows stops and the Achaeans drop back and reform into ranks.

"*Now*, sir," says the royal bastard's grandson. "Run now or die."

Hector runs.

Right now, the closest thing great Agamemnon has to a palace is a big hut inside the walls. Its slats and cloth shake to the Achaean victory chant. "Re*joice*, we conquer." At the end of each syllable, spear butt or booted foot strikes soil and sword pommel strikes shield. The din is almost over-whelming, but Agamemnon seems not to mind.

It is just the two of them, now: Agamemnon and Odysseus. "So I guess the Gray-eyed One steered us straight again," says Agamemnon.

"Us?" Odysseus murmurs, raising an eyebrow.

"*Us*," says Agamemnon emphatically, reminding Odysseus of who is high king and who is not. "Through you, of course," he adds diplomatically.

"Of course. Thank you." Odysseus hides his smile behind a wine bowl.

"You're welcome," says Agamemnon grandly. "Tell me, why didn't we kill them all, including that bastard Hector?"

"Because," says Odysseus tiredly, "this morning a thousand Trojan heroes left to sweep us into the sea. Tonight a hundred beaten men return, running back with their tails between their legs, including great Hector. They'll spread fear and humiliation through Troy like a plague. If we'd killed them all, the Trojans would say they'd all died heroes. A few survivors kill the myth. And, incidentally, they would have fought like gods to avenge a dead Hector. After today he may have a hard time getting his own bodyguard to follow him."

Agamemnon snorts. "As usual, I think you're right, but I don't know how you get there. Tell me—" he stops as the chief herald sweeps in. Though the man is forbidden by law to wear armor, he has a way of making silk and linen clatter. "You have something to tell us, herald?"

Odysseus raises both eyebrows in surprise as the herald drops to his knees. He thought the man so proud he would argue with the Boatman about the fee over the Styx, believing one of his noble lineage entitled to cross free. Nevertheless, this most eminent of men hits his knees today. "King Agamemnon," he says, "my lord. We have counted the dead."

Agamemnon, obviously enjoying this rare display of humility, won't look up as he mixes more water into the wine. "And?" he asks.

"Among our own men," says the herald, "no more than one hundred and ten."

"And?" says Odysseus.

"Among the Trojans," says the herald, "at least seven hundred and fifty."

"At least?" asks Odysseus.

"My lord," says the herald, "we cannot be sure. They died so many in places that they died four deep. We may not yet have turned back all the layers."

Agamemnon forgets the reverence due the dead and laughs. Odysseus remembers his duty enough to hide his smile in the wine bowl again. "Gentle herald," says Agamemnon, "return to your task and come again when it is done." The herald rises and makes his clothes crackle and squeal in his obeisance to them both as he withdraws.

"Well," says Agamemnon. "A hundred and ten to seven hundred and fifty. Not bad."

"No," says Odysseus. "Not bad at all."

Twilight. Lacademon stands at the edge of the ditch. He knows what he has to do and doesn't want to do it. He has been there since late afternoon, arriving an hour after the last Trojan crossed, whimpering like a baby but glad to have his life to take back to Troy. When the sun is just about to set, Sinon walks up behind him, and his heavy hand lands on Lacademon's shoulder. "Good work today, soldier," he says.

Lacademon does not speak.

"Lost some friends today," says Sinon. "We all did. They died like soldiers, remember that." That is the best Sinon can do. Lacademon knows this, and so reaches behind him with his right hand and pats the big paw on his left shoulder. Soon Sinon is gone, leaving Lacademon with what he has to do.

The ditch can be smelled at a hundred yards now. They say that there is so much blood at its bottom that it has become a real ditch, a sluice for fluid as well as a defensive work. This Lacademon believes. The corpses with which it is now choked are so numerous and have died so bloodily that its whole length must be puddled a foot deep with their clotting gore. Most of the dead in the ditch died hours before, when the sun was still high; now their bloating bodies swell and heave and burst in the cooling air. The iron tang of blood lends its high-top note to the smell that a breeze now blows back to the Achaean camp. But worse than blood and the beginnings of putrescence is the cesspool reek of the battlefield. When men die, their bowels and bladders empty. Any place where a lot of men have died thus carries the scent of their last few meals.

Lacademon knows he hasn't much time. The carrion birds circling overhead smell what he smells and are not repulsed. The light will fail soon and he needs to see to do what he has to do, and he doesn't want to be out here after dark. The heralds have been at work for a while: half the bodies are out of the ditch and laid out on the ground. The noncombatants' muslin is spattered with mud and blood and shit. The Achaean dead are still clothed in their bronze, but the Trojans were stripped to their teeth before their pulses stopped.

Lacademon knows he is close to the spot where Cephales fell. Praying that the heralds have got him out of the ditch by now, he slowly walks the aisles of the dead, examining each fallen Achaean. At some, ruled out by the foreignness of armor or appearance, he barely glances. Others warrant closer inspection. After fifteen minutes, Lacademon, who thought he knew all the ways a man can die in war, is aghast at his former ignorance. Or perhaps he has never seen it all at once: headless corpse next to one disemboweled, face frozen in a scream, stiff arms gathering up looping guts; a warhammer's victim, oddly intact but for the newly-lopsided helmet and brains running from its nose, lying beside one leaden-faced, bled to death after an expert stroke had severed the tendons behind its knees; even one unfortunate who had somehow crawled to the edge of the ditch after a chariot had run him over and crushed his spine, for nothing else is heavy enough to dent armor like that.

After he has walked a hundred yards in either direction, he is sure that Cephales is still in the ditch. He groans. He thought so, anyway; he died too soon to be on top. He looks behind him and ahead to get his bearings. He is pretty sure that the main Achaean gate was just there and Troy was right here when Cephales fell. He takes a deep breath and goes over the lip of the ditch. Something squishes under his feet. Dying daylight and the trench's long shadows at first mercifully protect his eyes from what it is. Whatever it is, or whoever it was, emits a long bubbling fart as he steps forward.

His eyes have adjusted to the light. He is standing on a Trojan. A big fat bastard when alive, he guesses, now so bloated in death that his swollen body threatens to burst the straps of his breastplate. He lies on his back, glazed eyes glaring straight ahead, blackened lips skinned back

81

from his teeth in the last expression of life's hot rage. "Sorry," mumbles Lacademon.

The walls of the trench curve away in either direction. There can be no more than fifty dead remaining on the floor. Gingerly, he advances, murmuring apologies and prayers of supplication to those on whom he treads. After a dozen steps he comes to a man seated with his back resting on the Trojan side of the wall. His armor is gorgeous, the best bronze chased with silver, strapped with tooled leather. Forgetting his task for the moment, Lacademon pulls out his dagger and drops to one knee before him. First he expresses his condolences. "Sorry, soldier," he says. "Fortunes of war. Don't worry, tomorrow we'll burn you clean." Then he shells the Trojan like a boiled shrimp. Two quick pops and off come the greaves, leaving shins exposed and white in the dying light. Four more snaps, and the breastplate is free. Lacademon rises to his feet and bends forward to pull the armor from his silent prey. As he does so, he comes face to face with him.

The Trojan wore his hair in long braids, one on either side of his head, artfully draped forward onto his chest. That symmetry in life has been preserved in death: someone has split the Trojan's head down the middle so forcefully that the sides have actually fallen apart, the eyes separated by four inches, the nostrils by two. For an instant, Lacademon wonders if a good hard tug on the braids will separate the head altogether. Then he looks at the Trojan more closely. Blood and brain have run from the deep fissure bisecting his head to obscure his already distorted features, but Lacademon remembers earlier that day when he cleaved an elegant Trojan's skull.

Stony-faced, he roots among the dead, flipping over corpses as though kicking through autumn leaves. He finds Cephales buried face down in the mud. Having bled out all he held from his fatal wound, his skin is pale rather than livid in death, though the blood covers his front in black clots that Lacademon brushes away as best he can, reassuring the corpse that he will look good on his pyre. Once he has cleaned up Cephales, he turns back to the dead Trojan. "You killed my friend, fucker," he says. With either hand he grabs a braid and yanks. The scalp splits completely. Just as it frees itself from the skull, it pulls the shattered bone apart so that either half lands on the Trojan's shoulders. His mandible, freed, clanks down to his breastbone as his shattered brain, exposed and unsupported, spills forward onto his chest. The last of its cushioning fluid pours down to soak the thin linen tunic that the dead man wore under his armor.

Lacademon stands in front of the disfigured corpse. In either hand he has a hank of hair to which chunks of face adhere. He hurls each over the lip of the ditch towards Troy, then leans forward and wraps his arms around the Trojan corpse, almost burying his face in its brain and not caring. He raises the dead man to his shoulder and then hooks his arm between his legs, and after a few swings to build momentum, throws the body over the lip of the ditch as well. The Trojan lands a yard closer to home. In an hour, the little dogs that own the battlefield after dark will snap and squabble over shares of his meat.

Cephales he extracts with much greater care. He stands the dead man up against the Achaean side of the ditch, hoping death will keep him still. Rigor mortis, however, has come and gone, and the corpse disobediently slumps to the ground. Finally, Lacademon slings the dead man over one shoulder and the Trojan's armor over the other and crawls up and out on his belly. He drops both burdens as soon as he emerges. One of the heralds stares at him incuriously. "Nice armor," he says.

"Thanks," says Lacademon. "I'm taking the armor, but I'm leaving the body. What's your name?"

"Who wants to know?" says the herald.

"I do," says Lacademon. "Don't make me ask twice."

The herald considers. He is very tired and this is not the first such conversation he has had that day. He decides to leave out some steps. "Haphestes," he answers. "Haphestes, son of Polybion."

"Haphestes, son of Polybion," says Lacademon. "Nice name. See this body, Haphestes, son of Polybion?"

"I do," says Haphestes.

"Friend of mine. Seen anything like this before?"

"A thousand today," says Haphestes.

"A thousand today? *A thousand today*," Lacademon laughs. He strides forward easily, still laughing, man to man. He grabs Haphestes by the long, oiled curls swinging from the back of his head and drags him forward to thrust his face into Cephales' death mask. "Well, look at that," he says, careless of his sacrilege. "That's my friend! That's Lacademon's friend! And when I come back here tomorrow morning to see him burned, I'd better see him washed and all his armor, I mean *all* of it, piled in front of his pyre! And

83

I don't want to hear that anything went to the gods or the college of heralds!" Lacademon shakes Haphestes like a terrier a rat. "Do you understand me?"

"I'm a herald! Stop!" Haphestes squeaks.

"Do you understand me?"

"I understand," says Haphestes.

Lacademon drops the quivering herald. "Well, you'd better." He shoulders his armor and moves off.

No sooner has he left that he realizes that his job is half undone. He spins on his heel and heads back to the ditch, shooting a glare at the crouching herald. "I meant that," he says.

It is now almost dark. The heralds are still working by torchlight; they will not leave Achaean dead to night scavengers. Lacademon remembers the reverence owed them and is almost polite when he asks to borrow a torch for a few minutes.

He slides back into the ditch, torch held high. If it goes out down here, he is afraid he will lose his mind. The stench of death is overwhelming. The silence of the dead is broken by an occasional rustle as a limb obeys a nerve fired one last time; sometimes trapped air escapes in what sounds like a living man's groan or belch. Illuminated only by torchlight, the ranks of the fallen look like an army invading from Hades: jaws agape in impossible screams, fingers splayed like talons on arms gone rigid. Lacademon is afraid that he will not find his place. Fortunately, removing Cephales and the Trojan has left an obvious gap among the corpses. Gritting his teeth, he starts turning over the dead; a dozen shrieking, mute faces. He tugs at an arm that comes loose and stale blood pulses weakly into his face. He gags and wipes his eyes and keeps working. He pulls aside a body whose face he recognizes: a Spartan who covered his back one day when they took a Trojan town. Lacademon closes the staring eyes and gaping jaw and gently straightens his limbs.

Finally, here it is, a dozen feet from where he found Cephales. A big leather rectangle, three layers of ox hide, oak framed, reinforced with bronze strips, a bronze boss at its center. He grabs its edges, raises it over his head, throws it over the top of the ditch, and scrambles up after it.

Back among the living he stands and tries to slip the shield over his shoulder; his hand fits easily into the lower strap. The shield flops forward, its broken upper thong flapping free. Lacademon's hand relaxes and the shield hits the ground. "I don't believe it," he says.

He stands there a minute. His shoulders shake and he does not recognize the sounds that are coming from his throat; they hurt on the way out. He fights to keep them inside, but they will not stay. Not until he tastes the tears does he know that he is crying. Humiliation only makes it worse. He bends to pick up the shield and almost falls. Finally, he succeeds. Clumsily, he carries it towards three torch-lit heralds who stare in astonishment as he approaches, sobbing like a child. "Hey," he finally says. "Hey. Do any of you guys know how to fix a shield?"

IN AGAMEMNON'S TENT

Beached, the black-prowed ship rocks as though it were on open sea, rolling to the waves of the Achaean victory chant. Achilles groans and grits his teeth. "Fuck," he says. "The bastards won without me."

Patroclus wraps his arms around him and kisses his shoulder. He lays his cheek against the hairy deltoid and pulls the silk sheets higher. "If they hadn't," he says, "we'd be dead now."

"The fuck we would," Achilles snarls, spinning in bed to bring himself face to face with Patroclus. Despite himself, Patroclus recoils just a little. Achilles' eyes are almost amber, like a great cat's, and when he is angry he no longer seems entirely human. "It's that crafty piece of shit, Odysseus. Figured out another fast one so we didn't have to fight man to man. But if we'd just fought man to man, like *men* instead of like a bunch of tricky Phoenician merchants, I would have come down out of this ship and saved the day. *Fuck!*" His fist slams into the pillow. Gently, Patroclus pushes Achilles flat onto his back and begins kissing his way down the ridged belly.

Agamemnon sits in his olivewood chair of state. For the moment, it is just he and Odysseus; the other lords will come soon. "I don't want to do it," says Agamemnon.

"I know you don't, lord," says Odysseus, sighing. "I wouldn't want to do it, either. But we've been over this: we could win without him, yes, but it will take a lot longer and our chance of winning is a lot worse without him."

Agamemnon settles himself in his chair. Reflexively, he glances over his shoulder for Menelaus, who is in his own tent, recuperating; earlier that day Odysseus walked him around the camp naked from the waist down to quell rumors that there was no longer a point to the war with Troy. "Well," says Agamemnon, "just tell me again. If he asks for her, it's not on the table, right?" He glances down. Briseis sits on a low stool, washing his feet with cool water scented with lemon.

"Not on the table, king," says Odysseus tiredly. Briseis looks up. It is the first time Odysseus has made eye contact with her. Up to this moment, she was just part of a problem that had so many pieces they could not be counted, but now he sees what all the fuss was about: black eyes big as a baby's hands, slightly slanted; an oval, straight-nosed face; the mouth small but full lipped. Her skin is as white as any skin exposed to Aegean sun can be, marred only by a light dusting of freckles that Odysseus suddenly finds absurdly endearing. As she stares, he wonders what her gaze means. Gratitude that he will keep her with her new master? Resentment that he will not bear her off to Achilles or back to her family? Odysseus realizes that he imagines himself the center of her universe like any fool, when he is just a forty-year-old man locking eyes with a pretty girl. He shakes his head, hard, and comes back to himself. A self that these days fucks only to clear his head so that he can better think about how to get out of here.

"All right," says Agamemnon, as usual ignoring the momentary discomfort of those around him. "All right, bring them in. Present it to me as though I haven't decided, and I'll agree. Maybe." He raises his chin to a regal angle and glares straight ahead, then lifts his royal right hand and crooks a finger.

A slave at the tent door admits the lords of Achaea in the first gathering of the high command since yesterday's battle. A dozen men troop in, barely dropping their giddy voices as they enter the royal presence. Most are wearing whatever they wore under their armor yesterday. Odysseus is pleased that Diomedes, at his suggestion, is the best dressed among them, in a festival robe whose yellow unfortunately highlights what look like fresh wine spills. At least he looks better than Teucer, who wears only a loincloth that has seen better days. Odysseus wonders wearily why he is surprised that those who aren't half drunk are completely drunk. Teucer is apparently in the latter category; he staggers forward and grabs Odysseus' head on either side with a big paw. As Odysseus tries to pull back, his head is yanked forward to receive a slobbering kiss on the bald spot at its crown. "Hey," yells Teucer. "Hey, Agamemnon! What other soldier can kiss his own head, huh?" He folds his arms over his stomach and doubles over with laughter. The other lords roar and pound each other on back and shoulders.

Diomedes, not to be outdone, steps forward to speak. Odysseus realizes with alarm that if he is the best dressed he is also the drunkest of the lot. "You know what I said last night?" he bellows. "You know what I said to my driver just before I passed out? I'll tell you what I said."

The lords lean forward, grinning. Odysseus will not dare a glance at the king. "I said, 'If Odysseus was here right now, I'd lick his fucking asshole! And I'll bet that's what the king is doing right now!'"

After their initial shriek some of the brighter and soberer lords realize that Agamemnon might not find this all that amusing. Odysseus risks a look at the king, whose eyes are glazed and whose neck tendons are so widely splayed in the effort to control his rage that his head looks like a pyramid. "My lords! My lords!" cries Odysseus, sweeping forward from the king's left. "Let me be the first to thank the king for having allowed me to share in his victory!" Achaean, he will neither cringe nor crawl, but bows before the king.

The other lords, no matter how stupefied by wine or nature, see the writing on the wall. One by one they follow suit. "Uh, right, thanks," says Teucer, bowing.

"Good work, lord," says Telamonian Ajax, nodding like a fool.

"That goes double for me," says Locrian Ajax, stepping forward to pat the king on the shoulder.

"Right! Right!" says Diomedes, stumbling up like a wine barrel on legs. "Hey, I'd've licked your worst horse's asshole last night, lord," he roars, pinching Agamemnon on the cheek. He turns to face the assembled aristocracy. "Hey, you guys! Let's hear it for the fucking *king* now!" He pumps fists and stamps feet. "Aga*mem*non! Aga*mem*non!"

The lords take up the chant. Odysseus looks out through the corner of his eye at the king. As he watches, Agamemnon's tendons recede into his neck and his rigid face relaxes. While his lords roar like bulls, he even cracks a grin, first frozen, then genuine and open. He extends his arms and rises to his feet. Open-armed, he beckons the Achaean lords to him. The nobility, laughing and weeping with emotion and uncut wine, rush to his embrace; to touch his robe, his hand, his cheek—to hug one another. They link arms, they kiss one another's cheeks, they fondle one another's backs and backsides. They stand like a flock of sheep huddled against the wind, with only one, Odysseus, standing a little beyond, a little out of reach, laughing and clapping shoulder or back, but never quite entering the circle.

Eventually, Agamemnon, laughing with tears streaming down his face, takes two steps back and almost falls over his chair. His laughter redoubles, but he seats himself and raises his hands, palms out. "My lords," he says. "My lords! Please! Quiet! Thank you! Thank you for this great victory. Lord Odysseus would speak, and as some of you have said, Lord Odysseus is worth listening to!"

Odysseus flinches. Not exactly the introduction he was hoping for. He glances at the king, who glances slyly back. "All right, smart boy," Agamemnon's face says, "let's see you sell this crowd now."

"Thank you, king," says Odysseus. The lords are beaming at him expectantly; they're ready to hear something good from Athena's favorite son. "Thank you again, lord, for having let us share in your victory, and for letting us continue to share in the spoils that you will surely win when we gain Troy!" The lords cheer at this. "And lord, though your victory was great, we cannot forget those who fell winning it." The kinglets murmur and even Agamemnon must cast eyes to the ground in reverence for the dead. "Their sacrifice demands further sacrifice from us, not just in the blood that none of us here, nor any of our men, fear to shed in your cause and ours." The lords look suitably solemn, so Odysseus plunges towards the point. "Not in blood, my lords, but in pride. And not pride offered to truce-breaking Troy, but in pride offered to one of our own. One who has spilled his blood for us and with us and who has risked his life twice for each time we risked our own. Lords, we must ask Achilles to rejoin us."

Not a sound from the lords. Until Diomedes belches and says, "Sure. Why not?"

Odysseus wants to groan aloud but knows it had to start sometime. The lords are silent for another instant, then erupt all at once.

Teucer: "Him? Let that arrogant son of a bitch stay cuddled up with his boyfriend while I'm fucking Andromache!"

Telamonian Ajax: "That cocksucker? Where the fuck was he when the Trojans crossed the ditch?"

Locrian Ajax: "I'd say fuck him, but he'd like it too much."

Old Nestor: "When I was young we'd've died before letting a treacherous cunt like that eat with our dogs."

But Idomeneus, louder than the rest: "What for? What for?"

Soon the other lords take up the question, and Odysseus raises his hands for silence. "My lords," he says. "We have—our king has—won a great victory, but we know that men in victory think themselves immortal and that one victory leads inevitably to another. Yet our experience teaches otherwise: the immortal gods love nothing better but to trip up the proud. So in our just pride, let us not forget the hard facts. One is that we have been here nearly ten years and Troy still stands." The lords growl. Odysseus raises his hand, palm out. "Lords, please. Peace. That Troy stands is nothing to our pride, that we still live is the deepest offense to Troy's."

Sober, the lords would have had a hard time following. Odysseus spells it out. "When we came here, we were outnumbered five to one, and reinforcements have barely kept even with losses. Yet we face an enemy in its own land, behind the tallest walls in the world, fifty thousand strong, their sons growing big enough to replace the fathers we have slain and *still* we live on their shores a mile from their gates, do we not? And *still* we sack their towns, outnumbered as we are, do we not? And deprived of our best fighter and his best men, confronted by *their* best fighter and *his* best men, do we not slaughter them like animals and send the survivors whimpering back in shame?"

The lords grin and nod. This is more like it. "So, lords, our pride must be great at just having survived on these shores. But are we here just to survive? Did we come here just to live in tents for nine years and throw back the best the Trojans could throw at us? Or did we come here to win Troy?"

The high command shifts and stirs and begins its mutter, *Troy, Troy.* "And so, lords, to tip the balance back so that it favors us, not just our survival but our victory, should we not bring to bear our very best?"

"Yes," the murmur runs. "Troy, the best for Troy."

"And lords, is Achilles not our best?"

"Yes," they say. "Achilles for Troy."

"And so, lords, should we not recruit Achilles to fight again?"

Odysseus hoped for shouts of agreement, but knows that that was too much to hope for. He is satisfied with the thoughtful nods he gets, the little muttered conversations between nobles with heads bowed. Teucer steps forward. "Odysseus," he says. "Uh . . . wait a second, am I wrong or did we kill a thousand Trojans yesterday? I see I'm right. All right. So what's the rush to get the boy wonder back? I mean, I saw Hector shitting his loincloth and running like a rabbit while Achilles was inside the wall, in his ship, fucking his buddy. So with a thousand Trojans dead what do we need him for?"

Odysseus smiles and nods. "Good question. Great question. Thanks for asking. As you say, there are a thousand Trojans in Hades now who weren't there the day before yesterday, which only leaves forty-nine thousand against ten thousand of us. Which means, as I figure it, the odds have gone from five to one to worse than nine to two. Still not good."

Euclid is still a thousand years in the future. The lords move their lips and count on their fingers. "Can't be right," says one. "Huh?" says another, resorting to his toes. "Well, wait, if fifty to ten is five to one—I get it!"

The sun outside the tent is appreciably lower when the Achaean commanders have reached consensus on Odysseus' figures. "All right," says Teucer. "All right, things still aren't so rosy. So maybe we still need all the help we can get. I don't know what you guys think, but I say hey, if we can get him back, why not? But the problem seems to me to be the king. With all due respect," he adds hastily.

"With all due respect," Odysseus echoes. He turns to the king. "My lord," he says, "if the lords are inclined to accept Achilles, as they seem to be, what can you give him to salve his wounded pride? What in your kingship, in your leadership of us all, can you sacrifice? Not," he adds hastily, "that you have done anything to have wounded the pride of a reasonable man. But accepting things as they are, and accepting men as they are, what can you do, lord?"

"This I will do," says Agamemnon, obviously enjoying his royal diction. "I will give Achilles all that Briseis brought with her, and I will give him more. I will give him my own daughter in marriage once we are returned from Troy in victory. He may, I will say further, choose himself which of the daughters he takes." The lords gasp.

"Lord," says Odysseus. "King, my lord, we could not have asked more."

As they are leaving the tent, Agamemnon embraces Odysseus. "Remember," he whispers in his ear. "Remember, she's not on the table."

"Right," says Odysseus. "Any preference as to your daughters?"

"No," says Agamemnon. "Who cares?"

THE EMBASSY
TO ACHILLES

Hector and Priam are alone in the center of the citadel in the family's temple, the chapel royal, the holiest of holies, which only princes of the blood and eunuch priests may enter. It is a circular room, the navel of the Trojan world, the oldest part of the oldest building in Troy. Walls painted a thousand years ago with scenes from a heaven few modern Trojans and no Achaeans would recognize: serpents with men's bearded heads, winged bulls, fat women with forty breasts—gods that the Trojans took when they took the land on which their city was built and that their kings continue to honor alongside the nearly human pantheon that now rules the world. Along the painted walls are a hundred boxes of carved stone or ivory or sweet scented wood, each the size of a steamer trunk—ossuaries holding the ash and charred bone of Priam's royal predecessors.

The unmanned priests waddled away half an hour ago, chanting tonelessly in the singsong baby talk they say is the native language of the Illyrian plain. Their passing left the air heavy with musky smoke from their swinging censers. Priam stands beside the prostrate figure of his best son, spread-eagled before the chapel's central effigy: a god they now call Ares, but who once must have had another name, for he looks nothing like a god of Achaea. He is twice as tall as a man and four times as broad, bearded to the waist, with ivory eyes irised in crimson and a vermillion tongue half a yard long hanging from a gaping mouth. Around his neck is a chain of human skulls that Priam hopes are at least as old as Troy, but the hair still clinging to a few sometimes persuades him otherwise. In either hand the god holds a curved sword of a type Priam has never seen used in any human war, broader at the tip than at the haft. His extravagant erection is spiraled red and black with peeling paint fifty years old and hung with fresh garlands left yesterday.

While the priests were present, Hector would not abase himself. Once they were gone, he did, sprawling before the statue, weeping, pounding his forehead into the stone floor. Priam lets him. For a long time he looks at the effigy and thinks. Perhaps this is the problem: perhaps his people have let themselves believe they are Achaeans, when in fact they are not; they belong to this place and its gods, not the place across the sea from which they came so many years ago. Or perhaps the problem is not place but time. When the common ancestors of Achaea and Troy swept south, away from the fogs and rains and snows and retreating rivers of ice, the whole world was Trojan. Gods spoke daily to the men they guided, and a few kings, unquestioned intermediaries between the seen and unseen, ruled peoples so widely separated and thinly spread that their wars were no more than brief ceremonial feuds.

Their common past is the Trojan present, but Achaea's no more. When Paris returned from his travels with his new wife, Priam had thought him a liar when he described the dozens of kings who ruled Achaea. Priam could not understand how two kings could live two days' journey from one another, much less that many kings could stand in one another's presence. How could the gods' favor be spread so widely without disappearing entirely? Yet if the lesson of yesterday and the past nine years is to be learned, the favor has not been too freely given. Achaea and her many unequal kings have somehow retained Olympus' mandate, or Priam has lost it, which is why his best boy now sobs and grinds his forehead in temple dust.

"Hector," says Priam. "Hector. Son. Enough." Angered at his old man's thin voice, he remembers the day when he led armies, and speaks louder and deeper. "I said *enough*."

"*Not* enough," Hector sobs, so much the brokenhearted child that Priam's heart splits. "*Not* enough. I *ran*. I *ran away*." With that the sobbing doubles in volume and Hector cradles his head in folded arms.

94

Like any father, Priam has no idea of what to do. And like any father, he finally does the only thing he can think of: he drops to his knees and rests his hand on his son's head. "You did what the god said," he murmurs. "You're a good boy."

Hector turns and for an instant Priam is startled. His scarred face, rimmed with beard, is contorted just like that of the child he comforted a quarter century before when a toy bow suffered a broken string. "Am I, father?" asks Hector. "Am I?"

"Yes, son, you are. You are a good boy." Priam twines his fingers in Hector's sweat-soaked hair and shakes the great head gently. "Now get up. We have things to do."

"Sorry about yesterday," says Diomedes. He looks subdued or, more accurately, hung over. "I guess I fucked up again."

"You didn't fuck up," says Odysseus patiently. "You just spoke a little sooner than I'd hoped. Don't worry about it." He claps Diomedes on the shoulder. "Don't worry about it. How's your head, anyway?"

"Awful," says Diomedes. "I started drinking before Hector was halfway back to Troy and kept going until we went to see Agamemnon. But I'll be all right."

"I know you will, " says Odysseus. "Let's go get the others."

It's not the delegation Odysseus would have picked, but it wasn't up to him. It includes Telamonian Ajax, who isn't that bright, and Phoenix, Achilles' old teacher, who is an idiot. And, of course, Diomedes. "All right," says Odysseus. So far as he can tell, all but Phoenix are in the agonies of a hard battle followed by a day and a half's drunk. All but Phoenix are sweaty and ashen. Phoenix, on the other hand, is as perky as a pup. "All right," says Odysseus. "Why don't you let me do the talking?"

Telamonian Ajax and Diomedes nod. Phoenix speaks. "I have some influence with him, you know," he says. "He was my pupil. Perhaps I should speak first."

"Shut up," says Ajax. If his eyes stay open he will bleed to death through them.

"Pardon?" says Phoenix.

"I said shut up, you stupid fuck. If you speak once, I'll kill you."

"Oh," says Phoenix. "All right."

"We're agreed, then," says Odysseus. They move off.

☙

"Here they come," says Patroclus. "You were right."

"Of course I was," says Achilles. He positions himself on the bed and picks up the lyre. "Take a couple of minutes to let them in."

Patroclus leaves his post by the porthole and walks up the two steps out of the cabin and into the companionway. As he leaves, Achilles strikes the lyre and raises his voice in song: his latest composition.

O Aphrodite you Goddess of Love (twang)

With your wiles you govern Olympus above (twang)

Patroclus shakes his head and smiles as he clears the hatchway and gains the deck. Though his lover has Olympus' favor, it has been distributed unevenly; the Muses appear to have forgotten him.

The embassy is waiting. Diomedes and Telamonian Ajax look distinctly seedy—not surprising, as they've had a hard few days. Patroclus realizes that there may be another cause for their fatigue as the wind shifts and he catches the reek of stale vomit. He discreetly takes half a step to his left, avoiding the worst of the tavern blast. Phoenix looks fresh, his bright eyes vacant as ever, and Odysseus is Odysseus: his oddly unlined face set in its perpetual half smile like a funeral mask; short, thickset body furiously erect, as though posture alone will give him the height that nature denied him; white linen robe crisp as a priest's. Patroclus knows that on the palisade he saw action harder than any warrior, but he seems untouched by war, as he has in the decade since Agamemnon fetched him from Ithaca.

"My lords," says Patroclus. "You are most welcome. Will you have wine?"

"Sure," says Diomedes. "Hair of the dog, huh?" He begins to laugh but stops at Odysseus' glare.

"Lord Patroclus," says Odysseus, "you are most kind to greet us so and, of course, we gratefully accept your hospitality. Can we take our wine with Lord Achilles?"

"Of course," says Patroclus. "Please follow me."

The delegation has been waiting just at the gangway. As they walk the deck of the long, narrow ship, the few Myrmidons on board stare curiously.

96

The mutter running among them is not at all hostile; they want back in the war. Perhaps these envoys from Agamemnon will restore their crack at Troy.

It is only ten yards from midship to the stern hatch and Patroclus courteously stands aside while the delegation climbs down the ladder and waits at the cabin. They are not without entertainment: from behind the half-open hatch comes music.

So, by Aphrodite, be not deceived (twang)

Her wiles though many should not be believed (twang twang twang)

Patroclus feels Odysseus' gaze and meets his eye. The Ithacan's half smile remains frozen in its place, but his eyes crinkle. Patroclus smiles openly and shrugs. With a graceful apology he steps forward and opens the hatch to admit the lords.

Achilles is naked in bed, the sheet pulled up just below his navel and the lyre cradled in his left arm. He idly strokes it as the lords file in. They stand before him and still he lolls in bed. Odysseus hears Diomedes gasp and Telamonian Ajax growl at the impertinence. His head, always full of thoughts, holds two: first, why a man so obviously in love with himself would need another like Patroclus; second, whether just driving a knife through the bastard's heart now wouldn't simplify things enormously. But he is Odysseus, and he has a job to do. "My Lord Achilles. I had no idea you were so talented."

Achilles snorts and drops the lyre to the side of the bed. He laces his fingers behind his head and stretches lazily, fanning huge muscles as he does so. "Lord Odysseus," he says, "always with a mouth full of honey when he wants something, when he thinks he can talk his way into getting it. So what is it you want, my lord? Or better, what does your master want?"

The blood sings in Odysseus' ears. For an instant, he thinks: there is a dagger at my waist. If I laugh, he will not expect me to pull it; two steps forward and one stroke down, and I'll bathe in his blood. But he laughs without drawing bronze and even raises his arms to block Diomedes and Telamonian Ajax as they lurch forward to kill this impudent godlet.

"My master," says Odysseus, "is my duty. My master is the oath I swore. My master, Lord Achilles, is the same master as yours. My oath. *Our oath.* Or do you forget your oath in your rage?"

Phoenix chooses this moment to pipe up. "I thought I taught you better," he says sadly.

97

Achilles and Odysseus speak at once. *"What?"*

"I said, I thought I taught you better." Phoenix seems genuinely upset. "How can you lie in your bed when noble guests pay you a call? Are you ill, Achilles? You don't seem sick to me, boy."

Odysseus chews the inside of his cheek. He wants badly to laugh and then have this fool beheaded. Achilles doesn't seem to find any of this funny, particularly being called "boy." Coming back to himself, Odysseus decides that if Achilles kills Phoenix they will truly have no choice but to kill Achilles. He hastily runs the odds: two of the best warriors in the world—for Patroclus will come to his lover's aid—fresh, against three tired, middle-aged men, two of whom smell like old wineskins. They're less than even that he would leave the ship alive.

Before Odysseus can speak, Achilles acts. He throws his silk sheet aside and rolls off the big bed. Odysseus, Ajax, and Diomedes reach for their daggers and drop into a half crouch, weight forward on the balls of their feet, blades up before their faces, the three of them instinctively spreading wide, ready to cover one another. Phoenix just stands there and so does Patroclus. The second Odysseus sees this, he relaxes, though he maintains his defensive posture so as not to shame himself. Patroclus knows the big boy better than he does, after all.

Achilles laughs, the sound filling the cabin. "Sorry, my lords," he says. "Didn't mean to startle you. Just doing what teacher said." He stands by the side of the bed, naked, with his head touching the overhead. His hands are planted on his hips, his legs slightly spread, his shoulder muscles deliberately bunched. Odysseus wonders how anyone can be so thoroughly taken in by his own beauty, why Achilles needs anything but a mirror to make him complete. How the love and lust of men could have blinded him to the fact that there are others who see that mass of muscle and wonder not how it would feel to touch, but just how hard it would be to kill.

A group that, apparently, does not include Phoenix. "Oh, my beautiful boy," he coos. "How you have *grown.*"

Odysseus doesn't think Achilles can hear Ajax snarl. "I meant what I said, you old fool. One more word and you're dead."

Phoenix sighs but holds his peace. Achilles slowly struts before the delegation flexing, drumming his fingers idly against an abdomen hard as armor. Diomedes grunts and Odysseus glances over to see him roll his eyes. Odysseus dares a wink. "Sorry, I didn't have time to dress, my lords,"

Achilles says. He wanders to a porthole, showing his back, visibly tensing his buttocks. Odysseus tells himself that if he does not laugh through this display, he will start believing in the gods after all. Patroclus catches his eye, shrugs, and winks.

"So, my lords," Achilles booms, turning to face them. "What brings you here?"

"As I said," says Odysseus. "My duty and yours. Forget, for the moment, my duty and yours to the king, to the oaths we swore, you and I and each of us here. Think instead of our duty to the dead, to those who were young and alive when we left Aulis, to those who now wander through Hades, mouthless shadows of themselves, whose bodies we burned when we could and when not left to the dogs and birds. Think of those who died in the nine years we have been here, fighting with us, who looked to you and took courage to go on to the fights that left them food for the dogs and birds and the fires to which we fed them. Think of those who died two days ago while you lay safe and snug here in this ship, and those who lie dying now of wounds they suffered when great Achilles was not there to help them."

Achilles does not move; his eyes do not leave Odysseus', nor will Odysseus' leave his. But in his peripheral vision, Odysseus sees Patroclus, who has taken up position just behind his lover and to his right. Patroclus' face is wet with tears.

"Do you not hear their cries, Achilles? Did you not hear their cries when they died before the ditch? Did you not hear men crying, 'Achilles, Achilles'? Will you lie here in your great ship, in your silk bed, while men who died with your name on their lips are ferried across the River Styx wondering where you were when their souls slipped from their mouths into the sand and down to the Underworld? That is the duty of which I speak, Lord Achilles."

Even Achilles looks stunned. Patroclus is now weeping openly. At his right, Odysseus hears a barking cough and looks quickly to see Telamonian Ajax' face working with his effort to control himself.

Achilles speaks. "My lord," he says. His voice is even and low. "I honor and revere the Achaean dead with whom I fought and those with whom I have not, those who fell while you and Agamemnon tricked the Trojans to their deaths. But I think, what honor is there for me? Where is Achilles? Achilles, who led them in the first year, and the fifth, and the eighth. Achilles, whose name, as you say, was the last word of many brave men.

Achilles, for whom death was everywhere, just as it was for those who died, but who because his goddess mother protected him, lived anyway. And when your master—" Achilles sees Odysseus flinch and drives the point home "—your *master*, Lord Odysseus, stole my prize, *stole* her, stole what was mine, *mine*, *MINE*—" He stops himself. He is breathing so hard, Odysseus fears that he will use up all the air in the little cabin. Sweat is rolling down his ridged muscles and his eyes bulge from his head. But even possessed by his fury, Achilles can try to speak like a man. "I ask, Lord Odysseus, where were they when I was shamed? The dead, I will tell you, didn't rise up and say, 'This is wrong.' And unless I'm mistaken, the living were quiet, too. As were you, my lords."

He scans the delegation with his eyes full of hate. "Which of you here said to the king, 'Lord, this is wrong'? Who said, 'My lord, think of Achilles and what he has done for us'? Where was the lord who said, 'King Agamemnon, this shames one who has done you nothing but honor'? So it looks to me, my lords, as though you sat by and watched me be shamed. You watched my honor be dragged through the dust. Yet you come to me now and speak to me of my honor? Well, whatever honor I had, you and your big friend took away when you stole my prize."

Odysseus has not dropped his gaze from the bulging eyes. This is hard because he is afraid; he does not want to fail. He also does not want to die. Achilles' beard is flecked with spittle and it bristles in his rage, so he chooses his words carefully. "My lord," he says. "My lord, I do not come here to talk you out of your injury. Rather, I come to acknowledge it in sorrow and humility. And I come here not for myself, but for my king, our king, the King of Mycenae and High King of all the Achaeans. It is he who sends me, Lord Achilles, and it is he who would do reparation for all your hurts."

Achilles is silent a long time. Finally, he says, "Let's hear it, then."

Odysseus' iron smile increases a barely perceptible degree. "Thank you. First, so far as my Lord Agamemnon is concerned, if you will rejoin the fight, Troy is yours. When it is sacked, the first choice of its people is yours—women, boys, girls, men. As many as you can take, likewise horses and gear. As to its treasure, the greatest portion is yours as well. And the same is so with arms and armor; any trophy you desire is yours as of right."

"That's *if* Troy falls," Achilles observes acidly.

"My lord, if you rejoin the battle, there is no if."

"Right," says Achilles. "That's then. What about now?"

"Now," says Odysseus. "Now you have all that the girl Briseis brought with her, together with three bronze cauldrons and tripods from Agamemnon's own store, and any daughter of Agamemnon's you choose as your wife, sworn to you at a sacrifice to the gods."

"Well," says Achilles. "Well, well, well. Let's see. Sounds good, doesn't it, my Lord Patroclus?" He turns to face Patroclus, whose face remains impassive. He turns back to the delegation and strokes his beard in a parody of thought. "Hm. The best that Troy has to offer. If we sack it. If I live to sack it. Well, I'd get that, anyway. If I live. And if I don't, well, someone else gets it. Who, I wonder? Agamemnon? Hm. Could be. So if I don't live to sack Troy, what do I get? The girl's treasure, but not the girl. Hm. Looks to me as though Agamemnon's offering what I'd get anyway and half of what I should've got if *he* hadn't taken what was *mine*. Oh. Sorry." He raises his right hand, palm out. "I forgot about the tripods."

Odysseus is startled. If it weren't for the fact that the man is screaming, he'd sound entirely rational. He is angry with himself for offering all he had at the first opportunity. Now, what has he got to give? A couple of horses? A chariot? He'd probably have to beg Agamemnon for those. "My lord," he says. "Think of what the king offers, not the *things* he offers. The *what*. The essence. As you say, the king will give you half of what he took. What king does that? What king does that without showing the world that he has wronged a lord whom he would honor instead? And in acknowledging that wrong, his wrong, he honors you above any among us who have fought here at Troy. And you will ask as you must, 'Well, if he would erase that wrong, erase that shame he did me, why does he not return the girl as well?' And as to that, you must know, Lord Achilles, that the taking of the girl was not his will but Zeus', to compensate him for what he gave up when he surrendered *his* prize, Chryseis, daughter of Chryses the priest, to placate Apollo and stop the plague that was dropping us all like flies. In compensation, I tell you, for what *he* gave up for everyone's good."

Achilles looks as though he will speak, but Odysseus raises his own hand. "Sorry. And speaking of compensation, directed as he was by the Thunderer, he cannot give back what he took, so what has he offered instead? Another girl plundered from the Trojans? Another pussy and mouth and pair of tits who, if not rescued at a sack, would have become that night's fuck for anyone with a spear, then a toy for the mess tents, then at last a mess slave herself? Because that's what you lost in Briseis, Lord Achilles. No, instead he offers you his own daughter, *any* daughter. The King of Mycenae's daughter. The daughter of a king triumphant, not the daughter of the defeated headman of a tributary village. So I see what you say, Lord Achilles. Yet I must tell you that what you say is wrong."

Achilles smiles. A rare sight in itself; rarer still, because it seems genuinely humorous. "Lord Odysseus," he says. "Lord Odysseus of the honeyed mouth. I said it in anger a few minutes ago, but now I say it in admiration. That was very good. So good that I was almost persuaded, even knowing what I know that you don't know. But I'll tell you that now. Long ago, my mother, divine Thetis, told me that I could live long in Thessaly, or brief but gloriously here on the Illyrian plains. Back then I chose short life with honor. So if I accept the king's proposal, I stay at Troy to fight and die here, and thus won't enjoy any of the rich rewards he's offered. And I am dishonored here. Thus I can live a brief life in shame at Troy's walls, or a long life in equal shame at home; not a choice I have to think about."

"Good point," says Phoenix, just before Telamonian Ajax clubs him with a closed fist on the ear so hard he staggers.

Despite themselves, both Odysseus and Achilles laugh. "He's an idiot," says Achilles, "but sometimes even idiots are right."

Odysseus will say nothing, but his smile is back in place when he meets Achilles' eyes.

Achilles speaks again. "Tell Agamemnon to give his daughter to one who has kingly honor, not like my own, which is nothing. And thank you for coming, my lords."

Dismissed, the delegation mumbles courtesies and leaves.

They are a dozen yards from the ship before anyone speaks. "Nice try," says Diomedes.

"Not good enough," says Odysseus.

"Really nice try," says Telamonian Ajax. "Really."

"I couldn't have done better myself," says Phoenix. Telamonian Ajax knocks him sprawling to the ground.

☙

"Let me," says Patroclus. They sit on the edge of the big bed. The delegation left half an hour ago and neither has spoken since.

"Let you what?" says Achilles.

"Let me lead the Myrmidons. Let me join the fight. I won't if you say no, but I want to." He turns to face Achilles' glare.

"Why would you shame me so?"

"I wouldn't ask if I thought it would shame you. I wouldn't do it if I thought it would shame you. I think it would do you honor. To show the rest of the army that even though you have been so wronged that you can't join the fight yourself, not for Troy's gold, not for Agamemnon's daughter, still you won't hurt your friends by holding back your troops. You'll look like a man much bigger than Agamemnon." He slips his hand between Achilles legs and squeezes.

Achilles smiles. It is as tender as he can ever be. "And you want a shot at glory too, don't you?"

Patroclus smiles back and tightens his grip. "Yes. I would lie if I said no."

Achilles' face betrays no notice of Patroclus' hand, but his cock does. "If I say all right, will you remember two things?"

"Yes."

"First, Troy is mine. You can go to the walls but not over. Second, Hector is mine for a couple of reasons: only I can take him—if you try him, you'll die—and only I *should* take him. Will you agree to that?"

Patroclus' voice is a whisper. He can't believe this is happening. "Yes," he breathes, "my lord."

"All right," says Achilles. He stands. "If you're going in for me, you should wear this."

He steps to the big chest at the foot of the bed and flips the lid open. He bends and then stands with his breastplate and backplate held negligently one-handed.

Patroclus gasps. He stands, then drops to his knees and holds up his arms. Achilles raises the armor over Patroclus' head. It is the most beautiful metalwork in the world: fashioned of something stronger than bronze yet lighter. Its surface is curved and rippled to mirror the muscles of a man more than human, chased with scenes of gods, thunderstorms, and

103

waterfalls that, looked at through the corner of the eye in the right light, stand out from imprisoning metal and flow and glow like apparitions. The thongs joining back to front and side to side are not mere plaited leather, but woven silk braided together with strands of silver. As Achilles lowers it to slip over his upraised arms, Patroclus closes his eyes because he is afraid to see the inside of something made in heaven.

His eyes still closed, he feels its weight settle on his shoulders and is surprised that it is not heavier. It seems to weigh nothing at all. He feels Achilles cinch the side thongs tight and as the armor encases him, he feels strength radiate from it into his belly and loins and heart. Overcome, he bites his lip. As he fights his tears, silky leather cheek pads slide down his temples and cuddle just beneath his eyes. He bows his head with the sudden weight of the helmet, then raises it and opens his eyes to find his vision suddenly restricted by metal: flaring nosepiece below, the artificial brow above. As he begins to sob, his head quivers with the weight of Achilles' pure white horsehair plume.

"Well," says Achilles, standing in front of him naked, voice soft. "It fits."

Crying like a child, Patroclus throws his arms around Achilles' knees and buries his face in his thigh. Hard hands find his neck between armor and helmet and direct his face higher.

Phoenix's nose has stopped bleeding. "Are you sure you're all right?" asks Odysseus.

Phoenix nods, pressing to his face a big wad of fabric torn from Diomedes' festival robe. "I'm fine," he says around cloth and clot. Still, he hunches on the ground like a whipped dog.

"Good" says Odysseus. He straightens up and steps over to Telamonian Ajax. "Thanks," he says quietly.

"Don't mention it," says Telamonian Ajax.

The delegation is a sorry sight. Diomedes has had to throw up the two bowls of wine he gulped at Achilles' ship, and now looks as though he would pay Charon all he has to take him across the River and out of this life. Phoenix squats and will look at no one as he nurses what probably is a broken nose, and Telamonian Ajax looks absurdly proud of himself. It has been an hour since they left Achilles' black ship. Odysseus led them away from Agamemnon's tent rather than towards it; now they stand near the southern end of the palisade, almost in the surf, fifty yards from the nearest Achaean, who stares incuriously, fogbound in his own posttraumatic hangover.

"All right," says Odysseus. "I asked you to let me do all the talking. It didn't work. It's my fault."

"No way it's your fault," says Diomedes.

"Right," says Ajax. "Not your fault at all. It's the gods who made Achilles an arrogant bastard, not you."

"Thanks," says Odysseus. "But someone's got to take the heat for this. You stay here or wait an hour or so and go back to your own ships. I'll tell Agamemnon myself."

Ajax snarls. "Like fuck you will. I won't let you."

Odysseus smiles and shakes his head. "Again, thanks, but it's better this way." The others protest, but Odysseus is firm. Soon he has his way and makes off towards Agamemnon's tent—using the long way so he will run into as few as possible. Well, that worked at least, he thinks as he trudges along. Without the rest of the delegation standing there, he can put whatever spin on this he has to. He can't blame *them*, of course, but when he tells Agamemnon how it went, he will have been a lot firmer and Achilles a lot more defiant. Best not to have any witnesses handy. And when his version of events reaches their ears, he can, of course, deny it as the usual exaggerated gossip of the camp.

The bigger problem is Agamemnon himself. Odysseus' stomach clenches when he thinks of his reaction. Not that he's in any danger; the king needs him too much. He just hates kissing a half-smart tyrant's ass, and he knows he'll have some puckering to do. He imagines the exchange: *Well, Lord Odysseus, I guess the Gray-eyed One finally let you down, eh? Had to happen sometime. Well, next time you have a good idea, don't hesitate to let me know. And in the meantime, there's a really dirty little raid we have to take care of. And you're just the man for it.*

"Hey, it's Lord Odysseus!" The shout breaks his train of thought. Startled, he realizes that he is close to the pickets near Agamemnon's tent. "Hey, boys, let's hear it for Lord Odysseus!" A full-throated cheer erupts from a dozen soldiers and their captain rushes forward and claps him on the shoulder. "Great work, my lord! I'm proud to serve with you!"

Odysseus grins and nods and thanks the man. He is obviously still over-joyed by the triumph over Troy earlier in the week. Once he hears about the failure with Achilles, he will, of course, revise his opinion accordingly. Odysseus knows no emotion as short-lived as gratitude.

He resumes his trek to the tent, now just a few hundred yards distant. As he approaches, he is recognized with greater frequency and equal en-thusiasm. At first he thinks it is the last dregs of the heady wine of Hector's defeat. Soon, however, it is clear that the troops are even happier than the day they stripped a thousand Trojan dead down to their skins. Odysseus groans inwardly and outwardly beams: some fool has probably spread the word of his entirely imaginary success with Achilles. As he waves and nods to his admirers, he says to himself, "Athena, if you exist, if you ever spoke to me, speak to me now and get me out of this."

He reaches Agamemnon's tent: four soldiers and a slave stand at its flap, the soldiers grinning, the slave almost incontinent with joy. The slave falls at his feet and kisses them. Odysseus prays for an earthquake to open the ground and swallow him up. The slave scampers back into the tent, while the soldiers start a victory chant that is taken up all around. "Re-joice, we conquer! Rejoice, we conquer!" As Odysseus beams back into their grinning, happy faces, he thinks: I am so fucked.

The tent flap pops open and the slave flies out to be followed immedi-ately by his royal master, his face wreathed in smiles, the limping Menelaus at his side and a dozen lords and the girl Briseis just behind. Fucked, thinks Odysseus. Completely fucked. Up the ass by a wild boar.

"My lord, my lord, my lord." Agamemnon takes two steps forward and embraces him. A kiss on either cheek. "My Lord Odysseus. Who but you could have achieved this great thing?"

"Great thing?" Odysseus' voice comes out a squeak, so he covers it with a cough and says, "Great king!"

Agamemnon laughs, drapes his arm across Odysseus' shoulders, and turns him to face the cheering crowd. This can't possibly be worse, thinks Odysseus. All right, I'll play along and when they find out what's really going on, I'll tell them the treacherous bastard changed his mind.

"Great king!" laughs Agamemnon. He bellows to the crowd. "There is no great king without great lords, and none greater than Odysseus! For who but he would have done what no one expected? What no one could have foretold? What not even I could have wished for?"

Odysseus tries to look like a man trying to look humble. His downcast eyes scan the crowd around him for a clue. These idiots are laughing and clapping as though Achilles has not only rejoined the war, but promised each man a horse and a hand job. Wait a second, those are Myrmidons! What are Achilles' men doing here at Agamemnon's tent? And why are they laughing and giving him the thumbs-up?

He raises his eyes and studies Agamemnon's profile. What he sees confuses and reassures him equally: the man has never been good at faking anything, and he looks genuinely happy. "And so," booms Agamemnon, "when I send Lord Odysseus to do that which cannot be done, he does not that thing, but a thing which I would never have asked him to attempt! For when I tell him, bring Lord Achilles back to the fight, he brings not him, but all his men, with Lord Patroclus at their head in Achilles' armor! And who can doubt that Lord Achilles will long stand to be out of the fight when his men and his best of friends have joined it!"

Odysseus, thunderstruck, remembers the tears that ran down Patroclus' face when he conjured up the fallen to taunt Achilles. "Who indeed?" he shouts, laughing.

On the Scaean rampart stand Hector and Priam, alone. They face the Achaeans a mile distant, from whom come clatter and babble and something that, when the breeze shifts to bear intelligible sound, seems to be laughter and cries of joy. Hector speaks. "I think this is trouble," he says.

Priam nods. "I think it is."

Odysseus is wrapped in Agamemnon's bear hug. From out of the corner of his eye, he sees a hundred yards away the dust kicked up by a chariot. Through the dust he can see the silvery glint of armor no mere man should wear. "Patroclus is coming," he whispers into his king's ear, folding him in a reciprocal embrace.

"Right," the king whispers back. "Listen, the deal was Troy and my daughter for Achilles, not for Patroclus. Right?"

"Right," says Odysseus.

PATROCLUS
AT THE WALLS

Before, the armor seemed impossibly light. Now, it has negative weight, lifting him heavenward off the floor of the chariot and almost out of his boots. Patroclus is not sure whether it is the metal itself or what greets him as he rides from the long, black-prowed ship behind the divine horses. Men, seeing that pure white plume and sparkling metal, laugh and weep and drop to their knees hands extended, palms upward, in thanksgiving to the gods. "He's back," they cry. "Oh, Olympian Zeus, he's *back.*" And even when they recognize him beneath his lover's armor behind those fraudulent horses, their joy is undiminished. "Look," they say, "it's not him but Lord Patroclus in *his* armor! Well, can *he* be far behind? So follow him, boys, because that's where Lord Achilles wants us to be, and that's where Lord Achilles *will* be!"

And so Patroclus slows his horses. He tells himself it is because he wants to give all the Myrmidons a chance to form up behind him, which is true; it is also true that just this once he wants to bask in glory that is not exclusively derivative. Just this once he will be something more than Achilles' "great friend."

Patroclus came to Troy in obedience to an oath. He and Idomeneus and Philoctetes and all the others swore to uphold the rights of whoever won

108

Helen's hand. When Paris stole her and Agamemnon raised his vengeful standard, none of her unsuccessful suitors had any choice but to rally to the defense of Menelaus' bridal bed. Achilles, bound by no such sacrament, came merely for the fight. When he joined the cause, Achilles was in the first flower of his manhood, a mass of muscle with beard just beginning to fringe his jaw, a young god soon the darling of everyone in the army, adored for his courage as much as his beauty. Patroclus, though just a few years older, was already past his first youth. But Achilles remembered their shared boyhood, when wrestling matches had turned into sweaty, confused couplings. And soon, if Achilles was the army's darling, Patroclus was its envy.

But now Achilles is in his great ship, and for the moment, at least, it is Patroclus who is the army's sweetheart. As the god-matched horses draw him through the ranks, he raises his arm and grins in acknowledgment of the troops' adulation and thinks, *So this is what it's like to be Achilles.* And there is no jealousy in it; his work before the Trojan walls has won him respect just one notch short of Diomedes', and it never occurred to him that any man born of a mortal mother could have what Achilles gets every day just for being himself. But now it is he who receives it—adoration, as far removed from respect as sex from affection. And who can blame him, how can he blame himself, if just for the moment he bathes in it, feels the divine armor soak it in and radiate it back into his body amplified as he wraps the reins around his waist and raises both hands in the air, fingers outstretched, open to receive all the sudden, unexpected love?

The horses sense his wish and slow their pace to a walk. Around and behind him, the Myrmidons coalesce laughing and weeping. The chant of "Achilles! Achilles!" thunders through the camp and shakes the wooden palisades. Soon, however, another rhythm, more complex, intrudes. "Pa-*troc*-lus! Pa-*troc*-lus! Now follow Pa-*troc*-lus!"

Grinning and cheering himself, Patroclus brings his horses to a halt and turns in the chariot car to face the ranks. *His* ranks. Behind him are a thousand men, the best of Achaea. They are distinct from the rest of the Achaeans in every way: taller, broader, their armor better at its making and better maintained through a decade of war. Less than half are truly Achilles' men, born to the service of Peleus' house. The rest are freebooters from as far away as Sicily, hungry for war and eager to serve under the half-divine boy-god. "Hey boys!" he shouts. "Thanks for coming!"

The men laugh and roar. Coming from anyone else, this would have provoked silence at best, more likely uneasy growls. What general would address his troops this way? But this is Lord Patroclus, the sweet night to Achilles' hard day, who has sent a hundred Trojans down to meet their ancestors, yet still would sit and listen sympathetically to the lowest troopers' drunken worries about his wife's fidelity. From him this familiarity is welcome. The men cheer and beat their shields against the bronze greaves covering their knees.

"Thanks," shouts Patroclus. "Thanks again. Now..." he looks for words. Never before has he had to address troops like this. "Now..." The clatter of shields against shin armor lets up a little. Patroclus thinks he can hear the beginnings of a murmur running through the troops. Hey, he's a great guy, but not a goddess' son. Patroclus draws strength from his armor. "Now, on to Troy!"

The responsive cheer nearly blasts his helmet from his head. He knows he shouldn't have put it quite that way, but in the silence of his own mind some god spoke, and that must be the way it should be. He unwraps the reins from his waist and snaps the horses into action. As they lunge forward at a trot, he pulls his sword and raises it above his head, first perpendicular to the ground, then pointing forward to Ilion. "On to Troy!" Behind him a thousand voices repeat his cry, and for the first time in his life, he knows the taste of power.

Agamemnon is distressed. He knows enough not to show it and continues to stand there, beaming, as Achilles' massed horses and men stream ahead. He turns to Odysseus at his right, grins broadly, and speaks without moving his teeth. "The bastard's not coming here."

Odysseus smiles, looks down, and with his hand before his mouth says, "I know. He's going for the gate and Troy."

Agamemnon laughs grimly. "What the fuck does he think he can do?" he asks through clenched teeth. "Ignore his king and the army and take Troy with a thousand men and the golden boy's armor?" He laughs uproariously.

Odysseus is impressed. Laughing himself, he leans towards the king as though about to share an impossibly dirty joke. Agamemnon drapes an arm over his shoulder and drops his head near, his face a mask of mock gravity. "Lord," says Odysseus, "we're stuck. No choice. If he goes out there alone he dies and takes a big chunk of the army with him. If we go with him, we can minimize the damage and maybe, if we're lucky, kick ass. We have to follow as though this was all part of the plan, and it looks as though we have about ten minutes."

Agamemnon whoops with laughter and claps Odysseus on the back. "Oh, that's good! That's very good! 'Those sheep are all liars, anyway'!" He doubles over, slamming his fists into his knees as he roars. "But now to business. Heralds, hear me!" he cries, standing upright, arms held high. "Now is the time our secret plan must be in effect! My lords, to your men! To your chariots! Surprise is ours! Troy is ours! Put on your armor and follow Patroclus to Troy!"

There is half a minute of dead silence while men stand like statues. One by one, wine bowls drop from frozen hands. Next gasps, then chuckles, then a murmur that in seconds raises itself to the roar of men whose throats are parched for blood. It starts to form itself into words—*Troy, Patroclus*—but Odysseus knows his people's love for time-wasting display too well to allow it to grow into a chant that won't end until Patroclus is within arrow range of the Trojan walls.

"My lords, didn't you hear the king?" he thunders. "Surprise is all! To your men and on to Troy!"

Now the lords scramble. In seconds, Agamemnon and Odysseus are alone except for retainers. "Now what?" asks Agamemnon.

"Well," says Odysseus. "Loverboy has to stay out front, so do the Myrmidons. But flank them with chariots and get the light infantry behind them with archers with orders to cover the Myrmidons. And once we've got the heavy stuff there, battle should be well joined. So leave it to the unit commanders to do whatever seems right. Whatever happens, happens."

"Should we try for Troy? Today? We're not ready."

Odysseus considers for a second, but just a second. "Patroclus will probably try it. If he gets lucky, we follow. Otherwise, no. Someone there has to make the call." He considers again, but the problem is not military. "One of us should stay here. It should be you. I think we'll be all right but this could turn into a bloodbath. Someone has to get the survivors back."

"Does Athena tell you what will happen?"

"No," says Odysseus. "Just what to do."

"All right," says Agamemnon. "You go, but stay with the heavies until you don't have a choice." Odysseus nods and turns to leave. "And one more thing." Startled by the tone of command Odysseus turns to face the king, who now actually looks like a king. "Come back."

"I will," says Odysseus. However moved he may be, his bronze mask will not betray him. "I will, lord."

☙

Hector and Bizimarko are on the rampart over the Scaean Gate, resting their elbows on the stone. "Well," says Hector. "Whatever else, we got rid of Pandarus."

Bizimarko spits over the wall. Both follow the gob's meteoric path to the ground. It is long seconds before it hits; Troy's walls are high. "Right," says Bizimarko. "You know how I felt about that, prince. The guy got fucked."

"I know how you feel," says Hector. "We didn't have a lot of choice. We swore a truce; he broke it. We could have burned him alive just to make sure the gods knew we were sorry. At least he got to die like a soldier."

"Right," says Bizimarko sourly. "Hear he died like a pretty good soldier."

"That's what I hear, too," says Hector.

They stare in silence at the Achaean camp. "Lot of dust coming up from there," says Bizimarko.

"Sure is," says Hector. "Victory games, probably." As he speaks the words he remembers his flight across the ditch and feels his bowels curdle with shame.

"I don't hear any victory hymns," says Bizimarko. "Ten thousand men a mile away, you'd think you'd hear it."

"Bad wind," says Hector.

"Blowing our way. We should hear victory hymns." Bizimarko is no longer resting on his elbows. "By your leave, let's send some runners out to the pickets. Something isn't right."

"Don't jump at shadows, Bizimarko. They're too tired from beating us to try us again today."

"Maybe, my lord, but—lord, the gate is opening."

"Bringing out more dead to burn, Bizimarko."

112

"Moving pretty fast for that, lord."

Hector sees the chariots. "Taunting us with games, Bizimarko, under our noses in front of their own walls." His voice lacks conviction.

"I don't think so, lord," says Bizimarko, his voice suddenly cracking. "They're headed straight for us. And look who's in the lead!"

Hector stares and will not believe. A mile away is armor so bright that it shatters sunlight. It sparkles at the head of what looks like a column of chariots. Above it, Hector imagines a plume that he cannot possibly see at this range.

Bizimarko looks white. "He bleeds, man," says Hector. "Sound the alarm."

For over a minute the bedroom in the high tower has resonated with the gongs. Helen raises her head and Paris' cock slips from her lips. "Don't stop," he breathes. "Please. I'm close. I'll go as soon as you're done." Helen hesitates, but a rough hand forces her back down.

The bedroom door is flung open. Before Paris can reach for the dagger beneath his pillow, Hector is across the room. "Sorry. They're halfway here, Achilles at their head." For the first time he seems to take in the scene before him. His brother stretched out on his back, either hand locked on a bedpost; Helen, naked, kneeling between his spread legs, fingers wrapped around his erection, head turned towards Hector, wet lips pouting. "Sorry," says Hector. He leaves even faster than he entered.

Helen looks at her husband. Then she looks down at her hand. He is limp.

Patroclus realizes that this is not going to be as easy as he thought. Before today he has commanded only small units, bands of no more than fifty men who were usually within reach of his voice and example. Though he knew when he thought about it that what Achilles did with the Myrmidons was different, he hasn't really thought about it all that often. So when he and his thousand men pour through the gates and on towards Troy, he looks behind to admire his new command. Expecting orders, it immediately slows. Patroclus laughs nervously and cracks the reins.

The horses advance faster than the infantry can follow, and soon he has to slow to allow them to catch up. Looking behind again, he sees more troops pouring through the gates; the Achaean army is following him. His chest swells with pride, straining the thongs that Achilles has cinched so tight to make the divine armor fit. Behind a line of heavy infantry he sees a black plume behind matched black horses and thinks he can almost make out Athena's owl on Odysseus' breastplate. Delighted, he raises his right hand and waves.

The Myrmidons respond instantly. Troops fan out from the column and form up on the right. Patroclus starts to wave them back into echelon. Realizing that he will simply compound his mistake, he turns the gesture into a forward sweep of his arm. To Troy. The troops roar and he urges his horses into a fast walk. He'll get his lopsided flank back into line before they get into arrow range.

"What is he *doing*?" says Bizimarko. He stares incredulously at the advancing Achaeans, chariots flanked on the right only by a thin force of infantry.

"I don't know," says Hector. "He must have something behind the flank."

"Or nothing and he wants us to think he does."

"Could be." Hector is in full armor. Around him on the wall are all the war councilors, including his frustrated brother. Excluding, however, his father, who is still immured in the family temple with its former men.

"Lord," says Bizimarko. "Let me take some chariots and hit that flank, just so we know what's behind it. If there is anything behind it. Now."

"Not yet, Bizimarko. We need to know what the gods say. If Achilles is back in the war, something has happened on Olympus and we need to know what it is."

Bizimarko almost spits again, but thinks better of it, remembering Pandarus. The royal house looks dimly on sacrilege. "I hope the gods speak before those sons of bitches have ladders on the wall."

The war councilors shift and murmur angrily, their silks whispering and plumes nodding. Their angry mutters are cut short when Hector says, "I hope so, too."

Bizimarko grunts. "Pardon my back, noble lords," he says with sarcasm just light enough to be ignored without the royal bastard cousins' loss of face. "I'm going to the wall to see what's going on."

Artibex creaks forward and whispers in Hector's ear. "Was even his father noble?"

Hector spins and stares in astonishment at the rouged lizard face. "And his grandfather. As if that matters, Uncle, when the Achaeans may be an hour from fucking our wives."

"It matters, Hector," says Artibex, smiling and dipping a triple-plumed silver helmet no soldier could wear without laughing. "But his great-grandfather was not, was he?"

"No, Uncle," says Hector wearily. "No, I don't think he was."

"Ah," says Artibex with satisfaction. "So I thought. Well, that explains—"

"Prince Hector!" The shout from the wall stops Artibex midsentence. "Lord," cries Bizimarko, "look at this!" His arm spins wildly and his face is bisected by a grin.

"That explains a lot. *Quite* a lot," Artibex concludes, sniffing.

Hector grunts and with a quick bow to Artibex—several degrees less formal than what protocol prescribes, a fact not lost on his stunned uncle—bolts to the rampart. "What is it?" he asks.

"Look at Achilles."

"I'm looking. What should I see?"

"A man who can handle troops for one thing, lord. Since I've been here, he's stopped twice and had his rear chariots running into the infantry—ha! There he goes again!" As Hector watches, two bands of archers leave the column and with consummate military precision wheel and collide with one another. The man under the white plume waves his sword in obvious frustration.

"Mother of the world," says Hector. "Is he drunk?"

"Don't think so," says Bizimarko. "Is he acting like Achilles?"

"No."

"Would Achilles fuck up a nice simple advance like this on his worst day? Drunk or sober?"

"No," says Hector, slowly.

"And we think that's Achilles because it's his horses and his armor, right?"

"Right," says Hector, more slowly still.

"So why can't it be someone else wearing Achilles' armor and driving Achilles' horses? Like, for example, Patroclus?"

Hector stares at the advancing Achaeans. The advance guard of a thousand Myrmidons is less than half a mile away. Behind them is a much larger force, five thousand at least, among whose leaders Hector can easily pick out Odysseus, Teucer, Diomedes, both Ajaxes. But that larger force moves with discipline and seems careful to keep itself separate from the Myrmidons who now advance at a sprint. Or at least most of them do. A quarter of the force has inexplicably planted its shields and leveled javelins as though to repel a chariot charge from nowhere. Achilles, or whoever it is in his armor, has now actually veered away from the head of the column towards troops defending themselves from no one.

"Apollo the Charioteer," says Hector. "You're right."

"You're right I'm right," says Bizimarko. "Lord," he adds hastily, but in battle there is no rank but that of war. "Think that Patroclus or whoever he is just fucked up an order again and that's why those boys are ready to receive chariots we haven't sent. Yet."

"So it's not Achilles at all," says Hector.

Bizimarko almost sighs. "No, lord," he says at last. "It's not. Do we still need the gods' permission to act?"

Hector stares at the big archway connecting the citadel to the rampart through which he silently begs his father and the priests to come to tell him what to do. But the archway, convoluted painted stone, remains stubbornly empty. At last, Hector says, "What do you suggest?"

"Right now," says Bizimarko eagerly, "archers. Pour arrows into them. Let the Myrmidons hit the wall and break up. Keep pouring the arrows in while we get ready. Then hit them before the supporting force gets here."

Hector still stares at the archway. Still empty. Finally, he lifts his helmet from the crook of his elbow and settles its comforting weight on his head. "All right," he says. "Let's do it."

Odysseus grits his teeth as Patroclus inadvertently orders yet another precise maneuver. He almost spits on the ground but stops himself. He has an audience; the last thing he wants to do is show contempt for a man he is about to order other men to die defending.

The main Achaean force has been at a full stop for a quarter of an hour while Patroclus untangles his cock from his loincloth. From the looks of things it will be at least as long before it will move again. Odysseus steps out of the chariot car and squats before the dozen men sitting behind it. "All right," he says. "Listen up." His voice is a harsh rasp just loud enough to reach the back row. "The Gray-eyed Lady has spoken to me." The men murmur reverently and Odysseus is briefly ashamed. Briefly. "Olympus is unsettled. The gods are watching us. If we prevail today, the weight in the Thunderer's scales may finally shift enough so that he will give us Troy. You're my best, my very best, so I will speak to you as man to man." As he expected, the troops nudge each other and grin with pride. Odysseus wonders again at how cheaply lives can be bought.

"Lord Patroclus is a great fighter. A *great* fighter. But boys, I won't tell you anything you don't know when I say he's no Achilles." As he expects, a ripple of laughter runs through the men and he catches them with a glare. "A *great* fighter," he says again, and waits until the embarrassed silence has lasted just long enough. "Anyway, as She of the Gray Eyes tells me, if Lord Patroclus prevails, we may win the day, if not today, soon. But if he falls, Troy's friends on Olympus will lick the Thunderer's toes and say, 'Well, you see, Achaea isn't worthy to win.'" His men's silence screams through the din of war. "So we must save Lord Patroclus. *You* must save Lord Patroclus. I know you can do it. Will you?"

These are not the roaring louts who make up a new song every time a third-echelon commander tells them that Troy is bad. They have been with Odysseus from the start and their continuing survival, if nothing else, proves skill and steadiness. So rather than break into the usual cries and victory chants, they simply nod to one another and at last to Odysseus.

"Good," he says. "I knew you would." He considers adding the threat, And if he dies don't come back, but that would be folly of the worst kind. He knows these boys. If Patroclus dies, it will be because they couldn't save him. It does no good to shame any of them into wasting themselves in heroic suicide.

"All right," he says. "Do it."

The air is so thick with arrows that he can barely see the sun. Patroclus doesn't care.

Before they came under the walls, his skin under the armor was slick with sweat not from effort, but humiliation. He could not break wind with-

117

out the troops behind him hearing another command, another crazy, embarrassing mistake that took him long, agonizing minutes to unravel, mortified under the gaze of his enemies on the Scaean rampart and his friends behind.

But now it doesn't matter. His outriders have hit the Trojan skirmishers, and the first Achaeans have fallen with arrows in their throats in the rush to bring ladders to the wall. War is just war, equally chaotic whether directed by kingly Agamemnon or some slave from his kitchen. Patroclus actually laughs when a razor-edged arrow grazes his cheek and the iron taste of blood fills his mouth. He spins to rally the troops behind and sees that he is suddenly surrounded by Ithacans, quiet and tight, moving at a schooled jog trot. "Hey," he yells, "if we live through this, thank your lord!"

Silence from the bodyguard. Finally, the one whom Patroclus takes to be their leader, a thick-chested man with a beard going gray, says, "Mind those horses, lord, and maybe we will!"

Patroclus laughs a little wildly. Less than a hundred yards ahead is the wall itself, gray and scaly as elephant hide, here and there decorated by the graffiti of the few invaders who can write—"Leonidas was here" or "fuck Troy"—broken only by the huge bronze-bound oaken gates, pimpled by ten thousand arrow strikes and blackened by marauders' fire. It's thirty feet high, its upper reaches ragged with the crenellations that allow Trojan archers to rain down death on the Achaeans. But against that wall is now one ladder, as usual not quite the right size, its top five feet above the crest of the wall. The Trojans thrust it away. It falls and the Achaeans at its base hoot and cheer and lift it again. One of their number, which is fewer than the fingers on both hands, decides to try for an honor that will get a constellation named after him, and dies with an arrow in his eye before he has achieved the fifth rung.

This looks good to laughing Patroclus. He throws his reins to the Ithacans' leader. "Remember me to your lord!" he shouts and, still laughing, pulls his sword and runs for the ladder. He doesn't bother with the troops behind, nor does he think of them. Nor do the arrows bouncing off his glowing armor remind him of mortality. There is only the wall and the ladder up it and Troy beyond.

The survivors holding the base are about to run as he reaches it, but when they see the man cased in silver sprinting towards them, they plant its feet in the ground and bend their shoulders to steady it. Not breaking stride, Patroclus shouts, "Good men!" and a yard from the ladder leaps to catch the tenth rung in a single hand while holding his sword high. His feet scramble and find purchase, and he climbs nearly as fast as he can walk. The shame of the long advance and his ineptitude at managing a thousand men for a thousand yards dissolves, washed away in the surf of arrows clattering harmlessly against the metal his beloved's mother has had forged for him. He thinks to turn on the ladder and urge the Achaeans forward, but remembers where he is and remembers too that if the Achaeans won't follow him now, they deserve to die in the sea with their ships burning around them as the Trojans jeer.

Halfway now, and the surf of arrows is a tidal wave. Exposed skin, naked of divine bronze, takes its hits, but the Trojan arrows slice without striking bone or artery. He bleeds, and bleeds a lot. It is nothing that will slow his advance up to the plumed and painted men at the top of the wall who push the ladder back, only to have the hearties at its foot grunt and struggle to keep it planted.

Then he is at the top and it is like nothing he has ever seen or imagined seeing.

The rampart, object of a decade in which the Achaeans have spilled blood enough to float their ships, which no living Achaean has seen, is dominated by a dozen silly old men in play armor their great-grandchildren should wear; old men painted like harborside whores and stinking of the Phoenicians' most overpriced perfumes, gaping and shrieking at this bloody man on the ladder. Among them are two or three soldiers, including a bear in bronze who must be Hector. They strain crazily to push back the ladder on which Patroclus stands and wave furiously forward the archers on either side who have been pouring down death.

As the ladder shakes, he knows he must descend, but for a moment, he peeks around his shield. Troy. Within its ragged circle of thirty-foot walls, a mile across at its widest, palace is piled on palace, each noble's great house twined around an even greater house, golden-eaved temples abutting granaries big enough to feed Mycenae in its longest remembered siege. Zigzag stinking streets are choked with people tattooed, painted, scented, hung with un-Achaean amulets dedicated to gods once fed with the ashes of sacrificed firstborns.

The ladder wobbles again and Patroclus knows he must go. But before he does, he targets the oldest and most absurd of the scented reptiles on the rampart and throws his sword like an awkward spear. It spins harmlessly at the Trojan grandee, who drops to all fours in panic. "I'll be back!" he bellows. "I'll be back to kill you all!"

Patroclus is halfway up the ladder. It is his third attempt of the day. He hears behind him the shriek of horses, the curses of men, the crash of metal on metal that means battle has been joined. He does not look back. It is nothing to him; all that matters is the top of the ladder. If he heard his own mother screaming for help from below, he would not slow his progress, hand over hand, foot after foot. He is close; the rampart is two yards above. He laughs and weeps. Snot bubbles from his nose to join his tears and run into his beard. Old wounds acquired earlier that day break their crusts and ooze dark blood; new wounds, fresh from Trojan arrows pelting him like hail, pour bright thin red that mixes with his sweat and drips from his pumping elbows and knees. He has fought all day in the Aegean heat in armor that weighs half as much as he. He has tasted neither water nor wine since he rode from the Achaeans' wooden palisades five hours before. His heart pounds and flutters. The world he can see has constricted to a narrow circle, a tunnel of blue sky edged in one quadrant with Trojan stone.

Another rung. He squints up and tries to focus on his objective, which is hard to do with vision so distorted. He makes out motion and drops his head. Not a moment too soon; bronze strikes his helmet and makes his ears ring. A Trojan arrow. The reverberation stops, but he can hear nothing. He shakes his head. Still nothing from above or below. No scream of man, no twang of bow, no crash of metal on metal. Nothing. Did the arrow make him deaf? Has he climbed this high to become a cripple, an object of pity and mirth, hours after the gods made him the love of all men?

He shakes his head harder in wide swings, like a Cretan bull trying to throw its assailant. This is the kind of joke the gods love. He will not believe that they played it on him.

He looks over his shoulder at the battle before the wall, his tunnel vision suddenly panoramic. The war is spread before him, frozen, the armies locked

in a single silent instant of mutual annihilation, like a thousand flies in amber. He stares in disbelief, his jaw locked open like a snake that can swallow a meal larger than its head. No, he thinks. Fight, please fight. He knows what this sudden stillness means: the gods are very near, and he doesn't want to be very near the gods.

He looks up. On the rampart, a dozen archers take their aim but, inexplicably, won't let fly. A soldier has a rock raised over his head, his face split in a bellow none can hear, and the rock stays where it is. Patroclus counts the beats of his heart. One, two, three, and still the soldier does not throw, still the archers do not shoot. He stares hoping for motion, any motion, even if it proves fatal. Nothing. He gathers his courage and tries to move his right hand to take the next rung of the ladder. It remains where it is, frozen. He screams with fear and frustration, turns his head into his right armpit, and sobs like a baby.

LOOK AT ME, ACHAEAN.

He has no choice. His head snaps up as though his hair has been grabbed and yanked.

On the rampart is a boy, or a young man, naked, the promise of a man's muscle still buried by the last remnants of baby fat. Behind his head is a nimbus, an indistinct plasma glow shot through with lightning whose crackle can be felt but not heard. The boy plants his hands on his hips. His lips do not move, yet he speaks. TIME TO DIE. I WARNED YOU. ACHILLES WARNED YOU. BUT YOU WOULD NOT LISTEN. NOW. The boy on the rampart, Apollo the Lightbringer, bends forward and stretches out his right hand. He is still at least twenty feet away, but though his feet remain planted on the Trojan defenses, his fist suddenly fills Patroclus' vision. The fist spreads into an open hand, fingers outstretched. The middle finger curves down to meet the thumb. It curls within the thumb's embrace, building tension. The tendons of the divine boy's forearm stand out. The thumb moves aside and the finger, suddenly freed, snaps out and strikes Patroclus in the forehead.

It is as though he has been struck between the eyes with a war hammer. His grasp on the rungs loosens; his feet fly out from under him. As the world spins, he has just enough presence of mind to wrap his arms around the ladder's uprights, and so slides down, biceps lacerated by inch-long splinters. He strikes ground hard enough to throw him backwards, the divine armor suddenly mere metal clattering like impossibly heavy pots rattled in *a kitchen. Lying on his back, blood streaming from ears and nose and mouth, Patroclus looks up at the rampart just in time to see the laughing boy wink out of existence.*

A murmur runs through the Achaean ranks while Patroclus staggers to his feet. He stumbles towards the man closest, Crito, a Theban. Crito's instincts propel him a step forward, but then his mind speaks and he takes two steps back. The scream of Trojan horses and the bellow of Trojan voices reach both their ears, and Crito the Theban is gone. Patroclus is blind to the Trojan presence. He stands staring at the rampart, eyes fixed on where he last saw the boy, mouth agape, arms held out at his sides. The Trojan squadron a dozen yards away is silent. Then a Trojan runs forward, darting and feinting, hoping to attract his attention and a semblance of defense. Though barely out of boyhood, he carries a man's spear too big for him. "Hey, Patroclus," he yells. "Die like a man. Hector is coming. Come on, Patroclus, don't just stand there."

Patroclus tears his eyes from the wall and tries to focus on his tormentor. No good. When he moves his head, the world just spins and he flaps his arms to regain his balance. The boy can't miss this opportunity for immortality. "Hey, Patroclus," he cries, "remember it was Euphorbus the Trojan who sent you to Hades." The boy throws.

With sudden clarity, Patroclus notes the spear's flat descending arc. Whether the boy would have been good with a boy's spear is an open question; with a man's he is terrible. A throw intended for his heart at ten yards strikes his legs equidistant between knees and buttocks, sewing his hamstrings together. Suddenly knock-kneed, Patroclus falls to his side in the direction of the throw, and rolls onto his back.

He is surprised that there is no pain, more surprised that there is no fear. But he knew that he would die this way. More than anything else, he is curious as to just what it will feel like when it all ends. He turns his head again to the wall, hoping for one last glimpse of Apollo, hoping that he will compensate for sending him to his death by showing him what will come next. But the god is gone. Slowly, he becomes aware of the throb of muscle outraged by the sudden intrusion of a wooden shaft two inches thick. Next, he hears the crunch of heavy military boots on the sand near him.

Crunch left. Crunch right. Thick legs planted on either side. Above him is a man as big as any in the Achaean army, thicker in body even than Achilles, dressed in armor whose beauty is inferior to Patroclus' lover's only in that it is the work of mortal hands. The big body bends, bringing them almost head to head. "Patroclus. It's Hector. I've come to kill you."

Hector straightens up and poises his spear thicker than any sapling, his hands laced together on its shaft, its leaf-shaped bronze point an inch from Patroclus' exposed throat. "So, Patroclus," says Hector. "Is this how you thought it would end? Is this what Achilles had in mind when he sent you here? Did he say, 'Go to Troy and die in the sand'? No? Or did he say, 'Go to Troy and take it, rape their women and boys, melt the gold in their temples down into big, heavy bars we can take back to Thessaly, and then I will love you, Patroclus'? Is that what he said? Is that what he said when he sent you here to die under my spear?"

Hector plants a foot on Patroclus' chest. The pressure makes Patroclus wince and cough. Something is broken inside; black, clotted blood flows from his mouth and onto the glowing armor. The world has become very small again: a tight circle of light surrounded by purple dark, the visible circle entirely occupied by an open helmet framing a face scarred by half a generation of war. Knowing that he will speak next in Hades, Patroclus can ignore the weight of wood lacing his legs and the gurgle of blood in his throat. "Trojan," he says, "don't flatter yourself. Leave that to your painted ass lickers. I died at the hands of a god and boy who got lucky. Hector is no more than the dog who tears the throat from a man already dead."

Hector roars and drives the bronze point down. In his anger, he misses throat and spinal column and severs the big muscles of the neck. Patroclus speaks once more as the roaring dark gathers around. "I see your death, Hector, and it wears Achilles' face."

Hector has extracted the spear point from Patroclus' neck and poises to strike again, for the last time. "Maybe," he says. "But you see yours, too. Now." The point comes down hard through the throat, through the bones of the neck, and buries itself in the sand.

Blood fountains from Patroclus' mouth. His arms scissor crazily as his life drips through the soil and down through the earth into Hades. Hector stares hard at eyes rolled back in their sockets and pulls out his spear. As he wipes the point on his thigh, a runner approaches. "My lord," he says breathlessly, dropping to his knees. "Prince Hector, Diomedes is on our right. Bizimarko asks your help."

Hector hesitates. He wants the divine armor, wants to throw the body in it to the dogs as publicly as possible. But stripping the body will take time, and from the look on the runner's face, there isn't much of that. He nods. "All right." He thinks for a second. "Tell Lord Sarpedon to get over here and get this corpse back inside the city. Now."

The runner sprints away. Hector looks at the dead man for as long as he can spare. What is left of Patroclus rustles and twitches and bubbles in death's long aftermath. Hector tests his spear point. Still sharp enough to send a few more Achaeans to join him.

THE BATTLE FOR PATROCLUS

Achilles has abandoned his black-prowed ship for a silken tent. Odysseus leaves his chariot in his driver's hands and ignores the Myrmidons as he strides to its entrance; he is still in all his armor and flecked with evidence of battle. The sentries hesitate, but they do not bar his way.

Achilles is in bed, his back to him. Odysseus knows that he cannot be asleep. He knows that this is part of his game and he will not play it. Without pausing, he grasps Achilles' shoulder with a hand gloved in drying blood, and the Myrmidons on either side of the bed step forward as if to stop him. They see the bits of brain and hair on his helmet's cheek plates and think again. Achilles spins between his sheets and half sits up, as though wondering who among the army, royal or not, is fool enough to lay a hand on him. He tilts back his head and opens his mouth in the beginnings of a roar of outrage.

"Shut up," says Odysseus. He does not raise his voice.

"*What?* You dare?"

"I dare. He's dead."

Achilles' face goes slack.

Odysseus leans forward and speaks in a whisper: "He died at the walls of Troy. He died like a hero. He died in your armor. Menelaus is guarding the body now and he's completely cut off. I'm going to get him back."

125

Odysseus rises and half turns as though to leave. He sees that even though Achilles' face is limp, the great muscles in his belly have begun to twitch in a spasm that threatens to tear him apart. He turns back and leans forward again to say one word so low that even the Myrmidons cannot hear. Then he spins on his heel and leaves.

The tent flap drops. As it does, Odysseus hears Achilles howl the name of his lover's killer.

෬

The sun has been up a long time. Men gather under the shade cast by a ship; they have just been told that they will join the battle for a dead man. "Tell me again," says one. "Why the fuck are we doing this?"

Another, older, less concerned for the why of anything, grunts: "Get back Helen."

"So tell me again," says the first. "Why do we care who fucks Helen?"

Another still, joking nervously, says, "Ten years with the Trojans, she's so stretched out that Menelaus won't even graze the sides. Like fucking a bucket."

His friend: "Right. I hear Paris has a dick like an ax handle."

The older one: "Then you must be hoping he's still alive when we go over the walls."

All laugh. Then they dress in bronze and laugh no longer.

෬

Patroclus has been dead less than an hour. Eyes now milky stare at the heaven that has betrayed him; flies unconcerned with war lick the blood from the corners of his mouth. Soon, they will lay their eggs in eyes and mouth and wounds; their children will swarm a corpse already bloating beneath its bronze in the Illyrian heat.

Shamed Menelaus does not want to die—not yet. Not for Achilles' boyfriend, that's for sure. He refuses to die until he has heard Paris beg for his life, and Paris' father and brothers and mother—until he has seen his friends and their slaves fuck them. Then he will gather wood for his own pyre and leap into the flames and be glad. He has to live through the afternoon first, though, and to do that he must save a dead man. Menelaus

126

plants a foot on either side of the body and faces the Trojan line; the main force is still engaged with the Achaeans five hundred yards away. A raiding party, a dozen infantry and two chariots, approaches fast. Menelaus knows they will be here in fifteen minutes and prays that his own reinforcements will be here first.

A single skirmisher from the Trojan party sprints towards him, far ahead of the rest. Panting, he stops ten yards away and plants his spear butt in the sand. He is a boy, no more than fifteen. "I want that armor, Achaean. That's my man."

"Is he?" says Menelaus. "I don't think so."

The boy comes closer. "It is. I killed him."

"Did you? Looked like Hector to me, but you Trojans all look the same. Hector looks like a little boy with a spear."

"I killed him, Achaean. It was my spear that went through his legs."

"Oh. Well, come get him." Menelaus doesn't move. He shifts his weight but stays where he is.

The boy does, too. "I killed him. He's mine."

"So who are you, boy?" says Menelaus.

"Don't call me boy, Achaean. My name is Euphorbus, son of Artinarax."

"Oh. I've heard of you. Met your father this morning."

"Lucky you survived, Achaean," says the boy, moving in with his spear point weaving.

"Guess so," says Menelaus. "He didn't."

"What?"

"I killed your father, boy. This morning."

"You lie, Achaean," says the boy, his voice a notch shriller. "The Achaeans lie. All Achaeans lie."

"Right," says Menelaus. "Your father had two horses, one black, one roan?"

"Yes. He still does."

"Sorry, now I do. He had armor with an ox on the breast and a helmet with a plume dyed purple and red?"

"He still does," says the boy, voice quivering, waiting for the time to throw.

"Did. Mine now," says Menelaus, ignoring the point of the spear and watching the boy's feet. When his spear-side foot goes back he will throw. "I killed him this morning at close range, so I'm sure. The point of my spear went up under his jawbone and popped his helmet off his head. I

127

saw the piss run down his leg as he died. Sorry. Now come closer, boy, and I'll kill you, too."

The boy's aim would have been bad at the best of times, but now it is just wild. The spear arcs high, spending its power on the climb. It would have landed yards behind him, but Menelaus, laughing, backpedals like a clown and lazily lifts his shield to hear the spear clang harmlessly against the bronze and ox hide. Point broken, the spear clatters to the ground.

Euphorbus half stands, half crouches, aching to turn and run. Still too young to bear the weight of a man's armor, he is protected instead by thin strips of bronze plaited together with leather thongs. Menelaus thinks to let him go, to run back in shame to spread the word of the Spartan king's mercy. But no: the boy is Trojan. Menelaus imagines him as a baby, held aloft on his father's shoulder in Troy's thronged streets as Paris displayed his new bride, laughing gleefully with the rest of the crowd as Paris fondled a big, firm, stolen breast through the sheer silk of a robe Menelaus had given her.

Menelaus drops his spear and shield and draws his sword from the scabbard on his back. He advances at a jog that turns into a full run as the boy stands upright and holds out both arms as though to stop him, and screams, "No!"

Menelaus laughs. It's just what he wants: the upright body is a perfect target for what he has in mind. The sword goes down diagonally and horizontally right to left, opening a flap through the boy's pathetic armor and the muscle below. Menelaus backs up a few steps. The boy still stands, his arms still reach, and he looks down in stupid surprise as his bowels spill through his opened belly and onto the ground, yard after uncoiling yard glistening grayish pink, barely touched by the blood oozing from the wound.

The boy drops to his knees. Gagging and whimpering, he tries to gather up his intestines and stuff them back where they belong. Slick, they slip from his clumsy fingers and plop back to the ground. He rubs his hands in the dirt thinking that a little sand will improve his grip—no luck. The boy drops back onto his haunches, with fifteen feet of his own guts lying steaming before him. He knows he is dead, but that it will take a long time to die. He starts to sob. "Please," he says. "Please. Mercy." He turns his tearstained face to Menelaus. "I'm a soldier. Let me die clean."

"Oh," says Menelaus. "Of course." He reaches down and knocks off

128

the boy's helmet, little more than a leather cap with a few dozen bronze studs. He grabs the Trojan's greasy curls with his left hand and the sword in his right sweeps again and the head is off.

The headless trunk flips and capers in its pile of bowels. Twin jets from the neck stump soak Menelaus in blood; his mouth fills with its ferrous tang. He holds the head a foot from his own. There is light still in its eyes, and horror and grief on its face. "All right, soldier," says Menelaus. "Let me show you something." Laughing, he holds out the head so that Euphorbus can see his own dead body.

When he is sure that Euphorbus will never see anything again he drops the head into the slinking guts. He wipes his sword clean on his thigh and returns it to its sheath.

The Trojans are getting close.

Menelaus is gone. A boy's corpse, headless, is a few yards from Patroclus'; Trojans swarm both.

"Shit," says Odysseus. He crouches on the crest of the ridge overlooking the dead men. His driver crouches next to him.

"Yes? And?"

"Shit," Odysseus says again. "The Trojan in command, that's Sarpedon. Not exactly a pile of wildflowers. Harder than fuck to kill and he might take a lot of us trying." He points at the gated city a mile away, shimmering in the heat. "See the dust rising?"

"Yes," says the driver.

"Hector. Any money. And once Hector joins up with Sarpedon, we can kiss Patroclus goodbye. Maybe not such a bad thing," he adds, more to himself than the driver. Patroclus' body within the walls of Troy might get Achilles off his godlike ass.

"Lord?" says the driver.

Odysseus sighs. Long ago he gave up the idea of ever being able to talk to anyone about the things that go through his mind. "Well, we'll get Patroclus back," he says. "We just have to do it the way I explained." He drops to his belly and starts crawling backwards through the high grass. His driver does the same.

His boys are gathered just behind the crest of the ridge, prone as he told them. Just a few dozen; he has never had the luxury of wealth, of men or ships or money, just his mind and the things the other kings thought the gods murmured to it.

"All right," he says. His harsh whisper carries better than Diomedes' war cry, but no farther than to those who need to hear it. "You know what to do; let's do it now." Without another word he turns and rolls onto his belly and shimmies up through the tall grass, his shield held high on the left and his spear cradled on the right. He will not look behind to see if they follow, because he knows that once a king does so, he is king no longer. But he hears bronze-clad bodies slithering through the grass and is relieved.

They are at the crest. Sarpedon and his men are tugging at the corpse so hard that Odysseus wonders whether it will split apart. He rises to his knees and lifts his spear. There are whispers in the grass again. He dares to look a little to his left and right; a dozen men on either side have done the same. Sarpedon does not notice. Odysseus raises his spear again and gets to his feet; two dozen men do the same. They advance.

It is only a hundred yards to the dead man, all downhill. Odysseus does not have much time to think, but when he can, he is proud of his boys. They do just as he told: they lope downhill fast and spread wide, so that the archers will have to pick their targets and make their arrows count. Their pace makes them keep shields away from their bodies as they run, which takes nerve with the Trojans so close.

An astonished shout comes from the raiding party surrounding Patroclus. They have been spotted. Odysseus raises his spear and the boys increase their pace. Odysseus roars a single word. They slow and draw together, shields suddenly before them, spears at a forty-five-degree angle, moving at a jog no more than a yard from one another. Now the arrows start, enough to drop two men, one dead with a shaft through his throat and blood bubbling into the sand, another down staring amazed at feathers buried in his thigh. Sarpedon's men are still trying to rally.

"Now!" Odysseus bellows. Just as they were told, the boys close shoulder to shoulder. Their shields overlap like the scales of a snake, impenetrable. Their spears are leveled between the shields' narrow gaps. They advance at a jog, screaming.

Suddenly, the two forces are on top of one another. Odysseus can see nothing in the dust except the men at left and right and directly in front. Shrieking like a fury, he kills and kills; each opponent too slow or too eager to be a hero. The Trojans fight as though they are posing for the side of a wine jar, stretching to their full height, arms high, spears pointed down. Their armpits are thus exposed, open for the quick upward jab that penetrates lungs and heart. And Odysseus, fighting like a turtle crouched with shield held high and angled to cover most of his body, makes that jab half a dozen times and makes half a dozen widows before he is where he wants to be: over Patroclus. Divine armor gone, he is just another naked corpse.

Odysseus knows that his friends back at the ships would stand here and fight until nightfall. Not him. "Now!" he screams again, hoping that he can keep the anxiety out of his voice. He may have asked too much.

He hasn't. However drunk they are with blood, his boys do what they were told. Four of them fold in from the flanks, grab the body, and run for the ridge crest.

Achilles has the body cradled in his arms. He has smeared it with unguents that he says his mother the goddess gave him, oils that will hold at bay the worms until his beloved's killer is himself dead. He rocks back and forth crooning, like a mother with a fevered child. From time to time his lips find cheek or forehead. Once, his tongue slips into the unliving mouth and he recoils gagging and sobbing from the taste of old blood and new decay.

Around him stand four priests. One holds a censer streaming smoke; another, sheaves of wheat; the third, a bowl of blood from fresh sacrifice; the fourth, a wreath of laurel. They chant in a language so old that no one understands it, including themselves. Farther back are the Myrmidons in their ranks, spear points buried in the ground, eyes following, silent in respect for their lord's grief. Farther back still are the ranks of the army, noisier than the Myrmidons, but still oddly hushed for Achaeans.

Odysseus and Agamemnon stand fifty yards away on a little hill. They watch in silence. Finally, when he can stand no more, Odysseus rumbles and spits on the ground. He has no patience for the love of man for man. A boy now and then for variety, of course, and publicly raping the headman of a newly taken town is only good policy, but this extravagant display is unseemly. Agamemnon smiles sourly. "I know what you mean," he says. "Makes you wonder why he got so worked up about the girl, doesn't it?"

Odysseus smiles back. "Not really. That wasn't about fucking any more than the last nine years were about who fucks Helen. It was about pride, just like all of this." The sweep of his hand encompasses two hundred ships and ten thousand Achaeans. "Will your brother fuck Helen when we get her back? Will he make babies with her? Will he bounce her grandchildren on his knee and say, 'Well, *this* is what the war was for'?"

Agamemnon is silent, but his eyes don't drop from Odysseus'.

"Didn't think so. But remember this, king: pride is what brought us all here and keeps us here. Yours, yes, but that of every man here, too. Remember that next time your pride is hurt."

Agamemnon remains silent for a long time. At last he speaks. "They say his mother has given him new armor made on Olympus."

"Is that what they say?"

"It is. He pulled it out of the water this morning, bright as the sun."

Odysseus thinks to ask him whether it was possible that the new armor came out of a trunk, whether Achilles was just rinsing it off, but he decides better not. "Oh?"

"Yes. Nice to have a goddess for a mother." Agamemnon's eyes are now straight ahead so Odysseus can't read him. "Of course there are gods in my bloodline, too. Just a little farther back."

Odysseus steers the middle course. "Yes. That's why they watch over you."

Agamemnon nods solemnly. Odysseus knows that he is completely serious. "Yes," says the king. "What do you think happens next?"

"I think Hector did us a big favor. Too bad about Patroclus, of course, but now it looks like Achilles is back in the game."

Agamemnon nods again. "Yes, too bad. But it does look like god-boy is ready, doesn't it? By the way, nice work today."

"You're very kind." Odysseus looks at Agamemnon's laurel crown and wonders how it would fit him.

"No, really, it was brilliant. They say you got Sarpedon himself. Nice. Very nice. I couldn't have done better myself."

Odysseus, practiced, keeps a straight face. "As I say, you're very kind."

TWO MEN AT THE WALLS

No one will speak to Achilles; no one in his right mind would. All day he has sat at the foot of Patroclus' unlit pyre. The only company he will tolerate is that of the priests who flank it, droning away in the language that the Achaeans spoke when their minds first awakened in the north, when the ice rivers were still fresh memories to their grandfathers, whose own grandfathers had been no more than puppets in the hands of the gods, hunting and breeding with no more consciousness of purpose than the animals they slaughtered.

Achilles takes no comfort from the priests' incomprehensible bagpipe hum. Generally, he sits moaning. Every so often he shovels up dirt and rubs it in his hair and beard. Once he spies a pile of dog turds and shoves it into his mouth but spits it out gagging, though particles of shit cling to his face. Sometimes he joins the priests with music of his own: a low keening that oscillates above and below the audible to make the hairs stand up on the necks of all within its range. Once he makes as though to climb up onto the pyre with his beloved, only to be stopped by the restraining hand of a bronze-masked priest.

A Myrmidon, nobly born, the son of a companion of great Peleus, takes him food in a bowl and wine in a cup. Achilles has touched nothing since the news reached him the day before. Conscious of his peril, the Myrmidon does what no Achaean will do: he drops to his knees before another man, meal held high, head hung low. He waits long minutes until his arms tremble and the pain in his shoulders makes him groan. Presently, Achilles stirs from his mourning to take two quick steps forward and kick him in the face hard enough to break his neck. Fortunately, it is only his jaw that is shattered, and he has the sense to keep his cries of pain to himself until his friends have come forward to carry him off to the main Achaean camp.

෬

"You don't have a choice," says Odysseus again.

"I *want* a choice," Agamemnon snarls, bolting out of his chair of state and circling the narrow confines of the tent in his agitation. "If you're so smart, lord, why don't *you* give me a choice? One of your cunning Ithacan tricks? Or better still, ask the Gray-eyed One how to save a king from this kind of humiliation."

His face is now very close to Odysseus', so Odysseus must refrain from rolling his eyes and sighing, which at this point, after half an hour of the same thing over and over, is a little hard. Nevertheless, he restrains himself. "I have, lord. It is no humiliation for a king to do what he must."

Agamemnon barks with rage and spins away. He wheels back to face Odysseus. "Have you *seen* her? Of course you have. How can I give her up? She makes Aphrodite herself look like a harborside slut!" He rolls his eyes to heaven and extends his palms. "Sorry, didn't mean that. Sorry. But you know what I mean."

"I know what you mean, lord," says Odysseus tiredly. "I'm a man, too. And she is very beautiful. Very ripe, and very young. But with Achilles back, we can take Troy, and with Troy's gold you can buy yourself an entire Egyptian brothel. Think of that, lord. Black twins, double-jointed, raised as temple prostitutes—knowing things a Mycenaean girl, or even a Trojan, would kill herself for even thinking. Is that worth giving up a single prize?"

Agamemnon stares at him hard, eyes bugging out, mouth working. Then his mouth clamps shut and his eyes haze in thought. Suddenly, he grins; his laughter erupts. He wraps a startled Odysseus in a back-pounding embrace. He holds the Ithacan at arm's length, eyes streaming, and asks, "Double-jointed, you say? Twins?"

Odysseus nods. "Twins, king."

Agamemnon laughs again and kisses Odysseus on the check. "I can live with that," he says.

Odysseus' laugh is far more modest but equally genuine, if for different reasons. "Yes, lord. They're there to be had if you have enough gold, and the king who sacks Troy will have enough gold for that and more."

"The king who sacks Troy," says Agamemnon, dreamily. Then, with greater authority, voice deeper, and chin outthrust: "The king who sacks Troy. Yes." He pauses for a moment. "Listen. Problem."

"Yes?"

"I have to swear I didn't touch her, right?"

"Yes."

"Right. Well, that's the problem. I touched her. In fact, I fucked her brains out."

"Yes, lord," says Odysseus.

"Well, uh, well, won't Achilles know that? I mean, when he takes her?"

"King, I think we can make sure that the girl won't tell."

"That's not what I meant, and you know it," says Agamemnon, suddenly irritated. "I mean, I hate to think about that animal touching her, but face it, when he fucks her he'll know someone's been there before."

"I don't think so, lord," says Odysseus.

"*What?*"

"No offense," says Odysseus hastily. "What I mean is this: right now, do you think he's thinking about fucking anything except the man on the woodpile?"

"No."

"And do you think it's at least possible that given his tastes he'll never fuck her at all?"

"Yes. Zeus, Father of the World, what a waste."

"Yes. And if he does—lord, have you ever seen the war hammer on him?"

"Huh?"

"His cock."

"Well, yes, at games and whatnot. I mean, I couldn't help but notice."

"Right. If he ever does fuck her, don't you think she'll scream and bleed like a stuck pig?"

"Well, Lord Odysseus," says Agamemnon, "I stretched her out a little. I mean, I'm not exactly some Trojan pinprick."

135

"Yes, lord," says Odysseus. "But you see what I mean. He's barely human and something tells me that he's not going to read her love poems and give her little butterfly kisses on the neck before he rams that thing into her."

Agamemnon winces and Odysseus realizes he's said enough. "All right, all right. I'll swear I haven't touched her and he won't know. But Odysseus, my lord, I'll swear an oath to the gods that I haven't, and they'll know that's not true. How can I do that?"

Odysseus chews his lip as though he hasn't anticipated the question and planned his response. "Lord," he says, "did the gods not bring us here?"

"Of course."

"And did we not come here and spill our blood at the gods' command because their laws had been violated when Paris raped the wife of his host, your brother?"

"Yes." Agamemnon tries not to smile. He knows that Odysseus will tell him why he is right to do what he wants to do, anyway.

"And will not that great purpose be served when you swear an oath that will bring back to the war Achilles, without whom we cannot win?"

"Well, I don't know about can't—" Agamemnon begins, but he catches Odysseus' eyes and says, "Right. Can't."

"So is it not the will of the gods that you swear an oath to them who know it not to be true, so that you can achieve the purpose for which they have put us here? How can an oath be false when those to whom you swear it know it to be false? And how can it be a crime against the gods when you swear it to achieve their purpose?"

Agamemnon nods. "Just so we're clear," he says. "I'll do it, but the gods know you told me to do it."

Odysseus' smile is so slight that his beard barely twitches. "Yes," he says. "Of course."

ଜ

Achilles sits at the foot of the pyre. His arms are wrapped around knees that touch his chin; he rocks back and forth crooning to himself, a cradlesong never sung by the mother he never knew except in visions. Spread before him ignored are the elements of the armor that she says she brought from Hephaestus' forge still hot with the rage Aphrodite's crippled cuckold husband applies to all his work. They lie on a blanket looking

136

oddly like fragments of a man flayed alive: greaves instead of shins, cuirass instead of chest, helmet instead of head.

Achilles stops his little noises. He stops rocking. Beside the bronze anatomy is a sword that has just caught his eye. It looks like a static lightning bolt—the gods' chosen instrument of retribution. Its blade is just over two and a half feet, narrow at the base and swelling to three inches just before it tapers into the thrusting point, so that its center of balance is far forward like a cleaver. Edged only on the business side, no back edge for fancy fencing, this is a tool for killing. Its guard is a simple crosspiece, the grip beaded bronze.

Achilles rises to his feet. The priests behind him stop their droning, wondering whether he will again have to be prevented from cuddling up to a corpse. They resume their chant with renewed energy when he walks forward towards the armor, rather than back to the pyre.

Achilles stoops; the sword's grip might have been forged from his hand. Still bent double, he takes a deep breath. He knows what will happen if he lifts the sword. He will have no choice: he will swallow his pride, he will kill Hector, and he will die. Still bent, he thinks about what to do. He can turn away from the sword, the armor, and the war. He can light Patroclus' pyre and go back to Thessaly. That slimy fuck Agamemnon and smooth Odysseus will die here, and in doing so, they will expunge their offense to him. But they will die guarding the bones of his lover who lies unavenged.

Hand still curved around the hilt, his arms shake. His head roars. He does not know what to do.

The roaring of the thoughts in his skull is suddenly replaced with the roar of surf. Water laps around his ankles. His eyes start from his head. He is on a hill a mile from the sea, yet in his crouch, he can look down and see foam swirling between his feet. How is it that the greatest tidal wave in memory can have broken here without warning?

Against his better instincts, he looks up. His hill, crowned with Patroclus' pyre, is suddenly an island of a few hundred square feet, he and Patroclus its only occupants, the priests gone in the same wave that submerged both the Achaean camp and Troy itself. The whole world now is just an oddly flat and placid sea. Achilles wonders how nine years' war can be so easily re-solved in a sudden mutual catastrophe. He shakes his head from side to side as the recognition dawns that what he sees is not what is, at least in the world in which he lives and will die.

"Mother," he says. "Mother. What shall I do?"

This time the sea doesn't boil. No monster pulls him down into the depths to confront the divine. The surf laps at his feet. Splat. Splat. Splat. He listens. Soon the voice of the surf can be heard. TAKE UP THE SWORD, ACHILLES, it says. YOU WILL DIE HERE. YOU WILL DIE A HERO, SON. YOU WILL BE CALLED A HERO A YEAR AFTER YOU DIE, AND A THOUSAND YEARS, AND TEN THOUSAND. BUT TO DIE A HERO YOU MUST DIE.

"I don't want to die, Mother," says Achilles.

YOU WILL DIE ANYWAY, SON. OLD AND FAT IN THESSALY OR YOUNG AND BEAUTIFUL HERE.

"Will I always be a hero, Mother?"

ALWAYS.

"Then I will die here. Can I see you in the afterlife?"

NO, I'M SORRY, says the surf. YOU ARE MORTAL. THE IMMOR-TAL CANNOT VISIT THE DEAD. WE CAN HAVE NOTHING TO DO WITH DEATH AFTER IT HAS HAPPENED.

"Oh," says Achilles. "All right."

This time he sees it happen. The waters at his feet rush forward, covering him to the waist. The surrounding sea tilts like a table suddenly upended, and the water sluices away from him, miraculously without the tidal drag that should have swept him down and out. He backs up towards the pyre, and suddenly around him are the priests, mute and immobile, sodden and streaming. Still the invading sea rushes away, exposing hilltop, hill, the crests of the Trojan walls, the topmost spires of the Achaean ships. As the water recedes, it gains momentum, tidal surge becoming a foaming rapid that spreads from horizon to horizon. Retreating, it reveals that which it has covered; yet somehow, for all its momentum, it leaves standing the frozen men and stacked weapons that it should have swept away like leaves in a whirlpool. When it is still a hundred yards from the ordinary limit of high water, a dozen lightning bolts split the cloudless sky and a thunderclap drives his terrified face down into the suddenly dry sand of the hilltop.

☙

He raises his ringing head. The water is where it belongs and the men of Achaea go about their business in a bone-dry camp. Through the reverberations in his mind, he can just make out the droning of the priests.

Still on his knees, he takes the sword in his hand. He rises to his feet and holds it aloft. He turns to the nearest priest. "What are you waiting for?" he bellows. "Tell the king I'm ready."

෴

Odysseus has just come back to the delegation. Agamemnon waits with fifty of his greatest men and their immediate retainers, two hundred officers in best armor along with priests and garlanded oxen mercifully oblivious to their fates. And, of course, with Briseis, veiled and herself garlanded as sacrifice, surrounded by her own honor guard of beautiful captives who, if no longer technically virgins, are at least young enough to make the claim straight-faced.

"All right," says Odysseus to the king. "We're all set. The boy wonder knows his lines. Let's do it."

Agamemnon grunts; he is not enjoying this at all. With one backward glance at beflowered Briseis, he shouts words of command and raises an ivory staff. The delegation falls in behind him.

It takes nearly half an hour for the procession to reach the pyre-crowned hilltop where Achilles waits. As they climb slowed by their lowing heifers and the heavy gifts lugged by sweating slaves, Achilles stares straight down at Agamemnon, who sweats like one of his own bondsmen and looks anywhere but at Achilles.

They are at the crest, a dozen paces from Achilles. Odysseus admits to himself that on this day, at least, he actually looks half divine. Over a crisp linen tunic he wears the replacement armor his goddess mother bore him from the sea where Hephaestus quenched it white-hot from the fires of Olympus. Or, Odysseus suspects, the spare armor he kept just in case. But whatever its origin, it glows like something divine, different from the frozen light that cased Patroclus and now hangs a trophy in Troy's Chapel Royal. The breastplate is worked with gorgons' heads whose serpent hair can almost be seen to writhe and twine. An almost impossibly pure white, the helmet's horsehair crest peaks twice as high as any other officer's, so that from a distance, Achilles looks half again as tall as he is.

139

As the delegation approaches, Achilles takes off the helmet and carefully places it on the ground between his feet. Though Odysseus has never been a boy lover, much less a man lover, he appreciates for the first time why every third soldier in the army sobs himself to sleep to dream of Achilles. The man is good-looking, and he knows it. Or knew it. With Patroclus dead, he no longer struts. Grief has killed his vanity, and for the first time, Odysseus feels sorry for him.

Achilles speaks. "Welcome, King Agamemnon."

"Your hospitality honors me, Lord Achilles. I bring that which I should not have had and more. I bring the girl I took from you, publicly, in a fit of madness sent by the gods. When the gods make men mad, what can they do? All they can do when the madness has left is make right that which was wrong, and to do right by those who were wronged. And so I bring back to you, Achilles, the girl I took. And with her I give you a dozen horses and a dozen tripods and a dozen cauldrons. And I will swear that I never laid a hand on her, in lust or otherwise. This I do, Lord Achilles, to make right the wrong I have done you."

Achilles face has remained stony. "King," he says, "your gifts are yours to do with as you please. I wish the girl had fallen dead the second I saw her. What has she brought me but anger? And what has the anger done for either of us? My lover, my perfect friend, lies behind me, waiting for the touch of fire to turn him into ash and bone and memory. And how many other Achaeans died under Trojan hands while I nursed my rage? No, lord. Keep the girl, keep the horses, keep the cauldrons. I just want back in the war."

The lords rustle and murmur. Sensing the start of a cheer, Agamemnon spins to glare at them; his pride has taken enough of a beating for one day. He faces Achilles again. "My lord," he says, "no orator, no matter how skillful, would interrupt you, and certainly I could not. You speak from a generous heart, and a warlike heart, and words from such a heart must be heard." He turns back to the Achaean lords. Odysseus' forehead creases. This was not part of the plan. "And words from my heart must be heard as well, my lords. You selfish bastards have been bad-mouthing me behind my back for a solid month now. And don't think I don't know who you are! Well, listen up, fuckers. *The gods made me do what I did. And you know it.*"

He is almost screaming. There is spittle flying from his mouth. His robe of state, Tyrian purple embroidered around the hem with marigold yellow, is patched with sweat and stuck to his body under his arms and on his back. The laurel crown is crooked on his head, ready to fall. Odysseus scans the crowd anxiously, alert for any hint that the Achaean lords are growing disaffected at this display. But they stare goggle-eyed, not in shock, but in what looks almost like reverence. Odysseus steals a glance at Achilles, who is actually nodding solemnly.

Agamemnon isn't done. "And next time you think about talking shit about your king, remember that. Think about what you'd do when the gods scream inside your head. Would you ignore them? Of course not. I tell you, my lords, we're puppets in their hands, king or slave. And when they make us do harm, all we can do is try to make it right later. *So don't blame me!*"

He is silent and stares defiantly at the lords. The lords stare back. Odysseus tries to remember the last time an army killed its leader in the middle of a war. His mind races. The men would never follow Menelaus, and Menelaus would die before leading an army that killed his brother, which leaves him and Achilles. And Achilles hates him, and every Achaean has a hard-on at the prospect of Achilles back in the war. He must either get Agamemnon out of this or kill him and hope for Achilles' gratitude. Odysseus knows how far he can trust gratitude. He steps forward to explain what Agamemnon really meant, but Achilles speaks first.

"Agamemnon is right, my lords."

Odysseus drops his hand from his sword hilt. It's going to be all right.

Prince Hector is alone. He knows he is a dead man. He knows the dead are always singular. Thus he refused the offers of company from court and family when he mounted the Scaean rampart again to look at the Achaeans who will kill him. Foolishly, he hopes for one thick greasy plume of smoke, a pyre—the Achaeans incinerating his victim. If they burn Patroclus today, perhaps they will go tomorrow. His heart sinks when he sees so many smoke columns that it looks as though the Achaeans have built an ashy temple on the beach. That means sacrifice, which means more war, which means that Achilles will face him and that he will die.

Suddenly, he laughs. The freedom of utter hopelessness gives his heart wings. Before the sun sets, he will be on his own pyre and out of this war. Hector is tired. But in a few hours the defense of the realm will be some-one else's worry, his no more. Still smiling, he turns and descends the four short steps to the lower rampart. His family and the court await him, and mistaking his radiance for confidence, they break into applause. *Go, Hector.* He looks at them and sees what is to come. He has sacked cities himself: blood-smeared men coming over the walls crazed with the knowledge that they can kill, men too old for shame on their knees holding up suppliant hands only to have thirsty stone drink their blood, wives and daughters and young sons pierced wherever an angry cock can find room.

Smile frozen, he embraces his admirers. He agrees with whatever they say. "Yes, I'll drive them into the sea. Achilles? Dead! Patroclus just made me hungry. Yes, he'll fuck his boyfriend in Hades." He looks at his father in his high chair of state, toothless grin splitting his white beard, nodding and nodding as he accepts congratulations for having fathered such a son. Even Paris looks happy, relieved that it's finally about to be over and he can put it all behind him.

His squire hands him his helmet and he pulls it on. The weight of bronze and stink of sweat-soaked leather comfort him. He waves and the crowd cheers. The squire offers his two spears, each twelve feet long. He waves them away, graciously. Not just yet. Andromache is close: their youngest, Astyanax, in her arms. He inclines his head towards an alcove and winks at the crowd. They cheer again and laugh knowingly.

In the alcove, he stands not knowing what to say. She is used to this and waits. The baby rolls his eyes aimlessly and lights on his helmet. The towering scarlet plume terrifies the baby, and he cries. Hector and Andromache laugh. Remembering what is to happen, Hector falls silent. "I'm not coming back this time," he says.

"Of course you are," she says, but she lies and knows she lies because she pulls his child closer.

"No, not this time. Not ever again." There is the chatter of the court behind them growing louder, and the sudden clatter of the squire as he draws a respectful two steps closer as if to say, "Not to hurry you, lord, but here are your spears."

He fumbles with his armor. Out it comes: a knife, very sharp. "We are finished," he says. "When they come, take the children, then yourself. Whatever happens, don't let the Achaeans take you alive."

She is quiet. So is the baby.

"I'm telling you the truth," he says.

Still she does not speak, but she shifts the baby and takes the knife. "I know," she says. "Goodbye."

142

THE DEATH OF
HECTOR,
BREAKER OF HORSES

His hatred is like the ocean and he rides it like a ship. He rises as it swells; he falls when it sinks. It is the whole world without borders, land invisible even at its most distant edges. It is everything. It is all he needs. It carries him forward like a wave that will drown Troy. Behind him, a hundred yards to his rear, is the whole army of Achaea, seated and silent, spears buried point down in the sand, bows unstrung, horses hobbled, helmets resting between feet. Only a few of the lords, kings themselves, prohibited by their dignity from joining common soldiers, remain in their chariot cars. Even they have laid aside arms and armor: this is between two men.

Balanced on his hatred as it rolls him forward, he wonders at what he feels. Nothing at all. Nothing but the momentum of hatred that is now so great that it seems to be something apart from him altogether, too great to allow him to feel anything else, even the fear of which other men assume him to be incapable, but which dries the mouth and quivers the knee of even the bravest in the instant before the first arrows fly. Nor does he feel

143

the lust to kill; that too has been swallowed up, drowned in an emotion even more basic.

He does not need to look behind to sense the army's presence; nor would he. It doesn't matter. What lies behind is significant only in that it contains the pyre before which he will shred Hector's corpse as the fire consumes his beloved.

Before him is Troy, just about two hundred yards away now, the scaly gray walls an unbroken line across his field of vision, like a hundred elephants, trunks twined with tails. Atop them, tiny and bright and silly as monkeys, are Troy's nobles, little spots of springtime color in their girlish silks. The breeze shifts and blows towards him across this nine years' battlefield, and he imagines that somewhere behind leather and dung and horses and men long dead in the sun, he can just make out the scent of myrrh from the Scaean rampart.

He left the lines at a slow trot. Now he saws the reins and the horses walk. He is in arrow range, but it will be ten minutes at least before he will be close enough to be heard in Troy. Ten minutes is a long time to be a target, yet no arrows fall. He understands; the Trojans know what has to happen, too. He is surprised, though, that he hears so little from ahead or behind. Silence is not Achaean, and the Trojans are Achaean cousins. Nevertheless, all he hears comes from close by: the creak of the chariot harness, the thongs binding the armor to him as thin and tight as a blister, and the crunch of bronze-bound wheels in sandy Illyrian soil. Even the horses are silent.

It strikes him that he is the first man to have seen Troy this way: close and alone. Ever since the siege began, these hundred yards before the walls have been the killing field, sometimes twice a day, sometimes once a month, a no man's land occupied by whole armies or not at all. As the horses shamble towards shouting range, Achilles studies his terrain. Whoever built those walls made sure that the defenders atop would have a nice, flat field in front to lay down fire. Nine years of infantry boots and chariot wheels have pounded it flatter still. The last shreds of any shrub or sapling that could have provided cover were uprooted while the Achaean hulls were still glistening wet. The barrenness is broken only by debris and bones of the unburned dead. There is nothing to block a spear, nothing to hide behind. Good.

Hector has been penned up in the city for nine years. No matter how

144

many times he has ridden through those gates to fight, he has returned home to sleep soft. Achilles has lived on the beach. Achilles will run Hector into the ground here on the barren plain and kill him where his family can see.

He is now close enough to the wall to make out individuals, and he pulls back the reins. The horses stop. The right-hand gelding turns his great head, and for an instant, its eye, big and soft, meets Achilles'. He wonders dizzily whether the horse will speak, whether it will tell him who lives out the day. But it stays a horse, silent, until it snorts and farts and dungs the ground. Relieved that the gods have decided to leave him alone, Achilles jumps out of the chariot. He arms himself, slinging the sword diagonally across his back, hilt just above his right shoulder, out of the way but easy to draw, shield riding high on the left, a twelve-foot spear, bronze head on an ash shaft, in either hand.

Atop the wall, a hundred yards distant and a little to his right, he can make out a purple canopy around which clusters a particularly gorgeous crowd. Under it he sees, or imagines he sees, what might be Priam's white beard. He winks at the horses and trudges towards the wall.

Twenty-five yards and still no arrows. And that *is* a white beard under the canopy. Better still, to the beard's right is a helmet crest that could belong to only one man. Achilles smiles. The hatred creases his face and shows his teeth. The voice inside his head screams so loudly that at first he is confused that the men on the wall haven't heard it: *Time to die, Hector.*

His lungs fill and his mouth opens. It is time for them to hear his hatred speak.

"Let me go."

Hector turns from the rampart and stares at his brother. His mouth opens but he does not speak.

"Let me go instead. She's my wife. I started this. Let me finish it."

Hector picks up the surrounding courtiers in his peripheral vision without taking his eyes from his brother's. The nobles are shocked speechless as well, for different reasons. Some smile proudly; others' eyes well with tears at the young prince's foolhardy courage. The king himself has risen from his chair of state, unable to believe that this is happening. Hector can't believe it, either. That even now his brother is self-indulgent enough

145

to make a grandstand play like this, secure in the knowledge that it will be refused, equally secure that it will save his reputation and his shot at the throne if Hector bites the dust.

He has to play the game even if that is how he wastes the last hour of his life. Beaming, he advances on Paris with arms spread wide and folds him in a bear hug. Then he holds him at arm's length, a big, scarred paw tight on either shoulder. "Oh, brother," he says. "You are your father's son." He turns to the courtiers, simpering in their finery. "Is he not, my lords? Is this not Priam's true son?" The lords murmur their agreement. A few even applaud; a great deal coming from these painted old birds. "But brother," he says, bellowing into Paris' face so that they wouldn't miss a word four rows back, "this Achaean is mine. And if it should happen that I am his—" he raises his arms for silence at the chorus of, No, never, the gods are just "—then Priam's son will avenge Priam's son." As the crowd cheers and sobs, he embraces Paris. With his mouth to his brother's ear, he says just loud enough so that he can hear over the din, "You'd better hope I don't come back. Asshole."

At the Achaean lines, Agamemnon takes front and center. The army stretches a mile on either side, though in some places not two men deep. He has left his chariot to join the little knot of his lords, the most favored, in the best position to see what is to come. A slave advances with a camp stool and Agamemnon waves him away. He will stand like the others this once, for this. He does not talk. If this afternoon goes the wrong way, he might soon no longer be king, or more to the point, alive. The troops would not take well to Achilles' death, but the Trojans would. If Achilles falls, those gates will open and the Trojans will drive them into the sea. Odysseus and Diomedes are ready to ride to the flanks to cover a general retreat if things go the wrong way.

His silence makes the lords uneasy. As Achilles plods towards the walls, they drift away from their king and form their own little groups at a respectful distance. Only Menelaus remains at his brother's side. The silence stretches on. Finally, Menelaus speaks. "That should be me out there."

Agamemnon is too startled to speak. At last, he says, "What?"

146

"That should be me out there instead of Achilles. Fighting Hector." He pauses. His face works. "That's my wife."

"I know, I know." Agamemnon puts his hand on his brother's shoulder. "But he'd kill you and I couldn't stand that."

With Agamemnon's hand still on Menelaus' shoulder, they turn towards Achilles and Troy.

⌒

"Time to die, Hector."

This is the third time he has screamed it up to the crowd under the canopy. Each time, the lords in their pretty robes heaved and boiled like ants in a shattered hill, leaving only the man at their center motionless beneath his yard-high crest.

"Didn't hear me, Hector? I said it's time to die. Come down here and I'll kill you."

The lords roil as though their shattered anthill has been poked with a stick, but still Hector will not move.

"You're afraid, Hector. You're shitting yourself up there. You put a spear through Patroclus' throat when he was down already, but you won't face me on my feet. You're a coward. You can't help it. It's in your blood. Your thieving brother couldn't face Menelaus, either, and when's that miserable father of yours ever shown his face out here, anyway. Too old now, maybe, but not nine years ago. No, he's been hiding up there with his women and his eunuchs, just like you. Coward father to two coward sons."

The shattered anthill is now a split beehive whose angry buzz reaches him even at this distance. He is surprised that that is all that reaches him; he thought at least one of Troy's defenders would risk an arrow or a spear. But no, no matter what he says, this will remain between the two of them.

He can see the great crest incline towards the white beard under the canopy. Hector's head stays bent for a long time. Then it straightens as the white beard rises and its owner wraps his arms around his son. Achilles' eyes are good, but he doesn't trust what he thinks he sees. Hector under his great crest walks slowly from the canopy, Priam's arms still wrapped around him, the old man dragging behind his warrior son. Will the old man not let go? The apiary buzz is louder and higher, as though the courtier bees have grown even more anxious.

147

It rises to an insect shriek as a woman, dressed almost as richly as a man, pushes her way through the congested court. Achilles guesses her to be the queen, Hecuba, and wonders at her temerity at appearing among men without a single lady in waiting. And his eyes almost pop from his head when the regal figure plants herself in front of Hector as he drags his sobbing father along the rampart and pulls open her gown to let spill a decidedly matronly breast. The great warrior recoils, and if there were any room in Achilles' skull for anything but hate, he would laugh. Instead, he smiles his grim leather smile. If Hector's parents will humiliate him this way to keep him off the field they know their boy's a dead man. Good.

Hecuba is trying to force down Hector's head for one last suckle. This is too much. Hector roars and shakes off his father. He elbows his mother aside and disappears into the crowd on the rampart. Achilles won't let this pass. He plants his feet and throws back his head. "Running away, momma's boy? What, don't want the titty? Come on, baby, you wanted the titty this morning! Go on, baby, suck mommy's titty. Just don't scratch with your beard!"

He isn't sure, but Achilles thinks he can hear someone laughing on Troy's rampart. He continues: "Come on, baby, you love mommy's titty. So does daddy! Here, don't crowd, I have one for—"

Tortured oak screams as two hundred pounds of forged bronze bolt are drawn across the Scaean Gate. The crowd on the rampart cheers as Achilles at last falls silent. Behind him, the rumble of the Achaean army crests in a roar as the gate opens for Hector.

Hector can hear the muffled laughter as he plunges down the stone steps towards the gate. Not from the court, of that he is at least reasonably sure; just soldiers, but somehow that's worse.

His squire is half the length of the stairway behind him, puffing and clattering as he tries to catch up. Hector stands stock-still as though he is waiting. He isn't. His eyes are screwed shut, his teeth clenched, his chest heaving with swallowed sobs of humiliation and rage and one thing more: fear. He was all right until the old man threw his arms around him and planted his reeking, drooling, toothless mouth in his neck, blubbering like a baby, "Don't go, son, that man's an animal, he'll kill you and come for us." Gently at first, then less so, Hector tried to disentangle himself while the bastard half brothers and uncles painted like aunts stared in even measures of terror and amusement.

And just when things couldn't get any worse, his mother held out her breast. Emotions he can't name and won't feel stopped him in his tracks and the court couldn't decide whether to weep or giggle as she begged and crooned: "Please, son. My baby. Remember when I held you here and fed you from my own body?" For a long second, he couldn't tear his gaze from a brown nipple, big and rough as a walnut, gnawed ragged by his dozen siblings. He felt himself stir, and retching with rage and shame, he threw the old man aside and plunged down the stairs to meet whatever the gods send.

The squire is almost there, but time is crawling now and he has plenty of time to think, to wonder why his hands are so cold, why he feels like pissing, why his vision swims, how it will feel when cold bronze slides through his stomach and backbone and he stares into Achilles' laughing face as he levers out his spear for another jab, how it will feel to die with wife and son watching. The squire rattles up and stops a respectful half step away. "Lord," he says, "both spears?"

Hector tries to speak, but his mouth is so dry his tongue sticks to the roof of his mouth. With an effort, he pulls it away, but it remains useless for speech. He tries again. All that comes out is a strangled gargling.

The squire's eyes widen. "Lord," he asks, "are you all right?"

His fear no longer his secret, Hector panics. His breath comes in ragged gasps and his eyes roll. He is sure that he will die right there, but he doesn't. *The swimming world is suddenly split by soundless lightning. Before him stands his half brother, Deiphobos, his favorite among Priam's numberless litters, wreathed in light like a god, speaking without opening his mouth.* COME ON, BROTHER, I'LL CARRY YOUR SPEARS. I WON'T GET IN YOUR WAY. PLEASE, LET ME COME ALONG, AND IF IT'S YOUR TIME TO DIE, I WON'T LET YOU DIE ALONE.

Hector nods, near tears with gratitude. He takes the spears from the astonished squire who stares agape as his lord tries to hand them to someone who isn't there. The spears clatter to the packed dried mud of the courtyard. Hector picks them up, drops them again, and mumbles, "Right, I'll carry them, then."

By now, Hector and the squire have been joined by more than Hector's invisible brother; half the court waits on the steps above the gate yard. As Hector fumbles his way forward, they raise eyes and hands at this evidence of divine intervention. The names of a dozen deities flutter through the noble crowd like windblown trash; first one bastard cousin, then another reports sighting a fugitive god.

Hector is now at the gate itself. Still smiling and chatting to himself, he gestures to the soldiers manning the bolt. Metal and wood shriek. Hector looks over his shoulder at thin air and bellows, "Let's *get* the bastard!" Laughing to his unseen brother, he trots forward.

Achilles is waiting a hundred yards from the gate. In Hector's charged vision he grows to twice and three times the size of a man. As Achilles breaks into an easy jog towards him, Hector turns to face his brother, who is gone.

For an instant, Hector opens his mouth and starts to scream, but even as he fills his lungs he knows what has happened; his jaws shut and his aborted cry whistles through his nostrils instead. The terror returns with renewed energy. His limbs are as still and cold as the bronze that protects him, and from the feeling in the pit of his stomach, he might as well have eaten his helmet. The gods must truly hate him to have done this.

But wait, maybe not. Perhaps they wanted him out here to win honor and bring down the arrogant boy wonder as a lesson that all are mortal. Still with his back to Achilles and his eyes to the ground, panting in an effort to control his quivering diaphragm, he catalogues the sacrifices for which the gods are about to reward him. The thousand bulls, the ten thousand goats, half a million birds. His confidence renewed, he spins on his heel— spear in either hand, war cry on his lips—to face Achilles, who is now twenty yards away, spear poised over his right shoulder for a throw, knees pumping as he runs.

As he sees Hector turn, he leans forward and lengthens his stride, opening up into a full sprint so that when the javelin flies it will have that extra momentum that might carry it all the way through Hector to bury its point in Troy's bronze-bound oaken gate. Achilles howls and raises the spear to throw. Hector hears the scream and knows that it is his death. He drops the spears and turns to his right, and as he pivots, pushes off as though he were trying for the prize at funeral games. His heavy boots churn like a boy's bare feet.

Achilles has built up so much momentum that he can't turn in time. He overruns Hector's former position when Hector is already ten yards away and picking up speed. Snarling, Achilles twists and throws, but he overbalances and the spear goes hopelessly wide. His feet tangle and he falls. He is up again so fast that he barely touches the ground. He thinks to taunt the Trojan nobles on the wall with their hero's performance, but he won't waste time or breath while Hector lives—plenty of opportunity for that as he hacks the body to pieces for the hungry dogs.

Hector now has nearly fifty yards on him. Another fifty and he'll disappear around the curve of the wall. Not to worry, the hamstrings and glutes that haunt the army's dreams also pack a lot of power. In seconds, Achilles has halved the distance to his prey. Hector darts a look over his shoulder and, arms flailing, pours it on. Achilles laughs and easily closes by another five yards.

Bizimarko is on the wall. Priam behind him is slumped in his silver chair under the purple canopy sobbing like a baby, elbows on knees, head in hands. Hecuba, her big floppy breasts now decorously clothed, is seated beside her king silently, face as expressionless and rigid as a day-old corpse's. Neither is watching what Bizimarko has to see: Hector, his hero, their son, doing his pathetic laps around their city walls with a laughing madman in pursuit.

Bizimarko knows those laps around the walls. When he tries out men for a slot in the royal bodyguard, those who make the last cut are lined up in full armor and raced around Troy's vast circumference. The winner takes the vacancy. But even Bizimarko can expect only a single circuit. The city is a mile across at its widest point; as nearly as anyone has been able to figure—and he was an Egyptian, so he should know—an orbit around its walls is three miles.

Hector is scared enough to run that orbit not once, but twice, with a third beginning. Bizimarko watches the sprinting, stumbling figure and thinks about how much you have to love your life, or fear death, to do this with your family and friends watching. Can you even think ahead to an hour later when, if you survive, you have to walk back through the gate, your head spinning with excuses? Oh yes, I tired him out. Oh yes, I fooled him. I just acted as though I was shitting my loincloth to tire him out.

Bizimarko watches Hector and hopes that he will not survive. He remembers the times when fear of brave Hector's contempt was the only thing that drove him through the gate and into the waiting Achaean spears. He does not want a living Hector to remind him every day of how foolish he was to believe that any man was different from any other; that a prince of the blood could behave worse than a slave; that when the time was right, Bizimarko too could run.

He looks over his shoulder. Priam sobs as though his broken heart will never mend. Bizimarko smiles sourly. Priam's heart is broken not because his son will die today, spilling on thirsty sand the blood that should feed another forty years, but because Priam might be cheated of his last few weeks if the Achaeans finally take the city. And Hecuba's face looks like ice never seen in the Troad, not because she grieves her son, but because she knows she is too old to whore for Agamemnon, and so that if things turn wrong, she will end her days sweating over a kitchen cauldron.

Bizimarko turns back to racing Hector. He hopes that when his own time comes he will die like a man.

Three laps done, and he doesn't have a fourth.

When he was a boy training to be a soldier, he would run longer than this, barefoot, holding across his shoulders a log six inches thick and a yard long. But that was then; his legs have barely held him this last mile. He wobbles and stumbles. His breath comes in ragged gasps; his heart rate has become irregular. A hundred yards ahead are the Scaean Gate and his spears and shield, lying where he left them. Ten yards behind is Achilles, loping easily, grinning and waving in mockery as Hector glances over his shoulder. No choice.

He runs past his scattered weapons and uses the last of his speed to put some distance between himself and Achilles. When he can sprint no more, he jogs to a halt and turns to face the pursuer. "Hold it," he says.

Achilles digs in his heels and skids to a stop. He glares across a dozen yards. He still carries his spear, its point weaving like a python's head, ready to strike. "Hold it? *Hold it?* What the fuck are you talking about? Just stand there another second, all right? No. Don't stand there. Run, bitch, and I'll put this spear up your asshole."

Hector raises his hands, palms out. His chest aches and his vision swirls. He can no longer taste salt in the sweat pouring down his face and into his sodden beard, and he knows that isn't good. He also knows that unless one god directs his own spear and another deflects Achilles', he will be a dead man soon. "Just hold it. Don't worry, one of us dies today. I just want to make a deal, all right?"

"Make a deal with Patroclus."

Hector ducks his head in acknowledgment. "All right, I killed him. This is a war, right? Fair fight and I killed him."

"Fair fight your mother's ass. He was on his back with a spear in his legs, in *my* armor, cunt, and you stuck a spear in his throat and watched him die."

Hector starts to speak. He wants to explain that it wasn't that way at all. This whole war is a big misunderstanding, he wants to say. He wants to tell Achilles that every time he killed an Achaean it was some kind of accident. But before he can humiliate himself completely, he draws a breath. "Yes, he was on his back. And if he hadn't died he would have gone over the wall and killed me and my wife and my father and my children. He was a brave man and a good fighter, so I had to kill him." He waves his arm behind him at Troy's walls. "That's my home, Achaean. I'll die defending it. I'll kill you too if I can, just as you'll kill me if you can and go over that wall and do what Patroclus wanted to do.

"And that's the way it has to be. But just because this is war and one of us has to die, we don't have to die like animals. Here's the deal: once one of us is dead, the winner lets the loser's people come out and take the body. We have two days' truce for funeral games. If you agree, I swear by my own life and my children's that if I win your body won't be touched. I take my spear, I go inside. And if any one of my people wants to touch your corpse, I'll drink his blood faster than I drank yours. Fair?"

Achilles' face is immobile. His spear has stopped its snake's-head circling. Hector holds his breath. At last, Achilles speaks. "Fair? Sure it's fair." His voice is level and reasonable. "Fair as can be. That is, if there was any chance you'd kill me, I'd think about it." His voice is rising now. "But see, you truce-breaking, murdering Trojan goat fucker, there's no chance you'll kill me. I'm killing you. So no deal. Now *die.*"

Hector drops to hands and knees and scrabbles forward to grab his weapons. He rolls onto his back and lifts his shield just in time to block

Achilles' spear. His teeth rattle and his shoulder crunches with its impact. His left arm keeps the shield in place over his body, while his right crawls blindly searching for a javelin. For the first time since he left Troy's gates, he is conscious of the rampart. For an instant, time stops; his vision is unnaturally clear. On the walls are the whole court, his whole family, everyone he has known since birth. Perhaps he sees more than are actually there, all staring in disbelief as he is about to die like a clown under Achilles' spear. Mouths gape, not because he is dying, but because he is dying badly, because he is dying like a man rather than their hero. He wants to scream at them, "If you think it's so easy, why am I here and you there? Come down here and kill him for me." But he doesn't, and they don't.

Achilles runs past him to retrieve the spear that bounced harmlessly off his shield. As he recovers it, Hector staggers to his feet. Achilles half crouches, spear raised, searching out his target. Why prolong it? Hector drops shield and spear, spreads his arms wide, and tilts back his head, exposing his windpipe. He waits a long second staring at a sky impossibly blue before razor-edged bronze flies through his throat. It severs his spinal cord, and sends blood coursing down to fill lungs that have, at any rate, been paralyzed.

He falls backward and cannot believe he is still enough alive to hear bronze rattle and feel the shock of body on earth. He tries to move, more from curiosity than desire to be elsewhere. Nothing. The purple mist of which the poets speak is gathering. He did not expect it to roar in his ears. How could mist roar?

Achilles' face suddenly fills his vision. Hector tries to speak, to offer forgiveness, benediction, warrior to warrior. *I understand you had to do it.* His lips move. His diaphragm somehow pushes his gorged lungs; blood gushes from his mouth as his eyes lock with Achilles' and he struggles to say this last thing.

Achilles snorts and rattles and hocks phlegm. The hot mucous splatters against Hector's face. His vision dims; his bowels relax; he dies, his last words unspoken except perhaps as his first words in Hades.

Such is the death of Hector, breaker of horses.

FUNERAL GAMES

Helen is in her bedroom standing where she has stood for over an hour, equidistant between door and window, wondering which will bring her the news. She knows what is happening and why. Worse, she knows what will happen. And why.

For an hour she has studied the twining fronds painted on the wall, counted the petals on the lotuses, listened to what the wind blew through the window. First there was the buzz and bleat of the court on the rampart fifty yards away. Suddenly diminished, it was broken by pleading, initially of an old man and then an old woman, voices unsexed by age and need almost indistinguishable. Next, the shriek of the great gate opening, then the court's polyglot voice, rising occasionally in a cheer or groan.

Now there is silence, utter and complete, what her bones will hear when the earth is mounded over them. It's different, however, in that it ends shattered by a scream unrecognizable as human, at least by one who has never heard a father lose a son. It rises up to graze the registers in which bats converse, only to fall back into depths that make those who hear it wonder how it is possible to feel such misery and still live. At length it is joined by a low, melodious howl, like a hunting dog's, wordless unless you listen closely to hear the gods cursed by names public as well as those known only to the initiates of the most secret of Troy's royal cults. That would be Hecuba.

Helen stands with her back to the window. She stares at her shadow

155

cast among the painted flowers and prays that Aphrodite will this once visit her when she is alone and dry, that her shadow will appear with hers, that her hands will rest on her shoulders, that her strength will fill her heart rather than her loins. But no, not this time, not ever. Helen's shadow remains solitary. She quivers. Her hands squeeze breasts and drop to thighs, hoping to arouse herself enough to warrant a visit.

The door flies open and bangs against the wall. Her hands leap from crotch to face. Paris takes two long strides and stands in the center of the room a yard away. Always pale by Trojan standards, he is now corpse white. Yet despite his obvious terror, a smile plays around the corners of his mouth. "He's dead," he says.

She nods. Her fingers are pressed against her lips. She is thinking about Sparta. She wonders whether Menelaus will ship her back in chains, or whether he will keep up the pretense of her guiltless abduction. Regardless of what he decides will most save him shame, she knows that he will beat her senseless whenever they're alone and fuck her whenever his tiny cock is finally stiff.

"He's dead," Paris says again as though she hasn't heard. Incredibly, he begins to laugh. "He ran. Girl, you should have seen him run. My brother, my glorious brother." Still laughing, he shakes his head. "Three times around the walls, Achilles behind him the whole way, laughing at him. Laughing. And when my glorious brother couldn't run any more, he tried to make a deal so that we could burn him decently. And Achilles laughed at him again and he crawled on his knees, and then, after one throw, *just one throw,* he stood there and let Achilles kill him because he was too scared to fight, because he'd rather die than fight. So that's how my brother died."

Helen keeps her fingers to her lips for a long time. Finally, she says, "He was your best hope."

Paris pales even further. "'Your' best hope? *Your* best hope? How about 'our' best hope? Oh, I get it. I get it now. After *ten years* I get it! You want to go back to that little piece of Achaean shit, don't you? *After* my people die, *after* my brother dies, *after* you've sucked my dick and swallowed my come and begged me to lick your cunt, *after* I've licked it, *after* you've fucked me a hundred ways I didn't know about till I met you, *after* I've stopped worrying about how you knew about those hundred ways, *then* you say, 'Oh, well, he was *your* best hope.'"

156

Even at a yard the spittle hits her face. Her fingers are at her lips again, eyes downcast. This all sounds very familiar, somehow.

∽

Agamemnon pounds Odysseus' shoulder. "Did you see it? Did you *see* it?" He laughs as though the death of Hector is the best joke he's ever heard. His arm snakes around Odysseus' neck and he pulls his head towards him and kisses it on the crown. "Zeus, Father of us all! Hector dead! Hey, Odysseus, you're going bald!" Still laughing like a maniac, he spins towards Diomedes and the lesser lords, all of whom whoop and sob as though they are a full day's drunk at the firstborn son's wedding feast. "My lords! My lords! Lucky day for us, eh? Not so fucking lucky for Hector!" The lords shriek and pump fists in the air and hold wide their arms to welcome their king.

Odysseus stands back just a little, grinning and waving his own fists in the air. This is something he's never been able to understand: how a man's triumph becomes a common possession while his defeat remains private property. But understood or not, it's part of his world, and so he capers as though it was his own spear that split Hector's windpipe. And when Diomedes and Telamonian Ajax look up from the laughing, back-pounding, weeping pile of Achaean nobility to wave him to join, he sprints forward and dives in.

∽

Zartibax will not cry. Even here among the ships a mile from the lines, the cheers of the Achaean army are deafening and unambiguous. Hector is dead.

At fourteen he is the oldest of the dozen boys shackled together beneath Achilles' black-prowed ship. He is the only one old enough to have handled a spear in anger, even though he was taken in his first battle before he could even throw. But at least he was taken as a soldier. Unlike these others, stolen from their parents as the Achaean blitzkrieg ripped through the tributary villages that once were Troy's empire; some well born, others the children of farmers just one notch above slaves, all old enough to understand what the shouting means but too young to stop their tears.

157

Zartibax snorts his contempt. Scorn for these babies makes it easier to ignore the fear that eats into his stomach and fills the back of his throat with its raw bile. Joined with the fear is its twin, hope: Zartibax has heard that Achilles will not touch a child, so he has made sure that their captor has seen the newly sprouted hair between his legs. Perhaps Achilles will celebrate his victory with him and get him out of this pen.

The chain dragging behind him in the packed dust, he approaches Lacademon. Though none of the Achaeans are friendly, this one, perhaps because he is only a Myrmidon by adoption, taken in after his lord and all his friends were killed in the battle for the ships, seems to hate the Trojan boys a little less than the others. Lacademon is laughing and waving his spear in the air, so he doesn't hear the bronze links clank until Zartibax is directly behind him. Startled, he jumps and spins, spear point level and ready to thrust. "What the fuck do you want?"

"He's dead, isn't he? Hector."

"What do you think, bright boy? Think we're cheering because *our* big guy bought it? Yeah, it's an old Achaean custom. We're happy when we're losing. Hey, maybe you guys should try it." He laughs nastily. "You'd be fucking *delighted* right now."

Zartibax's lip trembles. He bites it hard. He doesn't know why the pain makes the tears stop, but it always does. "So he's dead, then." Then, defiantly, not caring whether Achilles takes him to his bed that night, he adds, "Is yes or no so hard?"

Lacademon reverses his spear so that he can grab it near the point to swing its butt into Zartibax's head to greatest advantage. But as he raises it above his shoulder and his muscles tense to strike, he sees that Zartibax neither flinches nor drops his eyes, and though clubbing the brains out of any Trojan boy would surely be satisfying, dignity and courage in death somehow spoil the whole thing. Slowly, he lowers the spear and plants the point in the packed sand. "Yes," he says. "The answer is yes. He's dead." He watches Zartibax closely. Zartibax can feel his eyes well and bites his lip so hard that a trickle of blood runs down the corner of his mouth. "Sorry, kid," says Lacademon, reaching for Zartibax's shoulder and then, realizing what he is about to do, scratching his own ear. "He died like a man."

"How do you know?"

"What?"

"I said, how do you know? He could have died like a woman, or a coward. You don't know." Seeing the spear pulled out of the ground for a swing, or worse, a thrust through his guts and a mumbled fable to Achilles about an escape attempt, he adds hastily, "But thanks for saying so."

Lacademon keeps his eyes locked with the boy's for a long time. Grudgingly, he lowers the spear again. "Yeah," he says. "Don't mention it. Listen," he says, sliding up to Zartibax and laying his arm across his shoulders. "Now that Hector's gone, peace be to him, I guess the war's going to be over soon. Right?"

"Maybe," says Zartibax, slowly.

"So I guess we won't be enemies any more. Right?"

"Maybe," says Zartibax, slower still.

"So if we're not enemies, I guess we can be friends, right?"

"Maybe," says Zartibax, so slowly that it sounds like a paragraph rather than a single word.

"So if we can be friends," says Lacademon, leaning forward so that his breath tickles Zartibax's ear, "it's all right to tell you what a good-looking boy you are, isn't it?"

Zartibax thinks. Lacademon smells like bad cheese. He will be gentle the first time and drunk every time thereafter, and he knows if he lets him once, there will be a thereafter, because he will be Lacademon's property. But Lacademon has a spear, and Lacademon can do him a lot of good right now. He looks at the soldier. "Maybe," he says.

"Maybe?" says Lacademon.

"Maybe," says Zartibax. Then, "Yes."

Achilles has seen more dead men than he can count. In fact, he saw more dead men than he could ever have counted before his first beard grew. But despite his familiarity with the recently departed, he will never be entirely comfortable with their mobility. Or volubility. He waits a long time after Hector falls to retrieve his spear. Until the river that ran down his twitching leg has dried invisibly in the sand in which it first puddled. Until his bowels stopped gurgling out whatever the Trojan great considered an appropriate potential last meal.

He stares at the dead man a long time. Hector's half-closed eyes show only whites. His mouth is slack, filled with black, clotting blood on which flies eagerly feast. His beard, ringleted and corkscrewed in the fashion of his people, is soaked equally with perfumed oil and the sweat and tears of his last hour. Sticking from the new mouth just opened in his throat like a yards-long tongue is the shaft of Achilles' spear, which Achilles grasps and twists to extract, his boot on the dead man's chest. As he pulls, the body spasms like a hooked fish and the clotted blood trickles from the dead man's mouth and nose. Hector struggles to sit, arms and legs flailing, and Achilles leaps backwards. The body, unrestrained, jackknifes up; the eyes open wide still showing nothing but white. The mouth works desperately, as though the dead man is eager to reveal the secrets of the Underworld while his body is yet unburned. And as his straining mouth gapes as though to shriek, all that comes out is a low drone, its frequency such that the hair rises on the back of Achilles' neck and along his arms and he cries out himself like a puppy.

From the walls of Troy, silent until now except for the occasional keening of the bereaved, comes what sounds like laughter. Achilles spins to face the ramparts. "Something funny?" he screams. "Something funny, you Trojan assholes? Want to see something funny? Even funnier than Hector dying like a fucking scared pig? Not like Patroclus, who died like a man. You want to see something funnier than your coward pig hero lying here dead?" He cups a hand to his ear and strains as though waiting for a reply. "You do? Good! A little something to lighten the mood! The hero takes a bath!"

In silence so absolute that he can hear not only the blood singing in his ears but the accompanying creak of joints battered by nine years of war, he turns to the corpse and plants a foot just under either of its armpits so his torso is directly over the unseeing face. He pulls up his kilt and takes his cock from the sweat-soaked loincloth. He looks over his right shoulder at the rampart. "Take a good look, Troy! You'll be seeing a lot of him soon!" Two-handed, he wags and snaps it. "Up your sons' assholes and in your mothers' mouths!"

On Olympus, when no gods speak, the silence must be equal. He does not stop to wonder why his own people are as quiet as the Trojans. Rather, he lets fly at Hector's face, the first piss he has taken since he rode out to meet his fate hours and hours before, the stream powerful and dark with the dehydration of his ten miles' run and fight to the death. He knocks a fly off Hector's eyebrow, he blasts crusted blood from the corners of his

160

mouth, he tries to write his name on his breastplate, a process compromised by near illiteracy and an emptying bladder.

Finished, he wags again, snapping the last drop in Hector's general direction. Tucking himself back into place he turns to the wall. "Ah. That's better, isn't it? Nice and clean now. But wait, he's sleeping! It's that nice warm bath. I know, I'll wake him up! From his position straddling the corpse he takes its flank. "Wake up, sleepyhead!" He kicks Hector hard in the ribs, so that the lifeless body jumps and groans. He kicks twice more, so hard that he can hear bone and cartilage shatter as ribs are driven into still lungs. Blood runs from Hector's mouth and nose. "Naptime's over!"

He circles to the corpse's head and kicks so hard that multiple vertebrae shatter and the skull lolls supported only by the already severed flesh of the neck. Achilles hops around the body, clutching his foot like a clown. "Ow, ow, ow! My toe! Oh, I get it—the helmet! Why didn't somebody tell me?" He drops his foot and with it the clown's demeanor. "Your hero's dead, motherfuckers. Now watch what I do with him."

He drops to one knee and in the same motion pulls his dagger from the top of a greave. He pops the thongs holding Hector's armor together with the practiced efficiency of a surgeon. He pulls the dead white meat out of the hard carapace as though he were eating a lobster. As the breastplate comes up and off, he slips and his right hand lands in a puddle of his own urine. He grunts, but before he can regain his balance, he feels the warm liquid rise from his palm to his wrist. Astonished, he sees the puddle spread and rise and become animated with tidal motion.

He is in water, hot and salty. Kneeling and bent as he is, it kisses the tip of his beard. Still on his knees, he straightens. Hector's gone, submerged, his existence evidenced only by the spear sticking out of water that suddenly extends to the horizon in every direction, the spear the only feature breaking the water's expanse.

The sudden ocean rises just to his waist, even though he is still on his knees. It is not in him to wonder why the sea is so shallow, first because it is not in him to wonder about anything at all, but mostly because he knows that he is not in the world, anyway.

161

He is not surprised when the water at the horizon boils and geysers. Her. She stays where she is. He had expected her to rush to her victorious boy like a joyous dolphin, but he smothers his disappointment. She is, after all, divine; who is he to expect her to come to him? He awaits her messenger to take him to her. Will he ride a whale this time? Will flying fish lift him and bounce him off the wave tops like a boy's skipping stone?

Still nothing. He begins to worry. Perhaps this is the world after all; perhaps something happened when he was face down over Hector's corpse; perhaps Troy and the army were swallowed up in opening earth and rushing seas and he just didn't notice.

The waves have stopped. The geyser has disappeared. There is no wind and the sea is flatter than any lake he has ever seen. Furious and terrified, he lifts one great leather-bound paw and strikes the water as though it is a boxer whose jaw he has sworn to break. Its surface shatters and foams, but without sound. He opens his mouth to shriek, but nothing comes out. In his terror, all he can hear is the pounding of the pulse in his own ears, and it speaks in his mother's voice.

DON'T
SON
DON'T
SON
DON'T
SON
DON'T
SON

He knows what she wants, or what she doesn't want, and for the first time where she might see, he rages at his mother. He tries to scream, but she will allow the silence to be broken only by the language of his blood. So his mouth gapes and his forehead is wreathed with vessels as he strains. Her words beat in his head; the only sound in the world as her heart was its only sound when he floated in that other sea, below that heart. Frustrated, he shows her that he will not obey. He pulls the spear from the water and plunges it down over and over again, like a fisherman stabbing at an elusive skate. His mouth works. "He killed my Patroclus. I don't care if it's wrong."

Blindly, he strikes the submerged corpse, sometimes burying the point in sand, other times bouncing it harmlessly off bronze, but often enough striking meat and bone, so that soon the water around them is crimson and the air carries the metallic scent of blood. Achilles expects her to appear, to stop him, but she will not; and his spear pumps up and down like a seamstress' needle, still in silence except for the voice in his veins. Finally exhausted, he stops and leans on the planted spear. He turns to the horizon where she first appeared and opens his mouth to try one last soundless scream. As he does, the water surrounding and supporting him drains away as though a plug has been pulled at the bottom of the world, and he tumbles backwards.

Achilles opens his eyes. He spreads his arms from his sides and works his fingers into the sand. Clearly, he is back in the world, his mother and her ocean gone.

He can hear now. From one side comes an angry murmur punctuated by shouts; he presumes it to be Troy. Why would the Achaeans be angry? But even the Achaean side is not silent. Not shouting, but its laughter and cries of triumph are less frequent and more subdued than he would expect. He looks to his left. The army is too distant for him to read faces, but there is less jubilant dancing than should have marked the death of Troy's hero, and a few too many men standing in little clumps, pointing in his direction.

The walls of Troy to his right are even more populous than during the fight with Hector. Achilles is close enough to pick out individuals clearly, all dressed in the ridiculous, effeminate riches of an empire whose borders have shrunk to a city's walls. One bugger with a scarlet-dyed beard pouring over his saffron silk robes shakes by the shoulder his neighbor, splendid in lavender with a towering headdress made of the plumes of a bird from no part of the world Achilles has seen or heard of. Both are so heavily made up that, even at this distance, Achilles can see the black tracks of kohl that tears have drawn across their rouged cheeks. Both turn to point and shake their fists at Achilles and his prize.

Now, in the Trojan murmur, lisping and accented as it is, Achilles can begin to make out individual words. He hears some of what he would have expected, what he dreamed about. "Woe is us," "We're done for," "Let's end it now before the Achaeans can," even an occasional "Poor Hector," though fallen heroes being what they are, not many of those. What surprises him are the cries of "Shame," "Blasphemy," "Desecration." For an instant, when the wind changes, he imagines he can hear the same once or twice blowing from his side in clear Mycenaean, not the giddy praise for which he hoped.

Finally, he looks at what he has won. Hector no longer looks the hero. Stripped of its bronze, his white flesh has been penetrated dozens of times; some individual injuries intersect. His abdomen looks as though it has been chewed. Blood is everywhere. Some of the wounds are neat; others look as though the weapon was twisted and dragged through his viscera, so that here and there a fragment of organ or loop of bowel protrudes.

Achilles stares. He was not alone in the other world, obviously.

Exhausted from mortal combat and contact with the divine, he thinks of abandoning his treasure and just going home. But he can't let Patroclus burn alone. He will feed parts of Hector into the pyre slowly, like a poor man with only a little wood to last a long winter's night. And he can't let the Trojan scum think they've scared him. He straightens his armor casually, as if in his courtyard in Thessaly. He takes off his helmet and wipes his brow. Helmet under his arm, he faces the walls and raises his free arm in mock salute. He thinks to scream another taunt and decides against it. What they'll see is more than enough.

He pulls stiffening Hector into a sitting position and gets his shoulder under his armpit. Grunting, he lifts the corpse and settles its weight across his back. Hector is a big man, but Achilles is bigger, and alive. Bending at the knees, he picks up his spear and Hector's massive corselet, bronze breast and back plates joined by leather thongs. They are all he can carry. Greaves, gorget, sword, and baldric all lie scattered. The helmet with its gorgeous crest that so recently struck terror in every Achaean heart whenever it was seen in battle lies a few yards away. Blood and mud now foul the plume.

Achilles cannot resist. Slow under his burden, he walks to the helmet. Carefully, like a fisherman again, he uses his spear point to lever it up. Successful after just a few tries, he holds it aloft and turns to Troy. "I'll be back for the rest, you sons of whores! Don't even think of touching it!"

The rampart is silent. Careful not to drop the helmet, Achilles shifts the dead weight across his shoulders. Carrying Hector like a shepherd a ram, he walks stiff-legged towards his chariot.

"What is he doing?" Diomedes' beard is still wet with tears of a joy that has long since fled his face. His lips quiver when he does not speak. His arm shakes when he raises it to point to the two men—one living, the other dead—now at Achilles' horses. "What is he *doing*?" he demands again.

Odysseus picks his words carefully. He knows that at this point he loses nothing by playing dumb. Even his worst enemies would never believe him stupid. "Right now," he says slowly, "it looks as though he's tying Hector to the tail of his car."

"That's not what I meant and you know it!" Diomedes bangs his fists on his knees in frustration. He straightens and leans into Odysseus' startled face; Odysseus knew the man to be pious, but didn't know how deep it ran. "Hector is *dead*. You can't *do* that to a dead man!" To Odysseus' astonishment, the big man bends double and begins to sob.

Half a dozen of Achaea's lords are with them. None is as upset as Diomedes, but none is happy, nor has any been in the past half hour as they watched Achilles macerate Hector's body and caught the rising tide of horror in their ranks. Telamonian Ajax drops an empty wineskin. "He's right," he says to no one in particular. "This isn't right."

"I don't know," says Teucer. "*I* wouldn't do this, that's for sure. But then, I didn't just kill Troy's best, now did I?"

"How can you say that?" Diomedes has risen from his nearly fetal crouch. There is spittle on his lips and his eyes look as though they will pop from his head and roll in the sand. "He's *dead*. There are *rules*."

"Right," says Teucer. "Of course."

Diomedes is undeterred. "Can't you hear the gods? Aren't they talking in your head? Aren't they telling you this is wrong?"

Locrian Ajax is nodding so fast that his head looks as though it will fall off. "Yes," he says. "Oh, yes." His eyes are crazier than Diomedes'. "The bodies of the dead are sacred. And Lady Hera, who I just saw, just now, is angry."

The other lords mutter. "Listen," says Odysseus, "you're right. This isn't right. The boy wonder's acting like an asshole. What a surprise, eh?" To his relief he hears a grunt of agreement and even a weak chuckle. "And yes, the gods are angry." Swallowing his distaste, he goes on with what he knows they expect. "Gray-eyed Athena warned me that he would do this, but she reminded me as well that the gods will have each man answer for his own sins."

165

Locrian Ajax speaks. His brief contact with the sacred seems to have left him with a philosophical bent. "So why do we expect them to punish Troy for Paris' wrongs?"

Odysseus laughs and winks at the other lords. "Hey, what are you, Ajax, a Minoan or something?" The other lords laugh, too. "First of all, *we're* punishing the Trojans, right? It's the gods' will, but we're doing the heavy lifting. And anyway, when Zeus, the father of us all, takes out his scales and weighs the fates of whole peoples instead of just two guys, well, face it, there's good and evil on both sides." The lords look solemn and nod, brows furrowed. Odysseus knows that he has reached the limit of their sophistication. "So let Achilles commit his outrages and leave him to his fate. And let's not forget, we still need him, Hector dead or not. What do you say?"

The kinglets are silent for a moment, some studying the sky or the palms of their own hands as they think, others with their lips moving as they converse with interior gods. One by one they nod.

Teucer speaks. "Okay. You're right. We'll leave him alone. But you can see a lot of our guys aren't happy. What do we do about them?"

"Well, you can't tell them what I told you," Odysseus says conspiratorially. "These are not educated men. They won't get it. Instead, simply tell them that Hector is the champion of those who broke the holiest laws, hospitality and the oath. What's happened to his body is the gods' punishment and an example to the rest of us. Remind them that Achilles is half divine, and the privilege of punishment is his alone. I don't want these mopes deciding they can shit on any dead Trojan they find, because next thing you know, they'll be shitting on us."

Diomedes wipes the spittle from the corners of his mouth with the heel of his hand. "Okay," he says. Odysseus is relieved. With him on board it's safe to assume that he can help Achilles get away with his vicious stupidity in spite of himself, and so avoid a religious war within the army. He smiles sourly. He may still see Ithaca before he's a grandfather.

Achilles cracks the reins. His heaven-born pair starts off at a walk. He snaps the leather again and they pick up the pace just a little, the slowest trot. Behind him, he hears a satisfying thump-thump-thump. He smiles happily; it is Hector's head bouncing as his body is dragged by its heels through the dust and dung behind the war chariot.

Achilles croons tunelessly to himself, half dirge, half love song. Soon he'll feed this Trojan meat into the fire and his Patroclus' soul can be released.

☙

Zartibax walks gingerly towards the prisoners' pen, Lacademon's heavy paw on his shoulder. Lacademon pulls out the peg that holds the jerry-built gate in place and holds it open for Zartibax. The other boys stare; most giggle. One, next oldest to Zartibax, scowls and spits into the packed dirt and turns his back. Zartibax feels hot blood rush to his face. Okay, big man, he thinks.

The boys stand and titter. He will not walk into the little compound, not like this. The pressure on his shoulder increases to a squeeze. The hand then leaves the shoulder and touches the side of his head. Fingers graze his cheek. Zartibax' lips move in silent prayer. Please don't let him kiss me, not here, not in front of the guys.

His prayer is answered. The rough hand slides up to the top of his head and tousles his hair, then moves to his back and gently pushes him forward. Without a choice, Zartibax goes into the compound glaring at the boys suddenly silent, looking anywhere but at him. The next oldest is still strutting contemptuously, presenting his back.

Well, well, well, thinks Zartibax. How convenient.

☙

After crowing Achilles rode nine times around Troy's walls, Hector's body splayed and bouncing with each bump, arms spread and flailing, long hair now dust-crusted and sweeping the road, the Trojans finally aroused to something like manhood, howling from their walls and showering their perimeter with spears and arrows. Just something like manhood: their gates remain shut, no matter what odds they could throw against Achilles. Over the whistle of arrows, the rattle of the chariot, the horses' hooves drumbeat, he nevertheless hears the pounding of his heart. He will not listen to its message.

167

On the wall under the purple canopy, Hecuba lies face down on her belly at the throne's feet, fists beating the carpeted stone. Priam is motionless, hunched head in hands with his elbows on his knees, sometimes whining like a full-bladdered hound at a door.

"The dogs will eat my balls," he says.

No one speaks. Hecuba's fists continue their tattoo. The courtiers stand like impossibly brilliant marble.

"The dogs will eat my balls," he says again, louder. The courtiers are no doubt silent because they can pretend not to have heard. He'll fix that. Leaping to his feet as fast as a man of sixty can, a man of sixty ossified by malaria and a diet of meat and wine and millions of squirming parasites and the countless trauma of war. He raises arms whose shoulders creak so loud that Athena's own owl on Olympus must turn its startled head to wonder at the noise. *The dogs will eat my balls.*

The courtiers turn to face him uneasily, not knowing what to do. What if the king is mad? What if he is not? Will there be a regency? Who will be the regent? What will happen to those who don't flock to him now, today, yesterday? What will happen to those who did when the king's madness is seen as mere grief? When even this aged king, powerful in his right senses, marks those who were a little too eager to embrace a succession suddenly vacated by his biggest and best boy? So the courtiers stir like a grove of willows in bud, bending to a fresh breeze not yet too powerful.

Arms still outstretched, Priam shouts: "Hear me. *Hear me.* I am not mad." A few of the bastard half cousins twice removed twitch in disappointment, past favors to Paris again mere acts of grace. "But I am old, and my son, my best son, is dead. My defender, your defender. You, all of you, can meet your deaths in war if that is what the gods decide, but if this city falls, I am too old to die defending it. And thus I'll meet my death at the hand of some Achaean foot soldier, a man whose father I would have turned down at a slave auction, who laughs at me as he dashes my head against rock or slits my belly to watch bowels slide out or cuts my throat and sees my pleading as bubbles of blood on my paling lips. And my dead body will then lie among the unburied, and the dogs I hunted with, mad from starvation and no longer fed with scraps from my hands, will tear open what's left and rip away even these useless things." Priam pulls open his robe and clutches himself, fingers curled around his shrunken manhood.

The courtiers gasp. The king's genitals are ordinarily displayed at only the most private ceremonies. For him to wave them in the prevailing winds at the rampart where any slave can see is an appalling breach of protocol. And, given their decayed state, not the best politics.

Bantiphex, a lieutenant of the guard, is at Bizimarko's side. "This is bad," he whispers.

"Tell me about it," Bizimarko whispers back through the side of his mouth, his face still fixed on the god king he's sworn on his children's lives to defend.

"No," says Bantiphex, "I mean it. This is terrible. The boys aren't exactly happy about Hector, especially Hector being dragged around like a turd out of a puppy's ass." His face works and he spits it out. "Some of the boys are saying it's time to give someone else a crack at the throne. Not me," he adds hastily, "never me."

"Never you," says Bizimarko. "Who?"

"Just some of the boys," says Bantiphex. "I don't remember. Just something you hear. But listen, we'll talk about that later, all right? Just don't let the king give them any more arrows to their bows right now."

Bizimarko hesitates, but not for long. He's sworn to defend this family, even from themselves. He hands his spear to the page at his side. The baldric, heavy with its sword, comes over his neck and into the boy's hands. He takes a deep breath and walks forward. The statutory three steps from the king, he drops to his knees. Bronze clatters as he throws himself on his belly. The courtiers again gasp at this gesture of grief and sympathy from the most hardened of the king's men. There is no sound from the king who faces away, his hands still occupied with his withered privates. Face flat against rough stone, Bizimarko snakes his hands forward until they grasp the king's ankles. Some of the courtiers weep openly. Bizimarko, Troy's proudest and bravest after Hector, is groveling and clutching his king's feet like an Assyrian. Among them a murmur flies, heavy though it is with words like "loyalty" and "humility" and "example to us all."

The king, oblivious, is bent forward, apparently examining what he fears the dogs will soon be fighting over. Bizimarko snaps his right hand back half an inch, fast and hard. It is enough; the king topples. He rolls with his hands cupping his balls, knees drawn up to further protect them, his eyes rolling in confusion and mouth working in what Bizimarko guesses are the names of his treasonous hounds. Bizimarko leaps to his feet, protocol apparently ignored in this royal emergency. "Come on, you fucking apes!" he roars to the guard. "Get the king inside!" In seconds, half a dozen of his best have the king shoulder high and on trajectory to the citadel's cool interior. "Heat and grief," says Bizimarko to no one in particular, and even those who haven't heard nod in knowing assent.

He follows the babbling monarch. Just before the citadel swallows them, Bantiphex steps forward and grabs Bizimarko's biceps. Their eyes meet and Bantiphex winks. Bizimarko thinks about doing the same, but won't. He should have known about the treason in the ranks a long time ago. Before sundown, he'll have to torture out of Bantiphex the name of every man who wanted Priam out of the way.

An oath, after all, is an oath.

Bumpity-bumpity-*bump*. Achilles saws the reins and his god-matched pair stops. So does the rhythmic pounding of Hector's head. Achilles is a little surprised that, given the injuries to its connecting neck, the thing hasn't fallen off yet. On either side as far as he can see is the Achaean army. Cheering like madmen, yes, but not quite as loud as madmen should. And not quite every man cheers. Some wave spears halfheartedly, as though they're not sure how happy they should be; others, fewer, have spears planted point down before them, scowling at their supporting hands; one or two—Achilles will get names later—have their backs conspicuously turned to their returning savior.

Ahead are that bastard Agamemnon and his circle of tributary kings: Menelaus, Diomedes, both Ajaxes, Teucer, and honey-tongued Odysseus, his smile so ambiguous as to mean less than nothing. Agamemnon can't piss in the sand without a god's great-grandson shaking his dick for him. Though the other lords are in battle gear still, Agamemnon has managed to change into a robe both festive and regal, its grandeur calculated to remind Achilles that no matter how much foot licking went on to get Achilles out into the field, now that the job's done, Agamemnon is still who he is.

Achilles holds his reins languidly; he does not dismount.

Agamemnon stands where he is, arms outstretched and grinning his welcome for a very long time. Nothing happens. His grin grows strained. Out of its side, he says to Odysseus, "I'm the king, right?"

"Right, lord," says Odysseus.

"So why isn't he coming to me?"

"I think, lord," says Odysseus slowly, "that it's because he just killed Hector."

"What an asshole," says Agamemnon. "Do I look like a bigger asshole if I go to him?"

"No, lord," says Odysseus, "you look like the bigger man."

"Oh," says Agamemnon, "that's all right, then." Without another word he drops his arms and then raises them higher. "Great Achilles!" he bellows. The lords around him raise their voices in chorus, and the army follows. Not quite as loud as the lords, true, but it follows.

Agamemnon sweeps forward, his frozen grin suddenly thawed as the words pour out. "Achilles, my lord, king, my son, my boy, what have you done for us, for Achaea, for yourself? For us not just victory, but survival, life itself. For Achaea, glory, but a life and a glory that we enjoy solely as a reflection of *your* life, *your* glory. And so, Lord Achilles, greatest of the Achaeans, as we sing our victory paeans, we thank the gods not only for victory, *your* victory, but for *you*."

Odysseus is impressed. The man can kiss ass.

Achilles apparently is not. He stares at Agamemnon, a little smile playing with the corners of his lips. Agamemnon stares back, his grin again glacial. At last, Achilles speaks. "Thanks, lord," he says. "Nice of you." He reaches into his chariot side and pulls clear a javelin. For an instant, its lethal tip is pointed at Agamemnon's unarmored heart. Agamemnon is too schooled in kingship to allow his fear to show; if this is how he is to die, it is what it is, and if it is not, any tremor of hand or bead of sweat will plant the confident seed for his eventual assassin. But Odysseus, alarmed, drops hand to sword hilt and has the blade a half-inch out before he checks himself. He grinds his teeth in irritation. Why risk his own life defending his king without weighing the consequences?

The point leaves Agamemnon's sternum as Achilles spins gracefully to face the rear of his car. There Hector lies, invisible to the Achaean lords, crusted in clotting dust. The spear hovers over Achilles' knotted shoulder. A fraction of a second later, it finds its mark with the plonk of bronze part-

171

ing meat and shattering bone unmistakable to men whose lives have been spent in war.

Achilles stands, his back to his army and his king. He stays that way a long time, long enough for the grumbling lords to piece together where the spear has gone. Finally, he turns. He breaks open a bundle of spears—spare ammunition slung on the side of the chariot car. He holds up half a dozen in either hand, spears whose shafts are an inch and a half thick and four yards long, pointed with two feet of barbed bronze; spears any ordinary man would have thought too heavy to handle. But god-born Achilles hefts them easily, and shakes them so that their ash shafts and bronze heads clatter like dried stalks. "Come on, boys," he says. "Come *on*. Stick a spear into this dead Trojan bastard!"

The lords hesitate, hang back, murmur. Achilles roars. "What's the matter with you girls? He's fucking dead! He can't hurt you!" He shakes his spears again. "In the name of Ares himself, how could you look at your grandchildren saying, 'Oh Hector was so scary I couldn't even face him when he was dead'?" He raises the spears high, pectorals bulging from the edges of the god-made breastplate. "That is, if any of you pussies have grandchildren."

The lords of Achaea stare open-mouthed. No one—not even Achilles on any day but this—would have offered such insolence without first kissing his family goodbye. Nor would anyone have proposed the desecration of a noble corpse without first offering enough placatory sacrifices to drive the surrounding country into a generation of famine.

Teucer growls low in his throat and Odysseus trades a quick, alarmed glance with the king. Both turn to Achilles, mouths simultaneously opening to speak calming words, brains racing to find them before Achilles is ripped to shreds by his comrades, but Teucer is too quick. Howling like a dog he charges forward, elbowing aside Odysseus as he lunges to stop him, dodging Diomedes and ignoring Agamemnon's shrieked command to be still. He covers the dozen yards to Achilles' chariot at a dead sprint and tears a spear from the bundle Achilles still holds high in his right hand, barely disturbing the rest. Teucer backs away from the chariot, the spear poised over his shoulder, its bobbing point tracking Achilles' exposed throat.

Achilles' beard fissures into a grin. "Come on, you pussies," he cries again. "Drink his blood!"

Teucer's head snaps around wildly, turned first to taunting Achilles,

172

then back to the Achaean lords, then to the splayed corpse invisible to them behind the chariot. His eyes bulge and his mouth works as he speaks to something not seen. Odysseus realizes that while Teucer is no drunker than usual, that is still more than enough for anything. His eyes again meet Agamemnon's. Odysseus nods to the king; the king, mouth a hard, nods back and jerks his head towards Teucer. Odysseus pulls his sword free and starts his jog ahead. He knows he can take Teucer, despite the decade dividing them, unless a wild throw is really lucky. He hopes he will not die protecting Achilles from himself.

Teucer's jaw is snapping like a dying mackerel's. One second, perhaps two, and Odysseus will be on him. The sun is behind him, and Teucer is crazed with the god yammering inside his skull. It's an easy kill for which none will honor him. Odysseus briefly considers trying for a split skull or frank decapitation, but the high-stroked approach will expose him to the lucky spear thrust. So he will go in low, a quick jab to the legs to loosen Teucer's hamstrings and drop him sprawling to expose his fatal points. Teucer is poised and gibbering. Odysseus knows the idea that presently floods his head is better than that which preceded it, though he does not have time to know completely what it is. He drops his sword in the dust and brings his shield before him as he drives forward head down and knocks raving Teucer to the ground.

He stands, the shield still before him, measuring the distance to his sword if he needs it. Achilles' laughter rattles in his brain. Let him laugh. He's still alive; so is Teucer, and so is Odysseus.

Teucer shakes his head. Blood flies from his mouth and nostrils. Unsteadily, he regains his feet and recovers his dropped spear. Odysseus backs up three steps and half crouches, ready to sweep up his sword. Teucer stands swaying. His eyes first light on laughing Achilles, who waves his burdened arms up and down and puffs out his bronze-bound chest begging Teucer to try it. Teucer's eyes roll to Odysseus and then to the Achaean lords, thunderstruck silent. Suddenly, he laughs wildly and runs back to the rear of the chariot car. Blocked by Achilles now shaking with laughter, Odysseus can only see the butt of the spear pistoning up and down as Teucer lacerates Hector's remains. Through Achilles' merriment he can barely make out Teucer's mingled curses and prayers for forgiveness.

Achilles turns back to the Achaean lords and holds forward his spears.

"Hey," he says. "At least one of you has the balls to take on a dead man!"

Odysseus will now risk a glance behind him. The open-mouthed horror with which the lords met the violation of a royal corpse is gone. At once shamefaced and grinning like guilty boys, the lords are edging forward to take the blaspheming javelins. Only Agamemnon and Diomedes stand where they stood, Diomedes ashen with outraged piety, Agamemnon soaking his robe with sweat as his nobles leave his side.

The lords pass Odysseus avoiding his glance. Each takes a spear from Achilles, some kiss his hands. Soon, from behind the car a dozen spears dance up and down and the air reeks of blood, hard though it is to credit that Hector could have any left to shed.

For a moment, Odysseus wonders whether it would be a good idea to join in. He spits in the dust as soon as the words form in his head. He has his limits.

THE TROJAN BOYS

Achilles is on the hill that his love crowns. Already the men have begun to call it Patroclus' Hill. This pleases Achilles. He would be less pleased if he knew that others were calling it Mount Patroclus and nudging their friends when they did.

He circles the pyre slowly. His eyes are fixed on the body at its center, lying like a sleeping child in a cradle of split cordwood and kindling soon to be soaked down with oils and loaded with spices. His dreaming baby to hiss and swell and split open and char. Achilles will watch because he knows he must; he cannot avert his eyes from his lover's incineration, not with others watching him. But that moment is not yet. Now he can look at the Patroclus who was, the Patroclus he loved, the man he fucked and then curled with like one spoon in a pair made together.

Or at least something close to that Patroclus. His mother has kept her word. The unguents she had him take from his trunk did their work; so far, Patroclus has not made a home for the flies' children. Today, though, the Myrmidons posted at each corner of the pyre have had to work a little harder at brushing away the winged visitors, and Patroclus has, unquestionably, gone green. The Myrmidon honor guard no longer volunteers quite so eagerly; it is too hot to leave a man unburned this long. Whatever divine Thetis promised, she is obviously somewhere upwind.

Achilles continues his slow orbit. Today he thinks he will not again try to kiss those stiff lips skinned back from teeth clenched by a bandage

175

binding shut the jaw. Yesterday he did, and the Myrmidons, signaled by priests more terrified than they were outraged, pulled him off the pyre as his foot scrambled for purchase among the split logs. No, not today.

Today he circles a man he knows now to be dead and soon to be ash and crumbled bone, a man who is starting to stink. But however bad he may look, he looks a lot better than his killer. There will be no pyre for Hector. He lies a dozen yards away from Patroclus, dead three days, crusted still with road filth, his jaw frozen open as though in a scream. Eyes that would accuse Olympus if they had not been plucked out by carrion birds are now lidless black sockets. His hundred wounds swarm with maggots, his naked body swells and bloats.

On the first day, a Myrmidon, thinking that his lord had cried himself to sleep at Patroclus' feet, crept over to close the Trojan's then-intact eyes. He bent over the body and was whispering a prayer when Achilles' bronze-bound fist crashed into the base of his skull. Today he lies in the camp at the foot of the hill neither dead nor alive. No Achaean has touched the Trojan since.

Achilles stands over Hector's corpse. He hasn't kicked it yet today, nor has he pissed on it for two days, nor has he had to be stopped from dragging it to the lip of the cesspit at the edge of camp to pitch it into months of Achaean shit. Today he thinks that it will be better just to watch him rot day by day, to see a man whose pride of body was second only to his own turn into leather and bone and hanks of hair that only the hungriest dog would worry.

He turns back to the pyre. "Today, my love," he says.

Agamemnon, Menelaus, Diomedes, Teucer, and Odysseus are in the king's tent, none of them happy, none speaking.

Diomedes finally breaks the silence. "I can't believe it," he says. "I can't *believe* it."

"Believe it," says Agamemnon.

Teucer scratches his jaw. "Look," he says. "I have to agree with Diomedes. I mean, all right, I got a little out of control there when he dragged Hector back, but it's not like I was alone, right? Incidentally, thanks again, Odysseus; you could have cut my throat and no one would've blamed you. I owe you, big guy, don't think I don't know it. Okay?"

"Okay," says Odysseus.

"But anyway, this is different. Like Diomedes said, we're *Achaeans*. Achaeans don't do this. Sweet Mother Gaia, I don't think *Hittites* do this anymore, do they?"

"I don't think so," says Menelaus. It is the first time he's spoken. No one expects his silence to be broken again.

"Right," says Diomedes. "We can't let this happen. King, if you don't stop it, what will your name be worth when you are dead?"

Agamemnon's mouth opens and does not completely close. He doesn't really like thinking past the next day, and the time past his death may never have entered his mind before. He turns his bugging, hooked-carp eyes to Odysseus.

"Diomedes," says Odysseus, smooth as though he knows what is about to come out of his mouth, "you're right, we're Achaeans. We're *humans*. We fear the gods. So we can't let this happen. Or can we?"

He pauses. He knows he has their attention. "I've said this before and you've all agreed. Each man makes his own fate or endures what the Fates send. Just as the gods themselves must, which is why even Zeus, the father of us all, must cover his face in fear when the Fates speak. And Lord Achilles, born as he is of a goddess, knows this. But unlike us, he had a choice. He knew that resuming this war meant an early death here at Troy, and he chose. He chose this war and that early death. And this, my lords, is part of that fate. And that fate will follow him through this world and into Hades' dark hall. And who are we to spare him what he has chosen?"

The lords are silent. Agamemnon nods, wisely, as though Odysseus stole the words from his mouth. Odysseus lets them think. Even pious Diomedes seems to waver. It's time to seal the deal. "Anyway, my lords, we need him. This war isn't over yet, Hector dead or not. And I will speak the truth: if it got me back to Ithaca a day sooner, I'd let that animal fuck me up the ass." Silence, then a shout of astonished laughter. Now, thinks Odysseus, finish. "Okay," he says, "I was lying." Silence again. "But I'd let him fuck Teucer up the ass." Another silence, another eruption of laughter, from Teucer the loudest.

Five minutes later, they leave the tent. Achilles will have his way.

"No," says Lacademon. "I won't."

"Hera's cunt you won't," says Menander. He is a lieutenant of the Myrmidons, two reports down from great Achilles himself and, since Lacademon was orphaned by his unit's slaughter, his leader among the storm troopers.

"Right," says Lacademon. "By Hera's black-haired cunt, by Aphrodite's pink nipples, by Hades' thorny cock, *I won't.*"

Menander's face fills with blood. Beard split in a snarl, his hand drops to his sword hilt. Lacademon's does the same and both men take a step back. Their fellows, noticing, start to clap and cheer and form a ring. *Fight, fight.* And with these two, if either lives, it's because a god grabbed a sword out of an angry hand.

Lacademon measures the two yards between them. The other man is bigger and younger and he didn't get where he is by being easy to kill. Maybe if Lacademon starts to cry or something, he can get this fatal boy to drop his guard. But as he looks at his rage-swollen face and the muscles bulging outside his armor, heavier on the sword side, and counts the scars on face and shield arm, he sees this boy is no pushover. It is no more than ten seconds since they squared off and Lacademon knows with a heavy, sinking feeling in the pit of his stomach that he prays will not unman him when the time comes, that this is the one who will end it all, who will send him down to Hades. There's nothing to do but die like a man. He draws a deep breath, filling his lungs with life's sudden impossible richness, and pulls free his sword.

He does not notice that the clapping and cheers from the sidelines ended as soon as they began. Just as that last long, sweet breath is about to become his final war cry, he sees the big man in the crowd. The very big man standing with arms folded, no helmet covering hair the brightest gold that ever came from Thessaly, his breastplate swimming with animals, gods, waterfalls. He ignores the men around him. His face is amused.

"What, Lacademon?" says the big man. "What won't you do? What is there by Zeus' thunder, by Apollo's balls, that you won't do for me? What won't you do for Achilles?"

Lacademon stares. His war cry whistles out his nostrils and turns into a sob. He drops his sword and falls to his knees. Menander, with less reason for relief, merely returns his weapon to its scabbard. "Nothing, lord," cries Lacademon. He fights to control the quaver in his voice, but sees no shame that he can't. "There is nothing I wouldn't do for Achilles."

Zartibax is proud that he gets to lead the parade.

At dawn, Lacademon came for them, resplendent in freshly polished armor over a white linen tunic not too badly stained—even bathed, perhaps—his spruceness marred only by a sagging face and eyes red-rimmed from grief and the wine to drown it. Zartibax smiled for the first time with a little tenderness; he knew that Lacademon would miss him when he was back in Troy, and however crude a fuck he might have been, it was nice to know that Lacademon had cared.

And so, when Lacademon and a dozen Myrmidons equally grand entered the boys' corral with their hands looped with garlands, he could not resist. As Lacademon bent to drop the woven flowers over his head—Zartibax could not help but notice that he alone among the boys had a double necklace of the freshest blossoms—he rose on tiptoe to kiss the soldier's cheek just above the beard, where the skin was as leathery and lined as dried beef. Lacademon, astonished, made to embrace the boy. But before the others stopped him, he arrested himself. Just one quick sob, and he faced Zartibax with a shaky smile and a fast, teary wink.

So Zartibax leads his procession of prisoners heavy with flowers, booty of war bought back by its rightful owners. His chest is swollen with pride. The boys are his first command; Lacademon his first broken heart. The future looks bright.

The Myrmidons fall in on either side of the boys' column. They are silent, eyes straight ahead. Zartibax guesses that they might not be too happy with the giving up of prisoners so soon after their triumph over Hector. Well, that's war. The Achaean camp seems nearly empty. Zartibax wonders why until they leave the crude timber gate so different from the carved stone of his own city's portals, and turn onto a beaten trail leading up a low hill. Massed there is the whole army, five thousand men on either side of the trail, four deep all the way to a crest that Zartibax sees is topped with an unlit pyre and blazing tripods and the violet robes of priests and the blinding armor of Achaea's great nobles.

As they turn that corner onto the trail, there rises a great shout from the army, a roar so loud and deep that it is felt as much as heard. Zartibax stops dead, jaw dropped. Lacademon puts a rough paw on his shoulder and urges him forward, and so he stumbles ahead, stunned by the glory that he knows is not his, deafened by the cheers that he knows are not for him.

The trail is not wide, barely enough for the column of boys and their guards on either side. Zartibax sees the men his father and uncles have tried to kill for years, who have sent uncles down to Hades. And while he knows that his people and the Achaeans are cousins, and that they all worship the same gods—and Zeus himself knows that Achaean Lacademon acts like any other man—when they are all together like this, he sees how *different* they are. Their armor is different, their clothes are different, their unoiled hair and beards are different, their clumsy dancing is different, their *smell* is different. In that moment he hates them not for what they have done and tried to do to his people, but for who they are. And he swears to himself that once they are driven off the Illyrian plain, once their stragglers escape the ruins of their pathetic camp to sail weeping back to Achaea and whimper the tale of their defeat, he will beg King Priam or King Paris for leave to lead an army of all right-thinking men, Trojan and allied, to sack their different towns and rape their different women and boys and slaughter their different babies and lead the few who live back to Troy to be mocked in chains for their difference.

He is halfway up the trail as he swears genocide. He turns shining eyes and a proud face to the hilltop where he will be redeemed. Almost there now, where father and uncles and perhaps Priam himself will be waiting.

As they march, the Achaeans take up a chant, neither of victory nor of peace, but of sacrifice. Zartibax begins to understand as the drums and flutes pick up the sacerdotal rhythm, at once mournful and full of hope. Of course, the enemy is giving up these beautiful boys, himself first among them, to appease Troy and Olympus for the death of the hero Hector, beloved of all the gods.

At the crest of the hill, at its center, dominating vision, occupying half the space available, is the pyre. It is the biggest he has ever seen, two yards high at least and six yards on a side, carefully built, its base bundles of pine, dry and resinous; next quartered fruitwood, apple and cherry and plum; finally big split cedar logs. Kindling and tallow mortar the pyramid soaked with sweet-scented oils and burdened with linen bags of spice and incense, all ready to hide the stink of the burning dead. Atop it the noble corpse. From where he achieves the crest, Zartibax can see mostly the dead man's feet, but beyond them glimmers the bronze in which he is to become ash and even the white plume of his lover's helmet, which he will wear until his body crumbles away and the horsehair is smoke.

A dozen bronze tripods surround the pyre at its closest perimeter. They are nearly as tall as the pyre itself, their bowls the size of shields, each fluttering yards-long plumes of flame from the best oil. Around them are ringed a dozen priests robed in violet silk, hooting and moaning in a language last spoken when the competition of men with beasts was still in doubt, two eunuchs' sopranos giving grace to the garbled baritones of ten whole men.

And further outside that perimeter, under a purple silk canopy, are the lords of Achaea. Only one is without armor and around him all the others cluster in respectful ranks. Robed in rich funereal red, crowned with a king's laurel, he is a man of middle height, his beard mostly gray with age, eyes bagged, forehead creased, but movements still quick and forearms still corded with muscle. His eyes never still. Agamemnon.

Behind him stands a man almost as old and taller, thicker of body, but nevertheless seeming smaller as though he has condensed around some shame, helmet in the crook of his arm. His beard is oddly trimmed, upper lip shaved. His eyes are fixed at the middle distance or the ground. Menelaus.

To the king's left, closest to him in a group of half a dozen in bright-scoured armor, is a big man, not young, but younger than the king. A page immediately behind him holds the great ox-hide shield Zartibax learned in boyhood belongs to Diomedes. The prince's expression perplexes; in place of the hatred and rage he would have expected, Zartibax sees something like pity. There is only one man to the king's right, shorter than the king, shorter than most of the other lords, made to seem still shorter by a massive chest. His black-plumed helmet sits on the ground before him. His hard black eyes are fixed on the boys, his face devoid of any warlike expression. Odysseus. For an instant, he stares directly at Zartibax, his iron smile unchanging, his eyes dispassionate as a lizard's. For the first time that day, Zartibax feels fear, unreasoned on this day of his release.

The Myrmidon guard leads the boys past the royal pavilion and curving around the hilltop. As they spiral up towards the pyre itself, Zartibax is distracted by a swarm of flies buzzing angrily around a dead bull carelessly left on hallowed ground. He glances in its direction and Lacademon hisses in his ear. "Don't look, boy." Of course Zartibax's head snaps to

181

the carcass. It's not a bull, but a man. His body is bloated to twice its ordinary size and covered with banqueting maggots. His face is eyeless and purplish black with decay, his withered lips are skinned back from teeth through which a black swollen tongue protrudes.

Zartibax whimpers and gags. He has seen the unburned dead before many times, but never a hero of the Royal House, great-grandson of Olympian Zeus, rotting like a jackal's leavings. Before he can vomit, Lacademon's rough hand shakes his shoulder. "I told you not to look, boy," he says. "Remember him as he was, not like this." Gently, he pushes Zartibax forward. Zartibax is beginning to wonder how they can welcome the Trojan delegation that will ransom them home with Hector a stinking heap.

The boys snake around the pyre. From behind him, Zartibax hears high, childish sobbing and once a violent retch. The other boys have recognized Hector.

They stop. Zartibax can see that they have formed a ring around the pyre. High as it is, he can see only two boys on either side before the rest are obscured by the corpse-crowned kindling. Behind each boy is a Myrmidon guard, his sword drawn in salute. Behind the guards are the priests, and from where Zartibax stands, he can just see the canopy beneath which the king and his nobles must await Priam himself.

Any second now, thinks Zartibax.

A murmur arises from the massed Achaean ranks on the hill. The lords themselves shift, nervous, expectant. Zartibax stands as straight as he can, proud Trojan, but remains ready to grovel in the dust at the first sight of Troy's king. But it is not Troy's king who appears. Rather, it is a man whose family tree is a lot closer to Olympus. Two yards tall, unhelmeted head covered in hair like spun gold, breastplate blazing with stars and swimming with dolphins and sea beasts even more fabulous, he strides towards the nobles who, all but Odysseus and the king himself, almost curtsy. Odysseus merely salutes, equal to equal, and the godling's reverence to the king is so perfunctory as to make it appear that the king bows to him.

Minimal politeness dispensed with, the godling turns to the pyre. For one instant, his face is directly on Zartibax, who steps backwards as though struck in the chest, colliding with Lacademon behind, who throws an arm across his chest to steady him. Involuntarily, he gasps, "Achilles!"

And still staring straight at Zartibax, Achilles nods and raises his great right arm, holding it high for one long second. Zartibax steals a glance left, then right, to see whether his friends are as transfixed as he by the most beautiful man in the world, so he misses the arm's fall. But he sees the left arm of each Myrmidon guard snake across the breast of the boy in front of him, and sees the sword-bearing right arm descend to draw its bronze across the imprisoned boy's throat. He sees each boy's skinny legs kick and scissor before him as blood jets from severed arteries, and sees them kick less violently with each passing second as the jets of blood slow to trickles. Still uncomprehending, he turns to face Lacademon. As he does, he feels the big man's forearm tighten across his own chest and the bite of edged bronze in his conveniently exposed carotid. As his vision darkens with the first big spurt of red blood, he hears Lacademon whisper, voice fat with tears, "I'm so sorry. I love you. Forgive me."

And because death comes faster than any expect, he is still confused when he sees his legs dance beneath him and watches his bladder drain and feels the cold spread faster than fire from the tips of his fingers and toes up into his belly and finally into his heart where it freezes the drumbeat that has kept the rhythm of his life. In that sudden silence, the last little dim circle of light left in his eyes goes out. Though he feels Lacademon release him, he is gone before what is left hits the ground.

Bizimarko pounds on Paris' bedchamber door. "Lord, open!" he cries. "It's Bizimarko! In the name of all the gods, open!" They are the first words he has spoken, perhaps the first words spoken in Troy, since just moments after the heavy column of greasy smoke from Patroclus' pyre began its twisty climb to heaven heavier than it should have been. Since word reached Troy that Patroclus did not go to Hades alone; that twelve Trojan boys, their throats freshly slit, their limbs still twitching, kept him company as the flames ate his body. That Achaea had sunk back a thousand years to the times when men still bought the gods' favor with their own flesh.

Dead silent, the court watched the column climb and spread until its mushroom cap covered half the sky. That their children had been substituted for animals was the least of the abomination. Worse by far was their fear of what would happen next. The gods eat smoke, men, meat; every sacrifice is followed by feast. If the Achaeans are so far sunk as to do what they have done, who is to say that cannibalism is not next?

Bizimarko's fist is raw. He pulls his sword from the scabbard, sacrilege in the presence of the royal family, but this is no ordinary time, and pounds with its hilt on the heavy oaken door. On the third blow, the door flies open to Paris wrapped in a silken sheet, his face mottled red with rage. "What the fuck do *you* want?" he snarls.

"Sorry, my lord," says Bizimarko. He forces his eyes to meet the prince's. "Sorry, lord," he says again. It is much less than etiquette and his survival require, but almost more than his contempt will permit. "The king, your father."

"Yes?" Paris' irritation is unabated. Thinking, no doubt, that the king, his father, wants him to take Hector's place at yet another hopeful disembowelment of yet another hapless animal.

"The king, your father..." Bizimarko cannot speak. His face works in the unmistakable effort of a strong man struggling to suppress unseemly emotion.

"Yes?" Paris' tone has changed, as has his face. His voice is filled with wonder and delight. His scarlet rage has fled. He stands a full inch taller, regal, thinking himself the brand-new king of a city the gods might still inexplicably spare.

"Your father," says Bizimarko slowly, "is gone."

Paris nods slowly, eyes fixed on the middle distance like a Medean statue of a king minus the four-foot beard, bull's hooves, and wings. "How did it happen?"

"Just now," says Bizimarko. He has begun to understand and is beginning to enjoy himself. "We went to his chamber and he was... *gone.*"

"I see," says Paris. "A great father, a great man, and a great king."

"Yes, lord," says Bizimarko.

They stand in silence for a moment. Bizimarko with eyes downcast but not quite so far that he can't see a smile playing with the corners of Paris' mouth. Mastering himself, Paris fixes his face in lines of grief and authority. "Captain," he says. "You may be the first."

"The first, lord?" says Bizimarko. "The first to what?"

Paris smiles indulgently. "Oh, Bizimarko," he says. "Your grief is very great, as is mine, but you forget yourself," he says indulgently. "You must pay me homage as your king." Imperiously he raises his arm, finger

184

pointed down to the stone commanding obeisance. As he does so, the sheet, freed of restraint, falls to the ground. Paris ignores the fact that he is a naked man with a fading erection. "Kneel to your king."

"I will, lord," says Bizimarko. "As soon as he comes back."

Paris chuckles, though his face has begun to cloud. "Bizimarko," he says. "Captain, no man, king or otherwise, comes back from the dead."

"Who said he was dead?" Bizimarko pinches his thigh so hard that it draws blood. "I just said he was gone."

"*What?*"

"Sorry, lord," says Bizimarko. "Was I confusing? Oh, Zeus Almighty, I was. Oh, forgive this poor piece of gutter filth, how great your grief must be—" He makes as if to hit the floor, to roll in shame. A rough hand grabs the strap of his breastplate and pulls him upright.

"What? Speak you fucking fool or that tongue feeds dogs tomorrow!"

"Lord," says Bizimarko carefully. "My family is noble. My life is yours to take, but not my honor." Suddenly he remembers why none of this is funny.

"Right," says Paris. His cock actually seems to be retreating into his body. "Of course. Shock. Grief. First my brother, now this." He is actually stammering. He doesn't have the balls to kill Bizimarko before he gets the story out, so he had better make it look as good as he can. "All right, Captain," says Paris. "Where is my father, the king?"

"We don't know, lord," says Bizimarko. "He wasn't there when we went to wake him. The lords of the bedchamber said that they left him alone with his grief. There were three slaves in the room and they said that he kept talking about going to the Achaean camp to get back his son. They all told the same story, even though I tortured them separately. They said he went down the hidden passage to the wall. The one—forgive me, lord—that only the family and its slaves know about. And I tortured them until they showed me where it was. Or at least the one who survived showed me where it was."

Paris' face is again engorged. "Survived? How could you let him live after that?"

"Don't worry, lord," says Bizimarko hastily. "I broke his neck myself. And if you think I've compromised the family's security by knowing this, as I say, my life is yours." He draws his sword and hands it hilt first to Paris, pretty certain that he will survive the exchange, but not so certain

185

that when the prince's fingers wrap around the grip his stomach does not clench.

Paris withdraws his hand. "Our lives are the guards', Bizimarko," he says. "Keep your sword and your life." He holds Bizimarko's gaze for a long instant, reminding him that he could have taken the sword. "So," he says at last. "Where is he?"

"I don't know, lord," says Bizimarko. "He said he was going to get your brother. He may be on his way to the Achaean lines."

"So he may be dead already," says Paris.

"He may be, lord," says Bizimarko, trying to ignore the hope in Paris' voice. "With your permission, I'll send out light cavalry to try to find him."

Paris speaks as though he has not heard. "Until we've found the body, I imagine we'll need a regency, don't you?"

"That's not for me to say, prince." Bizimarko pauses respectfully. "The cavalry, lord?

"The cavalry," says Paris, "won't be necessary." He fixes Bizimarko with a regal stare. "The gods will protect the king, my father. The king, my father, is doing the work of the gods in retrieving my brother's body from those animals. They will let no harm come to him. If he returns—*when* he returns with my brother's body, it will be proof positive of the rightness of our cause. So we need not interfere, because if we did, it would appear that his body was retrieved through force of arms rather than divine right."

Bizimarko is aghast. Not that he has never heard men argue that their own desires were the gods'; he is shocked, rather, that the prince thinks the gods might endorse passive patricide. "Lord," he says, "of course you have a point, but can't we send out a few skirmishers at least to find out where he is?"

"No, Bizimarko," says Paris. Naked, fully flaccid, he crosses his arms in front of his hairless chest. "He's doing the gods' work. The gods will look after him. Have the Council come to me an hour after dark. And Bizimarko—" here he smiles, and Bizimarko almost gags at its forced sweetness "—I remember my friends. Do you understand, Captain?"

"I understand, lord," says Bizimarko. As he backs away from the princely presence, he begs the gods that Priam will return, or at least that he will die a clean soldier's death before he has to protect King Paris.

186

Priam thought that three flat miles would be easy, even in the dark, even at his age. After all, was it so long ago that his chariot swept across this plain at the head of Troy's triumphant army while his best boy, Hector, still a stripling, held the reins and Priam made his great ox-horn bow snap and sing as all who opposed him dropped with arrows planted in their throats and bellies? When the time for set battle came, he slapped his hand on young Hector's quivering shoulder and made the boy stop so that he could dismount and face a single champion, some barbarian giant, man to man. How Hector would quake, equally terrified to lose his father and have his father see his fear. But in those days, Priam's beard was barely gray and Hector had no beard at all, and in those days, when Priam and an opponent left their chariots, only Priam came back.

Priam smiles as he thinks of this. As he does, his foot catches a shattered chariot wheel and he plunges forward face first, arms thrown out too late, his fall broken by his jaw. He rolls onto his back and clutches his face, palms pressed to bleeding lips, his eyes leaking the easy, shameful tears of old age. He is filthy, his silk robe covered with mud, his hair and beard clotted with the muck of the battlefield. This is not the first time he has fallen and he is only halfway there. But he eventually reminds himself that he is, after all, halfway. He regains his feet and stiff-leggedly presses on.

The pyre is now glowing embers crosshatched by charred logs. Occasionally, one cracks and spits its resin and falls into the coals. Then, briefly, a ragged banner of fire shoots towards heaven, only to be extinguished a moment later. At the center of the grill lies a blackened skeleton cased in blackened bronze, tomorrow to be stripped of its scorched armor and crunched into fragments and powder and poured into a golden jar that Achilles and his heirs will adore until their line is extinct. Achilles sits with his back to the fire. Long ago, long before sunset, the lords and their army left him with his grief. The priests, less compassionate by nature, had to be urged to go. One still can be heard halfway down the hill, moaning as he nurses a broken femur.

Achilles' knees are drawn up to his chest; his arms are wrapped around his knees. It is cold, and with each hour that passes, the fire that consumes Patroclus warms him less and less. When the sun comes up, Patroclus will be gone and the fire will warm him not at all. He does not look behind him at the fire, no matter what noises it makes. Earlier he did, once, as the corpse popped open, a shriek issuing from its burning lungs. As Achilles leaped to his feet and spun to face it, Patroclus sat up in his flames and his right arm flew up as though to say, "Come with me," and it took five strong men to bring Achilles down before he launched himself onto the pyre. But that was earlier, when there remained strings of uncooked flesh on his lover's still wet bones. Much earlier. Now he will just sit with his back to the fire and feel what little warmth love will yet provide.

A hundred yards away a Myrmidon barks. Achilles does not raise his head, but eyes burning as hot as the coals behind him flick in the direction of the sound. "Who goes?" cries the Myrmidon.

No answer; the challenge is repeated. At that moment the wind shifts and carries with it what sounds like an old man's voice, indistinct at this range, but the Myrmidon is clearly audible. "Bull*shit*. And I'm Hera, Queen of Olympus. Straight answer, pops, or you're dog food."

Achilles raises his head now and stares at the sentry. Near him, barely visible in the light provided by the moon and dying pyre, is an old man, stooped, with a white beard nearly to his waist. Achilles knows him but refuses to believe his eyes. Without rising, he speaks. "Bring him. Now."

Both intruder and sentry turn to face Achilles. Despite a better look, he will not accept the evidence of his senses. The Myrmidon swings his spear around and nudges the old man in the small of his back. Slowly, they trudge up the hill. They stop a few yards away. Achilles remains seated. "Lord." The Myrmidon looks fretful. "I don't know how this clown made it this far. I'm sorry. The men down the hill will pay for it."

"That's all right," says Achilles.

"You're kind, lord," says the Myrmidon, "but this is inexcusable. Especially now. I'll—"

"You'll do nothing."

"Yes, lord. Anyway, this clown says he's King fucking Priam. I mean, *right*. Like he's come to pay his last respects to—"

"He is King Priam," says Achilles.

"Oh," says the Myrmidon. "Oh. Well, like I said, *right*. Uh, should I go get King Agamemnon and the other lords?"

"No."

"No. No, of course not. Just King Agamemnon, right?"

"No."

"Ah. Of course. Stupid of me. Just Lord Odysseus first. I understand. Ha. Well, I'll just send up another few boys to keep an eye on this bird, sorry, the king, and I'll—"

"No."

"Uh...no?"

"No." Achilles takes his eyes from Priam, who seems transfixed by the crumbling corpse on the fire, and faces the sentry, still without rising. "You'll resume your post and let no one pass. No one. And until I've told you otherwise, you will say nothing of what you've seen, what you've heard, or who's been here. Nothing. And if I learn that you have, I'll kill you myself and feed your body to pigs. Do you understand?"

"Yes, lord," says the Myrmidon.

"Repeat your orders, then."

"I resume my post and tell no one of what I've seen, what I've heard, or who's been here."

"And if you do?"

"You'll kill me yourself and feed my body to pigs." The Myrmidon is at the Achaean equivalent of attention, eyes fixed on the middle distance, his face immobile, his voice quivering.

"Do you believe I will?"

"Yes, lord," says the Myrmidon. "I'm certain."

"Then go, soldier, and do your duty."

The Myrmidon has recovered his composure. He backs away three steps, raises his spear in salute, turns like a grenadier, and marches back down the hill. Achilles waits until he is back at his post, spear butt planted in the dirt. He still does not look at Priam. Finally, he speaks. "Have a seat, my lord," he says. "Warm yourself at our fire." From where he sits with eyes averted, he cannot tell what Priam is doing, but he hears silk rustle and feels the warmth of a body beside his.

Long minutes pass. "Nice fire, isn't it?" says Achilles.

No response.

"Yes," says Achilles, "nice fire. They burn better when there's a lot of animal fat in them, you know. Funny thing. You don't like to think of people as animals, but they burn the same way, don't they? Like my Patroclus here." His voice is perfectly matter-of-fact. "I loved him. My father raised us as brothers. First I loved him as a brother, then I loved him as a lover.

189

I fought with him at my side these nine years. Then he took my place and your boy killed him. And now there he is, just like a fat bull sacrificed to Zeus."

"Men do burn just like animals," says Priam. "It is strange. Not so strange, is it, though, that Trojans burn just like Achaeans?"

"Not strange at all," says Achilles.

"No," says Priam thoughtfully. "Nor is it strange that boys burn just like men."

Achilles is silent for a bit. "Not exactly like men," he says. "Faster."

"True," says Priam in the same reasonable tone. "But they turn into bone and ash and grease just the same, don't they?"

"That they do," says Achilles.

They sit in silence for a long time before Priam breaks it. "Your mother is a goddess, I believe?"

"Yes," says Achilles. "Divine Thetis."

"Yes," says Priam, "so I heard. I wonder why the gods have mortal children."

"Why should they not?" asks Achilles, startled and a little irritated with himself for being so.

"Because in doing so they visit on themselves a curse even worse than mortality."

"How so?"

"Because to die is bad enough, to know that we must die is bad enough. But the gods compensate us for this bitter knowledge by giving us children. Death is like a black iron wall at which our lives' paths end, stretching to either horizon and up to the edge of heaven, so huge that we can see neither around nor above it. But children are like a little window in that never-ending wall through which we might see a little of what lies ahead. Not much, just to the next curve in the path, but enough to let in some light, to see some of the future, some sense that we will live even after we are dead. And when a child dies it is like that little window is slammed shut, and all we have is darkness." Priam pauses for a while. "So when the divine gods give life to mortal children, they do so knowing that they will outlive them, outlive them and their great-great-grandchildren, and in doing so they experience a thing worse even than death, over and over and over again."

Achilles still will not look at the man on his right. "I don't know, my

190

lord," he says. "I've never died and I have no children, so I can't compare."

Priam snorts softly. "Believe me here, Lord Achilles. Believe me. You have seen death as least as often as I. It is never good. Sometimes it's better than others: the arrow through the eye at the height of battle when you are dead before you hit the ground, the spear through the heart when you cough out gallons of blood and grow white and sag and are gone, those are not so bad. But even with the worst, the deep cut to the leg that turns green and stinks in camp so that you grow fevered and rage all night against enemies no one else can see until finally you are still, you are in the same place as those who fell like stones in battle to suffer no more. But I tell you, when a son dies, not in infancy or childhood, but fully grown, a leader of men himself, that is a death you suffer every morning from the instant you wake until you are asleep, and even then your suffering does not stop, because he comes to you in dreams, sometimes a boy holding his first bow, other times a bridegroom with his new wife. And from those dreams you awaken sobbing, and you promise Zeus that if only he will bring him back, you will die however he chooses, smothered in dung, disemboweled, a blinded slave tortured for amusement. Anything. Anything is better than the death of a son."

Achilles is silent. There is nothing he can say.

Priam speaks again. "Your father, Achilles, is mortal?"

"Yes," says Achilles.

"And he still lives?"

"Last I heard," says Achilles.

"I am happy for you," he says. "Though not so happy for him, because I know how he feels. How he feels every time the messengers run to him, saying, 'Lord, sails on the horizon.' I know how he pretends to be undisturbed, how his heart at once sings and sinks, thinking first, 'My son is returned,' then, 'They come to tell me my son is dead.' How he sits in his hall keeping his face a mask until the messengers say, 'Lord, the ships are at the dock. Lord, the ships come from Troy.' I know how his heart pounds and how he prays his men will not see his hands shake. How, when he goes down to the dock, he keeps his head up but will not look at the men on the ship for fear their heads will be bowed and two of them will hold between them a jar that has in it the ash and bone of the boy he held high to catch the sun's light on his very first dawn. And how, when he reaches

191

the dock and sees the men laugh and joke and clap each other on the shoulder as they offload the gold you have taken from us, sees the Myrmidons crippled by our spears and arrows coming back from the war to their farms, how his breath leaves him like the north wind in one big burst, and he almost faints with joy and then catches himself and laughs with relief and pleasure. I am not happy for your father, Achilles, for I am a father, too."

Achilles is silent.

Priam continues. "I did not come here to warm myself by your lover's pyre, Lord Achilles. I take no pleasure in his death, no more than I take pleasure in the deaths of the Trojan boys you used as kindling. I came to ask you, in your father's name, to give me back my son."

Achilles will not speak. The fire behind him crackles with the drippings of the dead. At last, he says, "When's the last time you ate, my lord?"

It is now Priam who is startled. "I don't remember."

"Neither do I. Hungry?"

Priam thinks before he answers. "Yes," he says. "Yes, I suppose I am."

"So am I."

Achilles whistles. The sentry on the hill below sprints to him and halts so sharply that his boot heels leave foot-long skid marks. "Lord!" he says, quivering erect. "I can be at Agamemnon's tent in—"

"The pigs are still hungry, soldier," says Achilles, "and so are we. Get us something."

"At once, lord," says the sentry. He is gone.

"My father is mortal, my lord," says Achilles, "and he is old. When I left he wept because he knew he would never again see me, one way or the other. I wept, too. I would weep now to think of him, but I can't. All my tears have been shed. They were shed when your boy killed my Patroclus. And now that I've killed your boy, I know I will die here. And if my father lives to see me again, what he will see is a big jar held high between two men with heads bowed. And I know that no matter how proud he is, he will weep then, not as he wept when I left, like a man, but that he will howl like an animal, and then soon after he will be dead himself, because he cannot long outlive that sight.

"I'm glad I killed your boy, King Priam. No disrespect, but he had it coming. It's a war. It's the way the gods made this world and the men who live in it."

"I know," says Priam. "It's a strange way they made it, and us, isn't it?"

"Maybe," says Achilles. "But it *is* the way they made it and us, and there's no point in wishing it were otherwise. So I'm glad I killed him. And when the time comes—again, no disrespect—I'll kill you and everyone in your city if I can. You understand that, don't you?"

"Of course," says Priam. "And you know if Zeus tips his balance our way, we'll kill you and all your army."

"Of course," says Achilles reasonably. "Otherwise, what would be the point of war? Someone has to win. When someone wins, another loses. The loser dies. No shame in that, is there?"

"None at all," says Priam.

"And one who wins and lives today, loses and dies tomorrow. And then there are no more tomorrows, and all that remains is the memory of how he met death. Is this not so?"

"It is," says Priam.

"My lord, I know that one day, probably soon, after all the days I've won, there will come a day I do not, and then the flames eat me and I go into a golden jar. No wife, no children will mourn me—only this army. Their grief and gratitude will last until they've eaten the last of the funeral feast. Only my old father will truly grieve, there on the dock when the boys hold up all that's left of me. All right, old man. I hated your son; I still do. I used to hate you, but I don't any more. You were brave to come here. You were right to remind me of my father. After we've eaten, take your son. But you must swear this: I will have what's left of him wrapped in scented cloth. There isn't much and it isn't pretty. Because I give you him out of respect for my own father, and because I wouldn't have him see me like that, you must swear not to look at him but just to burn him as he is. Swear."

"How can I?" says Priam. "How can I not look at my own son one last time?"

"Look," says Achilles. "Don't piss me off. I'm doing you a favor. Yes or no?"

"Yes," says Priam. "Of course, yes. I swear. On what shall we swear?"

Achilles looks down the hill. The sentry is returning burdened with bread and a bowl of stew and a jug of wine. "How about breakfast?" says Achilles.

IN
ODYSSEUS' TENT

Odysseus always rises early—earlier than anyone else in the army, though the army wakes at first light. He is dressed and outside before the sky is something other than pure black, when the dimmest stars have just disappeared, but the brightest is still present to contest the world with the sun for a few last moments. His men come to him then; the men who no one knows are his, the men who make the army believe that when Odysseus speaks with his perfect knowledge, it is because Athena whispered secrets in his ear.

They are gone now, their secrets told. It is the minute before dawn. The stars are gone. The sun has not yet come to bring color to the world, and so the world is shades of gray: silver above, lead below. He is back in the tent undressed, so that when Agamemnon comes and confronts him with the news, he can rub his eyes and say, "Yes, I knew," and tell Agamemnon details of which the king was unaware, and add casually that the Gray-eyed One came to him in a dream and that this is how he knows. Themselves slaves to inner voices, the lords of Achaea never question the messages Odysseus relays from Olympus.

Long ago, Odysseus thought his singularity a curse: that for some unimaginable sin, he alone among men was deprived of communion with the divine. Even as a boy, no matter how much he envied his friends the invisible companions he had long outgrown, he knew to keep his isolation secret. And soon he learned to fill the silence in his head. Bereft of sacred guidance, he had no choice but to watch the world and discover its workings for himself.

Lately he has come to wonder whether he is as entirely alone as he thinks. True, none of the warrior kings with whom he serves has ever hinted that their rages and jealousies are sent by anything but the gods, and all seem equally given to the trances of Olympian visitation. Odysseus has noticed, however, that other men seem slightly less receptive to possession. Not warriors or farmers, but shipbuilders and masons, as though frequent thought somehow renders the mind inhospitable to the gods. There have been times when he has seen such a man turn away from an excited account of a sacred hallucination with a look he thinks he understands. But he knows better than to talk. If there are others like him, they know as well as he the consequences of making their disbelief known.

Odysseus gets back into bed and composes himself for an hour's sleep. Agamemnon will be here soon.

Priam is halfway back to Troy. He walks just ahead of two slaves who drag a sledge and its burden of a man-sized bundle of sweet-scented linen. Man-sized but not man-shaped; the cloth hides the outlines of what appear to be limbs and a swollen center, as though what it contains is a chimera, an amalgam of man and bull. Whenever Priam looks behind him, he chews his lip and reminds himself that he is the king of Troy who has sworn an oath, and that he cannot look at what his son has become.

The slaves grunt and sweat. The ground has been broken by years of battle and the burden is heavy. One of them falls to his face and Priam tells them to rest. They drop their traces and as they do, the burden shifts and out of the twine-bound linen protrudes an arm, skeletal, hand nothing but bone and tendon, fingers splayed, forearm clothed in the remains of muscle and blackened flesh. Even from where he stands, Priam can see the busy maggots burrowing away from the dawn light.

I swore an oath, he thinks. On broken bread and stewed lamb and spilled wine. I cannot look.

195

But he can see what he sees. As the slaves sit panting between their traces, he drops to his knees and crawls sobbing to the out-flung arm. Rigor long since passed, it swings easily in his grasp as he presses the boney palm to his lips.

Agamemnon is gone, and with him Menelaus, Diomedes, and both Ajaxes. Goggle-eyed they told him the news: that Achilles at long last softened his heart harder than iron to let a father have his son. They asked him what it meant. He told them. Happy, they left.

The sun has been up for hours. Atop his little hill, Odysseus sits on his ox-hide stool. A bowl of wine cut nearly to water is in his hand. He raises it to his lips and looks toward Troy. From the city a thick column of fat-blackened smoke sends a prince to a Hades that Odysseus knows does not exist. Hector is gone.

Odysseus drains the bowl and looks to his right, down towards the ships, where the Myrmidon camp has suddenly become the busiest division in the army. Achilles is back.

Odysseus smiles. He will be home soon.

ACKNOWLEDGMENTS

First and foremost I have to thank Tom Perrotta and Richard Selzer, without whose generosity of time and spirit this would not have happened.

Equal gratitude is owed Lily Richards, my editor and publisher, whose insight and diligence made this book far better than it would otherwise have been.

I've been fortunate in the friends whose tireless and occasionally unfounded faith kept me at it: Pat Kaplan, Jill Cutler, Pamela Seighman, Eleni Markakis, Janette Blumberg, Philip Weber, and John Talbot.

Deepest appreciation is owed as well to the families into which I was born and into which I married. The present generation knows who they are; as to the next, I hope that I will be around when Jared, Alec, Evan, Emily, and Ellery are old enough for Uncle Terry's book.

And thanks finally to my mother, Bertha Hawkins, and my mother-in-law, Estelle Witt. May their names always be for a blessing.

9 781934 081204